ANDROMEDA BREAKTHROUGH

Books by Fred Hoyle

ASTRONOMY

The Nature of the Universe
Frontiers of Astronomy

CURRENT AFFAIRS

A Decade of Decision

PHILOSOPHY

Man and Materialism

FICTION

The Black Cloud
Ossian's Ride

By Fred Hoyle and Geoffrey Hoyle

Fifth Planet

By Fred Hoyle and John Elliot

A for Andromeda
Andromeda Breakthrough

ANDROMEDA BREAKTHROUGH

FRED HOYLE *and* JOHN ELLIOT

HARPER & ROW, PUBLISHERS

New York and Evanston

This book is based on the BBC television serial
of the same name and is published by arrangement
with the British Broadcasting Corporation

CONTENTS

1

OUTLOOK UNSETTLED

THE alarm signal buzzed quietly but insistently above Captain Pennington's head, a discreet echo of the bell jangling outside the guard room across the parade ground of the headquarters unit No. 173 Marine Commando.

Pennington groped for the bedlight switch and sat up. He stared uncomprehendingly at the vibrating clapper arm. In every officer's room were these little buzzers. They were painted red; they existed for No. 1 alert. It was accepted that a No. 1 would in reality mean only one thing: notification of the seven minutes the ballistics people had worked out as the breathing space before World War Three came and went.

Captain Pennington heaved himself out of bed. He was conscious of running feet as the Marine Commandos observed their long-taught procedure. The bedside phone rang as he was struggling into his denims.

"Major Quadring," came the abrupt, clipped voice. "Sorry about the panic measures. Orders from Whitehall. It's not the big thing, so ease up. But it's bad enough. Thorness. Major fire. Probably sabotage. Can't be sure that the trouble isn't sea-borne. Hence the S.O.S. to your boys."

"Thorness!" Pennington repeated. "But that's the king-pin of ——."

"Exactly. Save your mental reactions till later. Get over here within an hour. Four groups, with amphibians and frogmen, of course. I'll be at the gates to get you through. Tell your men not to fool around. The guards here won't be waiting to ask questions."

The phone clicked dead. Pennington checked his assault kit and ran from the officers' barrack hut into a night of soft-falling snow. He could make out shadowy figures of the men already

7

standing to by their trucks and amphibious vehicles, the engines ticking over. Not a light showed.

"Right," he called loudly through the darkness. "You'll be glad to know that this isn't it. Nor is it just a dummy run. Some real bother at the rocket station down at Thorness. I know no more than you, though we're going because there's probably a sea job to do. You can, of course, use headlights. I'll set the rate; we ought to average fifty. Keep the inter-com channel open till I order otherwise. Carry on!"

A Land Rover wheeled round and stopped beside him. He got in. Orders snapped out and the Marines got aboard their trucks. Pennington nodded to his driver and they roared through the gates.

They had a forty-five mile run from their base to the lonely promontory nosing into the Atlantic on which Thorness had been built as the nerve centre of Britain's rocket testing range. The whole area had been cleared of civilians, and the twisting, undulating road straightened and levelled for the articulated rocket carriers and fuel tankers. Pennington made the trip in precisely 55 minutes.

The main gates between the barbed-wire-festooned chain link fencing were shut. Guards with automatic guns stood under the floodlights. Dobermann Pincher dogs sat, immovable and alert, beside them. At the sound of the convoy Major Quadring came out of the concrete guard post with an N.C.O. Quadring was a lithe officer of middle-age, smartly dressed and unruffled. After a glimpse at the Commando identity marks on Pennington's vehicle he gave orders for the gates to be opened.

"Pull into the parking bay to the left," he said as Pennington jumped down. "Tell your chaps to relax, but to remain with the vehicles. Then come on in here. I'll put you in the picture. Over a cup of char—laced, of course."

Beyond the floodlights at the entrance, a double necklace of lamps edging the main road of the camp strung away into the misty night. The snow had stopped and what had fallen was melting into slush, so that the ground was dark, and the shapes of the camp buildings were dark, too, except where emergency lights were shining at windows.

Faintly inside the compound there was another smudge of light, where mobile lamps were trained on the main computer building, and a heavier pall—which was smoke—hung, smelling sulphurous, among the mist. Quadring led Pennington across the concrete into the guard hut.

Only in the light of the unshaded bulb of the guard room was it evident that Quadring was a worried man. His face was grey with fatigue and strain, and he tipped an over-liberal portion of rum into his own mug of tea.

"I'm sorry about a sortie on a night like this to this God-forsaken place. I think Whitehall and Highland Zone overdid it a bit with that No. 1 alarm and excursion, but then I'm only a simple soldier. They know better than I what's involved, though even to my un-technical mind this is a bloody business."

He refused Pennington's offer of a cigarette and began ramming tobacco into a blackened pipe. "The sea mist has closed in like a blanket down on the coastline. You drop from the station right into cotton wool. Not a damned inch in front of your nose. It'll lift with dawn, probably with rain or sleet. I tell you, it's a nice place.

"Someone or something attacked this place about four hours ago, and destroyed its brain. Which means, if my job here is as vital as they tell me, that old Lady Britannia is stripped of power, wealth, and about everything the politicians were banking on."

Pennington looked at him sceptically. "Frankly sir, you're over-dramatising things, aren't you? I mean, everyone knows Thorness is a rocket testing base, and where they run the computers which made those I.B.M. interceptions such a wow. Surely the machines aren't unique. The Yanks and the rest of N.A.T.O. . . ."

"The machines were unique," Quadring answered. "If you commandeered every computer in commercial or Government use in the country they wouldn't amount to more than a cash register compared with the scientific toy that's now a tangled mess of valves and wires and smouldering insulation. Nor does the rocket side matter all that much."

Pennington drained his rum and tea, easing himself on the hard wooden chair. "Of course, I've heard some pretty bizarre accounts of the sidelines here," he said with a grin. "It's pub gossip. That sort of thing was bound to start rumours."

"But nothing as good as the truth," Quadring said. "I've had an okay from G.D.1 to put you vaguely in the picture. Your boozing pals in the bar parlour haven't burbled anything about the Dawnay Experiment in their cups, have they?"

9

" The Dawnay Experiment? " Pennington repeated. " No sir."

" I'd never have believed my security was so good," the Major grinned.

He re-lit his pipe and sucked gratefully at it a while.

" This Dawnay woman's a sort of de-sexed biochemical genius from Edinburgh, though I admit I found her a pleasant person before she fell ill, through some infection from her own work, poor old girl. And so far as I can understand it, the computer helped her to synthesise chromosomes, which you no doubt learned when you were told about the birds and the bees being the seeds of life.

" She obviously hadn't much of a clue as to what it was all about, beyond the fact that the formulae spewed from the computer made sense. But the upshot was a human embryo."

" Human? "

" That's what they say. I agree it's a nice point. It grew like fun—or rather she did, for the organs of sex were there—and in four months she was 5 ft. 7 ins. tall and weighed 123 lb. The report is good on pointless and harmless facts."

Pennington tried to look amused. " Was this zombie, robot or whatever she was still in some sort of enlarged test tube, fixed in a clamp, or what? "

" Not a zombie by any means," Quadring retorted. " They called her human, because she looked human, behaved like a human, had human intelligence and human physical abilities. Though not, I gather, human instincts or emotions until she was taught them. In fact a rather pretty girl. I know. I've met her dozens of times."

" The people who know about all this and have to look after her must have a feeling of revulsion," Pennington said thoughtfully. " I mean a thing produced in a lab . . ."

" Don't kid yourself, and don't just take my word for it. Everyone accepts her as an attractive girl. But a very special girl. Dawnay built her, but she was only the artisan. The design came from the computer, and it saw to it that she was tailor-made for its purpose. She absorbs knowledge from the computer, and the machine needs her to programme it, or rather, did do so."

" Did? "

" She's gone."

" You mean she's disappeared? "

Quadring looked into the dark congealed mess in the bowl of his pipe. " That's exactly what I do mean."

Pennington laughed, a little too loudly. " Perhaps she didn't exist! I mean, I don't think one can really believe in a manufactured human being with a mental rapport with a computer."

" We service types aren't paid to think," said Quadring. " Right now, our job is to find her, and whoever destroyed the computer. It could hardly have been an outside job. It was done too expertly and quickly. The building was burning nicely by the time the patrols called me and had bashed through the locked doors and plied their extinguishers. Anyway, there wasn't a lot of point. The computer had been well and truly damaged with an axe before the arson. Security checks have told us one thing so far: the girl—she's called Andre, after Andromeda, the star or whatever it is that's alleged to have transmitted the dope for the computer—is missing, along with a scientist named John Fleming."

"Anything known about him? "

" He's marked with a query on the files. Nothing definite. But he's the usual sort of bright young genius who thinks he knows better than the Establishment. The story is that he'd fallen for the girl. And she sort of depended on him for advice the computer didn't or wouldn't give. They were certainly always together—at work and off it."

" So they might be together now? "

" Exactly. At first light, if the mist clears, you and your boys start looking. Some half-asleep guard down at the jetty thinks he saw a man and a woman get in a boat and head out to sea just before the alarm siren started."

" They could have landed anywhere along the coast by now," Pennington said.

" Not in that boat. It's known it hadn't more than a gallon of petrol. It's just a little outboard effort for pottering along the promontory to check the defences. They'd make one of the islets off the coast, no farther."

" What about a rendezvous out at sea? "

Quadring glanced at his companion. "A snatch by our old friend a Foreign Power? " He shrugged. "It could be. The Navy got the alarm along with you. Destroyers and aircraft by now will have started combing the Western approaches and away up North for too innocent-looking fishing trawlers and blatantly neutral tramps. But our radar watch would have picked up anything bigger than a rowing boat.

"My bet is they'll find nothing. Maybe you won't either. But with this sort of weather a little open boat isn't exactly healthy. The island makes the best of some poor bets."

Quadring stood up and looked through the window. "Time to get moving," he said. "And I've a tricky report to write on my incompetence to date."

There was an almost imperceptible lifting of the blackness of the sky when Pennington walked across to the parking lot. The men were smoking and talking in undertones. Pennington told them briefly that a couple of suspected saboteurs, a man and a girl, were believed to have escaped by boat either to land farther up the coast or on one of the islands in the vicinity.

"They're wanted alive—not dead," he finished. "So no rough stuff. They're not believed to be armed, and there's no real reason why they should be unpleasant. The girl is—er—a particularly vital witness. We'll get down to the jetty and arrange sweep and search routine from there."

They had to hang around at the water's edge for another half hour for daylight. The mist began slowly to lift like a vast curtain, exposing first the grey sullen sea and then, a couple of miles out, the lower slopes of the nearest island with patches of snow still smudged against the northern sides.

Their landing was an anti-climax. Pennington was in the leading amphibian when he saw the figure of a man standing motionless on the shingle beach of the island. He didn't move when the vehicle lumbered out of the water and pulled up beside him.

"My name's Fleming," he muttered. "I expected you."

He was a tallish, well-built man in his early thirties with a handsome but haggard face. His hair was wet and matted with sand, and his clothes torn and muddy. He stood quite still, as if exhausted.

"You must consider yourself under arrest," Pennington said. "And the girl who came with you?"

Fleming continued to stare out to sea. "I lost contact with her when I was looking for shelter. She wandered off. There are footmarks. They end at a cave entrance. There's a deep pool inside."

12

"She—she's killed herself? " Pennington demanded, mystified.

Fleming rounded on him. "They killed her. The whole damned circus which used her." He became calmer. "She was hurt, badly hurt. If she slipped into that water she wouldn't have had a chance. Her hands—well, her hands were—."

"We'll dive in the pool; drag it," said Pennington.

Fleming looked at him with something like pity. "You do that," he said. "Your bosses will demand their pound of flesh, drowned if they can't have it alive."

Pennington called to a Marine. "Take Dr. Fleming back to the mainland. Hand him over to Major Quadring. Tell the Major we're staying here to search the island."

The direct line between Thorness and the Ministry of Science in Whitehall had been busy since the news of the disaster to the computer had been flashed to the duty officer just after midnight.

The Minister himself had arrived at his office at the unheard-of hour of 9 a.m. He used a side door in case some observant reporter got the idea of a crisis. Rather to his annoyance, he found his Personal and Private Secretary, Brian Fothergill, already there, looking his usual calm and elegant self.

"Good morning, Minister," he said affably. "A nasty morning. The roads were quite icy."

"To hell with the icy roads," the Minister muttered pettishly. "What I want is some information about this Thorness business. Defence woke me at five. I didn't worry the P.M. for an hour. He took it badly, very badly. He's arranging a Cabinet for eleven. We must have useful material for him, Fothergill. If not a solution. I suppose we're still in as much of a fog as that bloody place in the Highland mists."

Fothergill delicately laid a neatly typed sheet of quarto on the Minister's desk. "Not completely, sir," he murmured, "as you will gather from this precis of the position. It's a preliminary, of course, all that I've been able to compile in the "—he glanced at his wafer-thin wrist watch—" seventy-five minutes since I inaugurated an investigation."

"For God's sake," snapped the Minister irritably, "drop that ghastly jargon. What you mean is that you've been nagging everyone for something to put down here. I hope you got the whole crew out of their beds."

The Minister read quickly through the report. " Good, good," he nodded, " as far as it goes. Which actually means bad, bad. Not your fault, Brian," he added hurriedly. " You are to be congratulated on the energy with which you have gone round in circles. But there are features of interest."

He re-read the report.

" The computer's gone. The girl's gone. The months of recording of the Andromeda equations by the radio-telescope at Bouldershaw Fell have gone. Somebody named Fleming whom I recall as an untidy and self-opinionated upstart has gone too. He gave me the impression when I met him that he drank. Which probably means he womanises too. I suspect that there's the usual tawdry sexual undercurrent in this debacle. However, that's a matter for M.I.6 and their confreres at the Yard. They must find them. More interesting is this note that our colleague Osborne visited Thorness yesterday evening."

He looked up and glanced blandly at Fothergill. " Where is Osborne? Missing, I presume? "

Fothergill permitted himself a moment's hesitation before he replied. " No, sir, I have located him. He caught the overnight sleeper which arrived at Euston half an hour ago. I took it upon myself to request his immediate presence here in your name."

" Quite right. And I'll put him through the hoop. These civil servants in the permanent jobs think themselves unanswerable to anyone." The Minister cleared his throat. He realised he was infringing convention in openly criticising the Department's Permanent Under Secretary to a junior.

" That will be all, Fothergill, for the moment. Show Osborne in as soon as he arrives. And don't let me be late for that 11 o'clock Cabinet. I shall need you at 10.30 to take my memorandum."

Fothergill faded noiselessly away. The Minister had time to ascertain a few more facts before Osborne was announced. As a senior civil servant the Under Secretary was permitted, even encouraged, to keep in personal contact with the Thorness project. But why this visit on the previous day? And why, as the Thorness guard room record book showed, had he signed in a visitor, name not given?

The thought of some espionage scandal directly affecting the Ministry of Science built up his fury to a zenith by the time Osborne entered immediately after he had knocked.

14

The Minister glowered at him. "Who was this chap you took to Thorness with you? " he asked without preamble.

"An assistant," Osborne answered shortly.

The Minister was determined to keep his temper if he could. " Why did you take him? " he demanded. "What did you need an assistant for on this nocturnal visit? "

Osborne seemed to discover something of tremendous interest on the Minister's desk. " It is essential for him to be in the picture," he murmured.

The Minister got up from his chair and crossed to the window. He felt uneasy at the calmness of this man, and knew that there would be little chance of getting at the truth unless he could disturb his calm. Right now the only person in danger of losing his temper was himself.

" He didn't leave a bomb, I suppose? "

He knew it was the wrong approach. Whatever unethical views Osborne might hold, he wasn't the kind to help in violence. "All right, of course he didn't," he went on hastily. " But you know what this means, don't you? "

He moved from the window and confronted Osborne. " We've lost our national capital, all of it. The computer's gone. The girl's gone. Even the original message which the Boulder-shaw telescope picked up has gone. There's no chance of starting again. From being a first class power, with the know-how for unassailable defence plus all the potential for industrial supremacy we're now relegated to a second-rate power; third-rate in fact."

Osborne turned his gaze from the desk and looked mildly at his inquisitor. His silence infuriated the Minister still more.

" Once in a million years," he pointed out, " or probably longer, a planet gets a Christmas present from another planet. And what does some dam' fool do? They go and burn it."

Once again he crossed to the window and looked down on the traffic in Whitehall.

" Were they fools? "

Osborne's comment was not more than a murmured question.

" We'll be back on American aid by the end of the year," the Minister retorted.

"At least America's a boss you can understand," Osborne suggested. " This Andromeda information we had to take on its face value. The results seemed splendid. But who understood

15

what it was all about? From somewhere in that dying and half-dead spiral nebula of Andromeda comes a briefing that makes no sense to anyone but a computer—and a freak girl; and maybe one honest-to-God human scientist."

" You mean Fleming," the Minister said.

Osborne ignored him. " Given that an intelligence in some recess of space sends us a stream of technical data which enables us obediently to make an anthromorphic creature to run its machine, who's honestly going to believe that the whole business is for our benefit and not theirs? "

The Minister lighted a cigarette. He could not help but be a little impressed with the argument. " Is that what Fleming thought? " he asked.

" That it was an attempted take-over? Yes. I'm not saying he did blow the computer to pieces, but if he did I for one don't blame him. I thank God it didn't fall into anyone else's hands."

The Minister was a simple-minded man. He disliked arguments about ethics. People were better off when they only did what they were told. " My country right or wrong, my mother drunk or sober " was a motto he had heard when he was a boy. He thought it rather good.

" Whose side are you on, Osborne? "

Osborne gave him a bland smile. " The losing one, usually, Minister."

His chief snorted in disgust. " I had hoped you would have had something useful to contribute. I was wrong. Perhaps Geers has bestirred himself enough to discover what the hell's been going on at the place he's supposed to be the director of."

The Minister switched on his intercom and told a secretary to get Thorness on the line. Osborne took it as a gesture of dismissal. He walked slowly from the office. He was privately rather surprised that he was still a free man. Never before in his precisely-planned and sedate career as a civil servant had he allowed his feelings to colour his sense of duty. Yet, in view of what had happened, he felt no regret whatever. He had, in fact, helped Fleming, and he was only concerned that no one should be able to prove it.

As he returned down the corridor to his own office he permitted himself a smile of amusement at a mental picture of Geers on this morning of crisis.

16

Geers was a careerist. As Director of Thorness he was the fair-haired glory boy of the Ministries of Defence and Science. He had adroitly swung over to enthusiasm for the Dawnay Experiment after several days of obstinate obstruction in favour of rocketry. Geers was a man who knew which side his bread was buttered. He had virtually achieved the pleasurable miracle of having it buttered on both sides.

But away up in Scotland Geers was now presenting the picture of a victimised and harassed autocrat. Despite the frantic messages to his quarters during the night he had dressed as slowly and as carefully as usual, his shirt collar uncomfortably stiff and his tie pulled tight into a small neat knot. But the impression of dignified pomposity which he considered essential for a key man in the nation's scientific technoracy was marred by the hunted look in his tired eyes behind their glasses, the black sheen of an inadequate shave, and the nervous tautness of his mouth.

He sat at his vast stainless steel desk, bereft of papers, but festooned with telephones, and glared at the visitors he had summoned—Fleming and Dawnay.

Madeleine Dawnay sat in the one easy chair near the window. Her rather mannish face was parchment yellow and her eyes were dull with fatigue and illness. She had pulled her dressing gown tightly round her emaciated body, missing the even warmth of the sick bay. Gratefully she sipped from a cup of coffee Geers' secretary had brought her.

Her eyes moved thoughtfully from Geers to Fleming, who lolled against the office partition. She said nothing, despite the glance of appeal Geers made to her.

"I've got the whole of Whitehall round my neck," Geers said plaintively. "The Minister of Defence is on the blower every five minutes, and half the senior staff at Science are badgering me, and I don't even know what happened."

Dawnay put her coffee carefully on the window sill. The slight physical action seemed an effort. "I don't know what's happened either," she said quietly.

"Osborne arrived at the station just after ten. With someone else. The public relations girl took them to the computer room. God knows why, but then I'm only the Director here. Afterwards, when Osborne and his guest had booked out, the duty operator locked up for the night."

17

"And Osborne went back to London? " Fleming looked better now; he had had a shave and a bath, and his usual casual slacks and wool shirt and sweater were at least moderately clean. He seemed now more despondent than tired, but there were strain marks around his eyes and at the corners of his mouth.

" Yes," said Geers. " No one else went in to the computer block after that, except the girl, Andromeda. After she'd been there some time the guard corporal thought he smelt burning. He went into the main control room and found the place a perfect shambles and full of smoke."

"And where was Andre? " Dawnay asked.

" Got out through the emergency exit, according to the corporal. Anyway, she or someone dropped a glove. A man's glove."

He turned and looked at Fleming, suddenly displaying a leather gauntlet taken from the desk drawer. " Yours."

Fleming did not trouble to look.

" So you know it all," Geers said. " Only two people know, you and the girl. The girl's dead."

Fleming nodded. With maddening slowness he repeated: " The girl's dead. So that's that."

" Not quite," said Geers angrily. " You have some questions to answer. You're the only person, Fleming, who wanted the computer destroyed. You always have. I can tell you that your security file is full of instances when you've shot off your mouth about it. In that I'm glad to say you're unique. Others have a better sense of loyalty, more vision."

Dawnay protested. " I think some of us were beginning to have doubts."

Geers turned and stared at her unbelievingly. He was about to speak when the intercom buzzed.

" Major Quadring is here, sir," came his secretary's voice. " He has the Marine Commando report on the island search."

" Right," Geers told her. " I'll see him in his office."

He rose and crossed to the door. " You're to stay here, Fleming," he ordered. Less brusquely he told Dawnay that he would try not to keep her much longer.

When the door closed Fleming moved across the office and stood close to Dawnay, looking out of the window.

" He's no business to drag you into all this," he said. " You're not well enough yet."

18

She laughed shortly. " I'm all right. I'm a tough old bird. I must be, or I wouldn't be here. But tell me, John, what really happened? You did it, didn't you? "

He kept on looking out of the window. " You don't want to be saddled with this."

" I don't," she agreed, " but as I'm involved whether I like it or not I'll just say that you can trust me if you want to trust anyone. Osborne must have smuggled you in. Then you and the girl destroyed it."

" The girl's dead."

There was a break in his voice which surprised her. In her experience John Fleming easily got emotional about principles, ideals, wrongs. But seldom about people.

"Anyway," she said quietly. " There's no one, no one, to give evidence against you."

Before he could answer Geers returned. He was grim but pleased with himself. Major Quadring had brought useful information.

Deliberately he took time to seat himself at his desk before he spoke.

" Right, Fleming; right," he barked.

" Right what? " enquired Fleming lazily.

" What happened when you got to the island? "

Fleming ambled around the desk. " Why ask me when obviously the snoops have told you? But I'll confirm what they have undoubtedly said. We got into the caves and I lost her. They're big caves. We had no torch. She blundered into a dead-end with a deep pool. That was it. Poor bloody kid."

Dawnay noted the break in his voice again. " I thought you held Andre wasn't human," she observed.

" Human enough to drown."

"Are you sure she fell in? " Geers asked suspiciously.

" Of course I'm sure," Fleming snapped. " Quadring told you that they'd found the bandages off her hands, didn't he? Or was that one bit of his smug little report he forgot to give? Or were those jolly Marines so dumb they didn't think them worth picking up? "

Geers studied Fleming in silence, taking his time so that he could be certain of noting any reaction. " I have news for you, Fleming, if it is news in your case. They've both dived and dragged the pool. There's no body."

There was no doubt about Fleming's surprise. "She must be in there," he shouted. "I traced her into that part of the caves. They've not dragged properly. There's no other way out. I searched thoroughly."

"So Quadring says," Geers murmured. His briskness had gone. He had hoped to bluster a confession from Fleming. But Fleming was obviously dumbfounded.

"She can't get off the island, and as it's been under constant survey since daylight that means she's somewhere in the caves. I'm going to look for myself. It's the only way to get things done in this damned situation."

"I'll take you," said Fleming firmly.

"No, that won't do," Geers retorted. "You're under arrest."

"Only on your instructions."

"Let him," Dawnay interrupted. "He knows the place. He wants to find Andre far more even than you."

With bad grace Geers agreed and the two men went off to get into warm clothes and seaboots.

Fleming was authorised to draw torches and a high-pressure lamp, and to fuel an outboard motor boat. Within half an hour they were crossing the two miles of angry water to the island. Neither said a word on the trip. Geers sat hunched in the middle of the boat staring at the silhouette of the rocky islet rising out of the mist. Fleming sat at the stern holding the tiller.

He beached the boat on the shingle right opposite the mouth of the cave.

Geers waded through the surf while Fleming heaved the boat clear of deep water. They clambered through the steep shingle at high tide mark and moved to the mouth of the cave. Gulls wheeled and called at this invasion of their private kingdom but the silence inside the cavern made a weird contrast to the screaming birds and the rhythmic hiss of the breaking waves.

"Sure this is the way you came?" Geers asked, moving cautiously forward in the wavering light of the lamp and Fleming's torch.

"Sure," grunted Fleming. "You automatically memorise this sort of thing just to make sure you don't forget the way out." He directed his beam of torchlight along a narrow sloping passage which curved to the right. "That's the way to the chamber with the pool. You can see the Commando's footsteps in the sand."

Geers began to move forward, shining the lamp on the

disturbed sand. He stopped abruptly when he sensed that Fleming was not following. " Where are you going? " he called.

Fleming was moving to the left. " I'm taking a look down this passage. There's another pool in here too."

" You think they dragged the wrong one? " Geers asked.

" No. Even Quadring and that Marine Officer aren't that stupid."

Geers turned back. " I don't know what your idea is, but I'm coming to see. We'll look at the other pool afterwards."

The passage dropped steeply, and the aperture became smaller. Fleming crouched low and moved steadily ahead. Geers, trying to keep up with him, caught his boot on a boulder and fell headlong. He grunted with pain as a jagged rock caught his shoulder.

Fleming turned and shone his torch on him. "Hurt yourself? It's tricky if you haven't done much caving. Wait here while I take a look at the pool. I won't be long."

Geers got up awkwardly and took a few steps back to the wider part of the passage. Fleming's footsteps echoed softly but clearly along the cave walls, getting fainter and fainter.

For a full minute there was the cold, dead silence of a lifeless world. Then, to his right in the direction of the main cavern, came the hard, clear sound of a stone moving across the rock face. It dropped with a dull plop into water. Geers froze into immobility, instinctively holding his breath. Another stone fell into the water, and then the rasp of several pebbles.

Geers' reaction was a mixture of excitement and fear. The fear won. He dared not move by himself. He yelled for Fleming.

His voice was a falsetto, and the urgency brought Fleming back as fast as he could clamber up the slope.

" Hi! " he said. " What's up? "

" Didn't you hear anything? Find anything? " Geers demanded.

" It's a deep pool, like the other. I think it's just behind the rock face of the main cavern. When you get deep pools like these in cave holes they are sometimes connected at the base —like a U tube. What goes in one may come out of the other."

" But nothing has? "

Fleming shook his head.

" No, but a body could be caught at the bottom. They'd better drag the second pool as well."

21

Geers shivered, though it was not as cold in the cave as outside. "Not a nice death, even for a creature," he muttered. More loudly he asked, "Did you throw stones into the pool?"

Fleming shone his torch on the other's face. "No," he answered. "Why do you ask?"

At that moment there again came the faint noise of moving pebbles. In the echoing and re-echoing of the tiniest sound it was almost impossible to identify the direction of the noise.

"There it is again. The noise. Stones moving," whispered Geers.

"Dislodged by me, and still not settled. It always happens."

Geers wasn't satisfied. He moved a step or so along the right hand passage, the light from his lamp swinging along the sides of the pool cavern. The rocks were wet and grey, with here and there pyrites glistening as the light caught them.

Fleming also switched on his torch and the beam reached right across the pool where the rock face curved gently into a rounded surface at the edge of the water. In a recess the light caught and held a blob of white.

"What is it?" whispered Geers, clutching at his companion's arm.

Fleming shook off Geers' hand and moved forward. The torch beam probed into the crevice.

"What is it?" Geers repeated urgently.

"Her, of course. Give me a hand to get her out."

Fleming eased forward, cautiously seeking a foothold on the slimy rock. Geers did not follow.

"At least play the light so I can see," Fleming shouted angrily.

When he reached Andre he thought she was dead. Her dress was saturated and clinging to her body. She felt stone cold as Fleming put his hands under the waist and shoulders to half-lift half-drag her back.

Difficult as the job was, he realised how little she weighed, how fragile this man-made *femina sapiens* was.

Gently he laid her on the dry sand at Geers' feet, leaning against the rock face while he gasped for air. Geers stood transfixed.

"Is she . . .?" he whispered, placing the lamp on the ground so it illuminated the girl's face. She looked like the death-figure of a young goddess, slim and fair and palely beautiful.

22

Fleming squatted down and pulled up an eyelid. The blue iris seemed sightless. There was no visible contraction as the light caught it. He groped on the ice-cold wrist for the sign of pulsation. There was a tremor of movement. He could not be sure whether it was in his own fingers or proof that Andre still lived.

" I'm not a doctor, so I can't be sure. But I think there's a flicker. She once said she had a better constructed heart than humans."

Fleming once more put his hands under her shoulders and pulled her to a sitting position. When the upper part of her body was upright her head fell forward. And she moaned.

" She is alive," shouted Geers exultantly.

" Just." With his free hand Fleming fumbled in his jacket pocket and pulled out a flask.

" Try a drop of the hard stuff, duckie," he said. With his teeth he unscrewed the cap.

" You shouldn't force her to drink alcohol. It's a fallacy that ——."

" To hell with your boy scouts' first aid rules! Here, my sweet," he murmured to the girl, " it's the real McCoy."

He let a few drops of whisky seep through Andre's pale, clenched lips.

Not daring to move, both men waited for the reaction. It came gradually. The lips relaxed and parted a little. The tongue tip emerged and moved across them.

Fleming gently brushed the matted blonde hair from her face. He was rewarded by a momentary flickering of the eyelids.

" That's it," he murmured close to her ear. " Now try to swallow a mouthful." He forced the mouth of the flask between her lips and against her teeth, tipping in a spoonful of spirit.

Andre gulped, spluttered and then swallowed it. Fleming could feel her body relaxing against his encircling arm.

" How did she get here? " Geers demanded.

" There must be a syphon between the two pools. She'd sink on one side and come up on the other. God knows how she managed to hang on the side and pull herself up. Not with those injuries."

He nodded towards Andre's hands, lying close together in her lap. They were grotesquely swollen and discoloured, the bloated whiteness of the back and knuckles contrasting horribly

23

with the seared flesh of the fingers where the computer had burnt them.

Geers shuddered. " Can we carry her out of here? " he asked doubtfully. " We must get her to the mainland as soon as we can. Then perhaps we'll find out the truth about this business."

The impatience in Geers' tone infuriated Fleming. " Give it a rest, can't you? The girl's half dead and all you can think of is putting her in thumbscrews."

He believed that Andre half understood what was being said. Her body tautened in his arms and she made a pathetic attempt to shift away.

Awkwardly Fleming struggled out of his duffle coat without releasing his hold on her and draped it around her shoulders. " You're okay," he reassured her. " It's all over now. We'll go away for a nice long holiday. You know who I am, don't you? "

Her clouded eyes opened wider and stared at his face. She nodded almost imperceptibly.

He felt ridiculously pleased. " Fine! I'm going to lift you up. Keep your hands just where they are and they won't get rubbed. Here we go! "

Geers made no attempt to help. He watched Fleming grasp Andre and lift her like a baby, shifting the weight until he had her held securely, her head against his shoulder.

Satisfied that they were leaving at last, Geers bent down to pick up the torch. Fleming was just behind him. With a quick shove from his boot he sent Geers sprawling. Then he kicked the lamp away. There was a tinkle of glass as it hit the rockface and the light went out.

Fleming laughed aloud. " Hold tight, darling, we're taking off," he whispered to Andre. Half crouching to avoid bumping the cave roof, he loped ahead helped by the fitful, jerking light from his own torch. Geers' wails of fright and fury echoed behind him.

Fleming reached the cave entrance with no more than one bad bump on his shoulder. There was a stretch of thirty yards to the boat. He noted with satisfaction that the tide had turned and the stern was already afloat.

He was wading in deep water before Geers stumbled from the cave entrance, bawling Fleming's name and alternately threatening punishment and appealing for him to wait.

Fleming lowered Andre into the bottom of the boat. She groaned pitifully as her hand struck a rowlock.

Fleming crouched over the motor. If only the damned thing would fire first time. Outboard engines were temperamental until they got heated up. He forced himself methodically to check choke and fuel control before he wrenched at the starter cord. He whipped it out with all his strength. The engine fired with a staccato burst of noise, spluttered, and then settled in to a steady rhythm.

With a kick over the side that filled his boot with sea water Fleming pushed off stern first. A couple of yards and there was room to veer. He gave the engine full throttle and the boat swung seawards. Geers was standing impotently up to his knees in water, shaking his arms and burbling incoherent imprecations. Fleming didn't trouble to turn round to look at him.

The sea was pretty calm while the island protected it from the ocean swell. He grabbed the chance to check the petrol reserve and to wrap his coat more tightly around Andre. She was either asleep or had lapsed into unconsciousness again.

The boat moved crabwise because of the current running through the narrows between the island and the mainland. On this course he was merely making a return trip right up to the jetty at Thorness.

The headlong flight had been without much reason. His objective had simply been to get Andre away from Geers and all that he represented in cold, efficient care and ruthless questioning.

Now he had time to think up a plan. But not much time. The sea was getting perceptibly rougher. They were hitting a swell. Foam frothed here and there on the crescents of the heaving water ahead. He made up his mind.

He turned the rudder to port and headed straight into the current. Emergency made his memory crystal clear. He could see this grey, misty waste of angry water as it was in the rare calm of a summer's day. He remembered the haphazard pattern of shoals, rocks and islets which had made the area forbidden territory to any sailor except a few crab fishermen even before the Admiralty cordoned it off as a rocket range.

Fleming was not unduly worried about crashing the boat. It wasn't capable of more than ten knots and was as manoeuvrable as a coracle. Though the half-hearted light of a winter's day was already lessening he felt sure that the noise of breaking waves and the swirl of foam would give him all the warning he needed of danger.

What he wanted was something a bit larger than a collection of rocks where maybe a long-deserted crofter's cottage or bird-watcher's eyrie existed. Such places were built to resist wind and cold; they were as strong as the rocks from which they were made. They would give him a breathing space while he thought out the next move. Not for the first time in his life he half-regretted acting precipitately.

A flurry of sleet hit him in the face. The gust of wind which accompanied it shook the boat, and a little water burst over the side, wetting Andre's face. She cried out and lifted her hand to brush away her matted hair. The touch of her hand on her forehead made her moan again.

Fleming opened the throttle still more. There was no point in conserving petrol. He had got to get her out of the boat before the storm grew worse or before nightfall. He wasn't certain which would come first.

For a full hour he sped northwards, straining his eyes and ears for a sign of land. There was nothing but the howl of the increasing wind and the expanse of the spume-flecked sea. Then, unmistakably, he heard the uneven roar of water crashing on to rocks and shingle. The sea became less broken, turning into a sullen, greenish swell. Beyond the broken mist a dark grey bulk loomed up—much darker than the twilight grey of the sky.

He throttled down and veered to starboard. With the currents and sporadic gale-force winds he had no real idea where he was. He had no intention, even now, of landing on the mainland, right into the arms of some official or meek and law-abiding citizen.

He steered a course a generous forty feet from the breaking waves. He tried to tell himself that he recognised the coast as one of the islands he had visited for recreation back in the summer, but he knew it was just self-persuasion. In such conditions all these islands looked much the same. All he could be certain of was that it was an island, a small one. Many gulls, disturbed by the noise of the boat as they settled down to roost for the night, wheeled around, with their piteous calling. Gulls preferred islands.

The rock face sloped abruptly downwards at the point where

the boat veered round until it was almost east of the land. Where the rocks met the water was a tiny beach, or rather a steep stretch of rounded stones, not more than twenty feet wide.

Without hesitation Fleming steered straight for it, running the boat half out of the water. There was a vicious jerk and the sound of tearing timber. The lower section of the boat had been stove in.

Fleming jumped over the side, feeling for a foothold. Then he caught hold of Andre and lifted her out. He laid her gently down on the stones above the water line and returned to the boat. He manhandled it round until it pointed seawards. Water was gurgling in fast. Tying the tiller midway, he set the throttle at full. The boat shot crazily away, the nose already down and the thrashing screw almost out of the water. He did not wait to see the boat go under; he lifted Andre once more and clambered as fast as he could to the higher ground beyond the stones.

There was a distinct track where the ground provided some shallow soil where coarse grass and stunted heather struggled to live.

Fleming was not surprised about this. He had expected it. For just at the moment the boat had swung towards the beach he had seen a dull yellow light a few hundred yards behind and above the landfall.

From the track the light had shape. It was a narrow vertical chink between some patterned curtains.

He did not care who lived there. Coastguard, radar operator, rocket trajectory observer, recluse. The main thing was to get warmth and help for the girl. She was now as lifeless in his arms as when he had first grabbed hold of her at the edge of the cavern pool.

2

COLD FRONT

THE Azaran Embassy was easily identified in the long row of Edwardian houses whose bed-sitter occupants liked to claim that they lived in Belgravia, while in fact the postal number was Pimlico. It was noticeable because its decaying and crumbling stucco had been repaired and given a coat of glossy cream paint. It also displayed a gaudy flag and a highly polished brass nameplate.

The interior was luxurious. The Ambassador's study was furnished with that refinement of taste and air of luxury possible only when money hardly matters. And Azaran, over the past few years, had floated to superficial and temporary prosperity on the small lake of oil British geologists had tapped beneath the desert.

Colonel Salim, Azaran's accredited representative to the Court of St. James's, had been the military strong man of his country's revolution. He had worked hard to make himself indispensable to the idealist whom fate and intrigue had made President, and his reward had been the best diplomatic post the President could offer. As a matter of fact, Azaran did not bother about the status of embassy in any other European country, but Britain, for the time being, was master of Azaran's economy.

Salim enjoyed living in the West more than he enjoyed switching from force to diplomacy. He was a hard man and something of a genuine idealist, but he had forgotten his religious precepts sufficiently to enjoy alcohol and he had tempered his fierce racial beliefs enough to develop a taste for Western women. Much more, he had been impressed with the practical uses to which Europeans put their wealth. In his country, wealth had to be gaudily displayed. But in the West it was exploited to buy something infinitely more desirable: power.

28

It was the prospect of unlimited power which kept Salim restlessly walking around his study on this grey winter's evening. He was getting rather soft with good living and a desk job. Fat was growing at his hips and in the jowl of his swarthy, handsome face. But he was still reasonably young. It was not merely vanity which told him that he was still impressive.

He turned eagerly when a manservant entered and announced, with a bow, that a Herr Kaufman wished to see him.

" Show him in," Salim ordered. Quickly he sat down at his desk and opened a file of papers.

The servant returned with the visitor. Kaufman was tall, and rigidly erect. Salim recognised him as a soldier; probably a Nazi junior ex-officer or N.C.O., possibly in a crack S.S. regiment. Salim did not mind that. There had been the occasion, back in 1943, when he had confidently assured Rommel's emissary that, when the time was ripe, he would bring the Azaran army over to the German side.

" Herr Kaufman," he exclaimed, extending his hand. " Take a pew." He was rather proud of his mastery of the English vernacular. It inspired a friendly attitude he had found.

Kaufman bowed slightly from the waist and smiled. His light blue eyes, enlarged by the thick lenses of his rimless gold spectacles, were appraising everything on the desk and around the room.

He continued smiling as he deferentially murmured that he had been ordered by his superiors to wait on the Ambassador.

" By Intel," nodded Salim. " What else were you told? "

Kaufman stared back unblinkingly. " Nothing else, your excellency."

Salim offered him a box of heavily chased silver. " Smoke? "

The other withdrew a case from his inner breast pocket. " These, if you don't mind.' He selected a small, almost black cheroot and lit it.

Salim got up and walked across the room to a table where some photographs of Azaran were displayed.

" Interested in archaelogy, Herr Kaufman? " he asked. " We are particularly rich in relics: Greek temples, Roman arenas, Turkish mosques, Crusader's castles, British anti-tank traps. They've all had a go at us." He turned and eyed Kaufman. "And now Intel. Your employers are taking a deep interest in my small and harmless little country."

Kaufman puffed out a cloud of smoke. It eddied over Salim, who made a gesture of distaste. "And if my employers are indeed keeping their commercial information up to date? As routine, of course. Is this important to you? "

Salim lowered his voice. " It's not unheard of for business interests to finance a breakaway state. And we propose to break with the British oil interests, Herr Kaufman. Their field has not been a very exciting one. We believe you will have more to offer than oil."

Kaufman thoughtfully shook the ash from his cigarello. " Our collateral? " he enquired.

Salim rubbed his hands together. " Let's be frank. You're a trading organisation. Probably the biggest commercial under-taking ever known. Just what cartels and groups are involved no Western government has been able to discover. Holding companies, secret understandings, private agreements, patent monopolies, offices registered in small and tolerant countries. But why need I tell you all this? You know it. You also know that with the Common Market and the increasing tendency for Governments to co-operate, the Intel organisation will find it harder to pursue its private way. Nobody very much likes such a successful enterprise."

" This may be true," Kaufman agreed.

" Your registered offices are in Switzerland," Salim went on. " I read with interest the other day that both the Canton and Federal Governments are getting impatient over income tax matters. They hint at laws enforcing investigation of accounts and so forth. Your directors seem usually to meet in Vienna, capital of a tolerant and non-committed country. But Austria would not, could not, afford to ignore pressure from her powerful neighbours. You are, in fact, an organisation without a home."

Kaufman seemed unimpressed. " We have offices in at least sixty countries. And influence in as many."

" The offices are merely trading posts, innocuous and politi-cally negligible. Your influence is in jeopardy."

Salim crossed to the map of the Middle East which was spread across half the rear wall of the study. " That little area painted red is my country. It could be the home sweet home for the headquarters of Intel. No interference. In return just some expert help for our own plans."

30

Once more Salim sat down. " What do you know of Thorness? "

Kaufman pondered for a moment.

" Thorness? " he repeated, as if the word meant nothing.

Salim made a gesture of impatience. " I have information that you have long been in touch with the British Government's experimental station at Thorness. Unofficially, of course. I believe that you could even explain an unfortunate fatality to one of the scientists there, named Bridger, but no matter. I mention it to show that I am not without knowledge of your current activities."

" They are no longer current," growled Kaufman. " The station has been virtually destroyed. The computer and everything associated with it were blown up and burned. That, at any rate, is what I have so far ascertained."

" Blown up? "

" That is correct."

Salim was non-plussed. His Court of St. James's manners disappeared as he waved away the cloud of Kaufman's cigar smoke. It was as if some latent violence in him had exploded.

" Please refrain from burning those filthy things in here. If you wish, go to the toilet and smoke there."

His visitor obediently stubbed out his cigarello. He seemed impervious to insults. " No thank you," said Kaufman after he had carefully extinguished all the burning remains. " But if you wish the interview to end . . .? "

Salim glanced at the file on his table. Everything had suddenly changed and what was expected of him now was something which he understood. Action. He re-read the copy of the appreciation of the situation he had dictated a few days earlier. A smile hovered round his mouth. The gods might after all be working in their mysterious way for his benefit, even with this Thorness debacle.

" There's a Professor Madeleine Dawnay at the station," he said. " I am offering her a post with our Government's biological research department immediately. And there's a Dr. John Fleming."

" A difficult person, Herr Doctor Fleming," muttered Kaufman. " It would not surprise me if he was involved in this tragedy for the British economy."

" Indeed," said Salim thoughtfully. " Anyway, you will agree

31

that he has a brilliant mind. I am informed that in fact he was the man who supervised the construction of the computer."

"That is true," agreed Kaufman. "Fleming has an astute and imaginative mind. He is disliked by most of his colleagues."

"But the Government of Azaran would like him," Salim murmured. He was quite calm again, almost silky. He smiled at Kaufman. "Indeed, it is my belief that my President would confirm his offer to Intel only on the understanding that it was a package deal, as they like to say over here; the package including Fleming. As a loyal employee of Intel, you have some ideas?"

Kaufman withdrew his cigarello case, thought better of it, and carefully replaced it in his pocket. "It would be difficult, costly," he muttered. "If my theory about sabotage is correct Herr Fleming will already be under arrest."

"Your directors undoubtedly prefer facts to theories," Salim observed. "Perhaps you should return to Scotland and continue your investigations. Phone me regularly to report progress. Guardedly, of course. Remember I am a diplomat."

Kaufman stood up, bowed stiffly, and took his leave. "You may rely on me, your excellency," he said.

As he neared the cottage Fleming moved more cautiously. Anxious as he was to get Andre under shelter he had no intention of walking straight into the arms of the enemy. He shifted off the narrow track and approached through the unkempt garden at the side.

It was a typical crofter's home of the Western Isles—ugly, squat, but solid. Wooden shutters suggested a cosiness inside. It was a broken shutter which had allowed the lamp light to stream out.

Fleming sidled up to the window. The tattered cretonne had been carelessly pulled across the tiny panes. Inside he could see a man sitting at a table. His pale, ascetic face had a simple youthfulness about it which was denied by his shock of greying hair and the criss-cross lines around his eyes. Fleming judged him to be in his forties or maybe fifties. The polo-necked sweater he wore was good but very old. His expressive hands were gesticulating, his long fingers grasping a pencil which he waved in the air in a to-and-fro rhythm, and he was talking, evidently to himself.

32

Fleming pressed his face closer to the glass to look around the rest of the room. It was a jumble of old, heavy furniture, and there were books everywhere. But there was no one else. The unpainted door on the far side was shut tight. Fleming felt satisfied that this was a reasonably safe refuge. He knocked loudly on the heavy oaken door.

A chair scraped on bare boards and a rather high-pitched bleating voice asked who was there. The door remained closed.

"Let us in, please," Fleming bawled as loud as he could. "It's urgent!"

A bolt moved protestingly in its runners. There was the click of a latch and the door opened a couple of inches.

"Who are you? What do you want?" A grey eye peered into the gloom.

Fleming pushed the door with his shoulder. "Just let us in first, uncle," he said. "Explanations later."

The man let the door swing open. He stood aside as Fleming strode in. He peered suspiciously but hopelessly at the unconscious girl in Fleming's arms.

"You're not a nephew of mine," he said uncertainly. "And I'm nearly sure I've never met the young lady."

He shut the door with a little fatuous, old-maidish gesture of resignation.

"No," agreed Fleming, crossing to the stone fireplace where a peat fire smoked sullenly but warmly. "Uncle's an old runic greeting." He laid Andre gently on a sofa drawn close to the fireplace.

The man's eyes lighted up with interest. "Runic, you say? I've never ——— " His voice tailed away.

Fleming removed his soaking coat, and threw it on a vast and half-collapsing easy chair. "Can we stay for a bit?" he asked.

The man hovered around helplessly. "I suppose so," he said without enthusiasm. "Where have you come from?"

Fleming was occupied in removing Andre's coat, pulling gently at the sleeves so as not to touch her hands. "The sea," he said shortly. "By boat. It's gone now. Smashed, I hope."

The man poked at the logs, sending up a cascade of sparks. "I must confess I find you difficult to understand," he observed.

Fleming straightened up and grinned. "I'm sorry. We're a bit flaked. Tough weather for a sea trip."

The other man was looking at Andre. He sort of shivered as he saw the shapeless, purplish flesh around her fingers.

"What has happened to your friend's hands?" he enquired diffidently, as if ashamed of ungracious curiosity.

"She burnt them. Touched some high voltage wiring. You haven't anything hot, have you? Soup?"

"Only out of a tin." The man drew a deep breath, ashamed of his attitude. "I'll get it. You must forgive me," he went on, smiling almost boyishly. "It's just you were so unexpected. My name's Preen. Adrian Preen. I — er — write." He glanced longingly at the table with the sheets of large, scrawling writing. "I'll get the soup." He went through the rear door, closing it carefully behind him.

Andre shuddered, moaned, and opened her eyes. Fleming knelt down beside her. "How do you feel?" he whispered.

Her eyes were vacant, but she was able to turn her head and look at him. She even smiled. "I'm better now," she murmured. "My hands throb. What has happened?"

"We're running away," he said, caressing her hair. "We started running two nights ago when we bust up the computer. Remember?"

She frowned and shook her head. "Computer? What computer? I can't remember anything."

"It'll come back," he assured her. "Don't worry your head about it." He got up and crossed to the table, glancing at the manuscript. "Sir Gawain and the Green Knight," he read aloud. "This is a rum do. I hoped for a shepherd, but we've found a sheep. Wonder how he manages to make a living with this stuff?"

He was interrupted by the click of the latch and he stood away from the table. Preen returned with a couple of steaming bowls on a tray. He grabbed a stool and placed the tray on it alongside Andre. "Condensed tomato, I'm afraid," he said apologetically.

"That'll be fine," Fleming said. He took a spoon and began feeding Andre, who sipped hungrily at the thick, red liquid. "What's the name of this island?" Fleming went on to Preen. "Soay?"

"It's just off Soay and very much smaller."

"Then you're on your own?"

Preen nodded. "And at your mercy." Hastily he apologised. "That was crude of me. But you were a surprise, you know.

Anyway, I'll leave you and your friend to enjoy the soup. Might I enquire your name?"

" Fleming, John Fleming." He did not volunteer Andre's.

" I ask only out of courtesy," said Preen mildly. " Since I'm your host. You'll have to stay here, naturally. There's nowhere else to go. That's why I chose this island."

" But why isn't really answered, is it?" Fleming suggested.

Preen hesitated, looking embarrassed. " I came because it's safe, or comparatively so. I used to protest against the Bomb and so forth, but I got tired of exposing lunacy and decided it was more sensible to opt out."

Fleming gulped down the last of his own soup. " That makes three of us," he grinned. " But when the bombs drop and you're the last oasis of life and learning how are you going to ward off the pirates, all frightened, starving, and full of radiation sickness?"

With an air of conspiratorial triumph Preen walked over to a heavy old chest which served as a window seat. From it he removed a short automatic rifle.

" Splendid," laughed Fleming. " We'll sleep safe tonight. I take it that we can all doss down somehow and get some sleep? It's been a busy day."

Preen showed unexpected resources. He had his own bed in the shelf alcove beside the fire. From another cupboard he produced heavy wool rugs. Andre was tucked in, the fire was made up, and Fleming wrapped himself up and lay down on the floor beside the sofa. Preen shot the bolts on the door and turned out the paraffin lamp. Fleming vaguely heard the indeterminate noises of his host undressing and going to bed before a sleep of utter exhaustion swept over his brain and body.

It had been three hours before the continued absence of Geers and Fleming aroused misgivings, and a Marine Commando launch went to the islet to investigate.

By the time action could be taken to locate the fugitives night had fallen and the weather had become almost impossible.

Geers, ill with his miserable wait on the island and sick with apprehension about the repercussions in London, sat at his desk drinking a hot toddy and blusteringly ordering Quadring and Pennington to do something. But he could not put off for very long the unpleasant task of phoning Whitehall with news of the latest debacle.

The Minister of Science took the call himself. He remained completely silent while Geers babbled on about the bad luck of the whole business in general and the unforgivable treachery of Fleming in particular. The great man's silky comments before he hung up were worse than the most sarcastic reprimand.

" Most unfortunate," he said softly. " You have my complete sympathy in a situation where you seemed to be surrounded by incompetents and traitors. You may leave it to me to put the best construction on it to the Old Man. He's unusually disturbed about all this, which is so uncharacteristic. Not going to Chequers. Staying at No. 10. And you know how he loathes the place since it's been done up. I do hope I can get his P.A. Such an excellent buffer when the P.M.'s in one of his captious moods. Well, goodbye. Keep in touch."

The Minister did get the P.A. He could be more forthright with him. "Just had a call from Thorness, Willie," he said. "They found the girl, and then the bloody fools promptly lost her. Now Fleming appears to have abducted her. So romantic, isn't it? Geers has bawled futile orders to every R.A.F. and Navy station from Carlisle to Scapa. I suppose masses of ships and planes and little men with radar sets are now rushing about like mad. Met. reports Gale Force 9, and storms of both the moisturised and electrical variety. The pursuers won't have much luck, and I don't feel this is a situation where praying for miracles would be listened to. But officially, Willie, I'm asking that you'll tell the Old Man that we're leaving no stone unturned, exploring every avenue. You know, the usual pap. Oh, I've decided to send Osborne back to Thorness so we get some coherent facts, and also to broach something else that's cropped up. He put up a bit of a black so he'll be all the more anxious to please. He's a sound chap at heart."

Osborne was sent for in the early hours of the morning and despatched to Thorness at first light by air. He was in Geers' office by noon. The Director had grabbed a few hours' sleep on a make-shift bed in the night duty officer's room. For the first time in his life he was conscious of looking dishevelled and grubby. He had disliked Osborne from the start. The fact that the man was still entrusted with a job which was nothing less than a check-up on his own efficiency made him dislike him still more.

"No news from the searchers, of course," questioned Osborne, taking a chair without invitation.

Geers shook his head. "We'll just have to wait and hope. It's my fault," he mumbled. " I should never —— "

" It doesn't really matter whose fault it is," said Osborne kindly. " It's happened. How's Madeleine Dawnay?"

Geers looked at him suspiciously, wondering about this new topic. " Much better," he replied. " The electrical burns she got from the computer weren't in themselves particularly bad. It was using that damned enzyme formulated from the machine. Or rather some error her morons made in compounding it. Fortunately Madeleine had the mental power to check it and see the mistake. From then it was easy: a miracle cure which will revolutionise our burns units and indeed all plastic surgery. One last priceless benefit from that machine the vandals have smashed."

" I'm glad—about Madeleine, I mean," said Osborne. He paused thoughtfully. " There's nothing more for her to do here, is there? Now the computer's wrecked?"

Geers shrugged. " Nothing much left for any of us," he said. " I wonder where the devil Quadring's got to? He should have some news of what's happening. Good or bad."

Osborne ignored this. " We've had a request for her from the Azaran Government."

" Who?"

" From Colonel Salim, in fact. The Azarani ambassador."

" No, I mean who have they asked for?"

" Dawnay, whom we've been talking about," said Osborne impatiently. "A formal request passed to us last night via the Foreign Office. They want a bio-chemist."

" What the hell for?" Geers demanded. Then, resignedly: " It's up to her, if she wants to go. I've other things to worry about."

"Ask her," Osborne replied. "And either you or she can phone the Ministry. Don't defer a decision too long. These little oil states love protocol. Mustn't suggest discourtesy by ignoring their enquiry."

"All right," grunted Geers.

The phone rang and he snatched it from the cradle. He listened to the brief message and then replaced the receiver, smiling with relief and satisfaction.

" They've located some wreckage. Splintered wood and so on. Registration number on one piece. It's the boat Fleming took; no doubt of that. No sign of bodies so far. Take some time for them to come up, of course. They hadn't a hope in hell." There was no tinge of regret in his voice. Geers was not mourning the presumed death of two colleagues.

" Whereabouts was the wreckage?" Osborne enquired.

Geers glanced at some figures he had jotted on his memo pad during the phone call. " They give Victor Sugar 7458 as the approximation." He went to the wall map of the Thorness rocket lanes and prodded with a finger at a spot on the grid lines.

"About there. A little south from Barra and east from South Uist. Shoal water. Only someone as crazy as Fleming would have risked it in such bad visibility. But the Navy will go on looking, just as a routine formality."

The two men sat in silence for a time. " I'll see if the canteen can manage some lunch," said Osborne. Geers nodded. He made no move to accompany him.

It was a day of abnormally high temperature for so early in the year. The air was saturated with moisture and the mist turned to a steady rain over the land. Out at sea visibility went from bad to worse. Even for Western Scotland, the weather was breaking every kind of record. Fleming normally ignored the climate, but now he found it oddly in tune with the melodrama of the crisis at Thorness.

Clambering around the island, he heard the occasional impatient whoop-whoop of a destroyer's siren and the regular throb of dieseled launches cruising slowly. Once or twice raucous voices cursed cheerily as the search parties tried to find some humour in their boring, pointless task.

He had told Preen he needed exercise and would collect firewood. He had said nothing about the possibility of a major search for Andre and himself. Preen was patently anxious not to enquire too closely into what the whole escape was about, though Fleming suspected that a man who had been a C.N.D. marcher would not have ignored Thorness or the possibility that a man and a girl fleeing for their lives on a winter's evening might be connected with the place and with nefarious reasons for getting away from it.

But Fleming was not really worried about Preen. The streak of anarchy in the man's make-up practically guaranteed that he would not pompously blether about a citizen's duty and so forth. By almost fantastic good fortune they had found a well-nigh perfect ally.

Fleming was far more preoccupied about Andre. He suspected that even her formulated constitution, free from the defects of heredity which were the birth-wrong of every human being, could not battle against the poisonous sepsis in her hands. Somehow he would have to get skilled help for her.

All that day the patrol boats cruised off the island. Late in the afternoon the mist thinned sufficiently for a couple of R.A.F. helicopters to nose around. Fleming was outside when he heard them. Alarmed, he ran back to the cottage. He grabbed a couple of green logs which were smoking on the fire and doused them in a rainwater butt at the back door.

" The choppers may sweep over here," he explained quickly to Preen. " Though I doubt it; a bit tricky to mess around in lousy visibility at zero feet with this hunk of granite in the way. Still, there's no future in arousing their curiosity with a smoking chimney."

Preen mumbled something incoherent and retired to the ingle nook with an obscure volume of Middle English texts to annotate. He had done his best to suppress his misgivings about the continued presence of his visitors, but he left Fleming in no doubt that he would be glad when they were gone.

Andre was sitting placidly on the sofa. She had gone out with Fleming after the makeshift lunch Preen had devised and walked a few steps. The effort had quickly tired her, and she seemed afraid of the loneliness. Fleming carried her back to the cottage.

He was getting more and more worried about her; not only was she physically exhausted and in severe pain but her mind seemed to be more or less a blank. He had noted how she seemed to be unable to make any spontaneous effort except for the basic ones of walking, drinking and eating.

Preen had rustled up some boiled sweets and when he had offered her the tin she had simply stared at it, not recognising their purpose. Fleming had put one in his own mouth and sucked it noisily before she got the idea.

Now, with one ear alert for the sound of the helicopters, Fleming sat beside her, his arm protectively along the back of the sofa and his hand touching her shoulders. " What do you remember of all that's happened?" he asked gently.

She gave him the look of a bewildered child. " It's all jumbled," she murmured. " I ran. Then I fell. In water."

She tried to clasp her hands and drew in her breath sharply at the stab of agony.

Fleming got up, rummaging on the mantelshelf above the half-dead fire for some scissors Preen kept there among a conglomeration of useful articles. " I don't think these rags I put round your hands last night were a very good idea. There's a lot of suppuration. I'll have to cut them away."

With almost feminine gentleness he began to cut into the material, trying to ease it off. He bent over her hands so she could not see them, and he talked quickly to help her ignore the pain.

" Before the running—you remember nothing?" he asked.

She spoke hesitantly, not only because she was searching for memories but in the effort to prevent herself crying out at the throbbing darts of agony. " There was a camp, a kind of camp, with low concrete buildings and huts. We were there, and lots of other people."

Fleming had got most of the matted linen off one hand. What was revealed wasn't pretty. " The machine?" he asked. " Do you remember a machine?"

" Yes," she said, nodding to herself. " It was big and grey. There was always a low hum, and often a lot of clicking. Those were the figures emerging. Everything was in numbers." She frowned and her mouth puckered, as if she was going to cry with frustration. " It's the numbers I can't remember."

" Good," said Fleming. " We can get along without the numbers. They don't mean anything any more to you or anyone. Those numbers were evil; they —— "

He stopped abruptly. The bandage on the other hand had come away easily—too easily. A whole crust of matter came with it. Underneath there wasn't pink, healing flesh, but the ominous purple of necrosis. He could not recognise gangrene, but he had some idea about septicaemia. He bared Andre's arm past her elbow. The sleeve of her dress could not be pushed further up. The arm was swollen, and the main artery stood out dark on the white skin.

" Preen," he said quietly. " Just come over and look at this, will you?"

Their host unwillingly laid down his book and walked across.

40

He glanced down and then abruptly shut his eyes, swaying a little with nausea.

" My dear! " he whispered, " how can you stand it?"

Fleming got up and took Preen across the room to the window. It was quiet outside, with the familiar mist eddying back in whorls from the sea. No helicopter engine marred the silence.

" I hate asking you for another favour," he said, " but could I borrow your boat?"

" Why?" Preen demanded suspiciously. " Where do you want to go with it?"

" To the mainland."

" It isn't seaworthy enough."

"All right, to Skye then," said Fleming impatiently. " I could arrange a meeting on Skye."

" You want to find a doctor, I suppose? Bring him here? That poor girl's hand. . . ." He swallowed down another surge of nausea.

" Not a doctor, something better. I'll not bring anyone here; I promise you."

Preen rather sullenly agreed to loan the boat. Once the decision was made he was anxious for Fleming to go. The sooner he went the sooner he'd be back. And then perhaps he could see some possibility of getting rid of his visitors so that he could be left alone in peace.

He accompanied Fleming down to the little beach where his launch was kept under the shelter of a leaning rock. A jerry-can of petrol stood close by. While they prepared the boat for sea Preen tried to apologise once more for his attitude. He said he would do his best to look after the girl.

" Fine," said Fleming with more optimism than he actually felt. " I shouldn't be gone more than twenty-four hours at the very most. Now, if you can brief me on the course for Skye."

Preen gave a landsman's vague instructions. " The current and what wind there is are always north-west. If you keep heading that way you'll pick up the light buoys at the entry to Loch Harport in under half an hour. I always beach at the end of the loch, where there's a little hamlet with a general shop."

" How far from there to Portree?"

" Over the hills not above ten miles; much longer if you manage to go by road, but you might get a lift in daylight."

41

Fleming glanced at his watch. " I'll walk," he said. " My torch still has plenty of life in it. Should make it well before dawn."

He did. He hung around the outskirts of the little town until people were moving around and it was safe to go to the airport without attracting attention. He got a snack there after checking that the next flight for Oban wasn't due to take off for half an hour.

Then he went to a phone booth. Thorness was an unlisted number and the local exchange was manually operated. He thought he noticed a hesitancy when the operator repeated the number and asked what number he was calling from. It was a risk he had to take. Unless the local police were very quick off the mark and unless Quadring was even quicker in alerting them he'd be away on the plane before anything happened.

He knew, of course, that calls to Thorness were monitored at the station as a matter of routine. In the present crisis this was doubly certain. He had to hope that the tapping was just the usual tape recording for checking later, and not some super snoop who sat in a cubicle eavesdropping on everyone.

Rather to his surprise the call went through in under a minute. He recognised the P.B.X. operator at the station.

" Professor Dawnay," he murmured as quietly as he could. " Professor Madeleine Dawnay. Sick quarters."

" She may be in her room. I'll check."

The operator's voice was in the usual impersonal and efficient tone. Fleming listened closely for any tell-tale click of an extension coming into circuit. There was none.

" Dawnay."

He was surprised how mannish her voice sounded as she gave her name. But he recognised her all right.

" How are you, Madeleine?" he asked.

He heard her intake of breath, and half-speak exclamation his name. It was no more than the J sound. She repressed it instantly. Fleming smiled.

" I phoned to say I hope you're in the pink as it leaves me at present," he said lightly. More slowly and distinctly he went on, " but I'm worried about one health matter. What does one do for burns? You are so expert on them. Not for me, you understand."

For a second or two he thought she had hung up. But eventually she said quietly. " Where?"

42

" Oban. Solo by B.E.A. I shan't have too much time before I must catch a return plane."

" You're a fool," she said calmly. " But as soon as I can. In the airport building."

His flight took barely twenty minutes. He had to wait nearly an hour before Dawnay arrived. He saw her get out of a taxi while he stood looking out of the window in the men's lavatory. He noticed a second car behind hers, and he waited to see who alighted from it. There were three passengers: a middle-aged couple and a small boy, with a couple of suitcases. So that was all right. She hadn't been followed.

He walked leisurely into the foyer and studied a travel poster.

" You're mad to come," he heard her whisper behind him. " But I've got the stuff."

He half turned round and nodded to a hot drink machine in a deserted corner. They walked over to it.

" Tea, coffee, or cocoa?" he asked, handing her a drinking carton, while he fished in his pocket for coins.

" It all tastes the same," she smiled. She took the carton and at the same time passed a little white cardboard box to him. He slipped it in his pocket before he pushed the coin into the slot.

" Thanks," he said. " It's the healing enzyme this time, I hope. Not the one that nearly polished you off."

Dawnay sipped her drink and made a wry face. " They call it coffee. . . . Yes, this lot is all right, I'll guarantee that. It's the original formula the computer gave when she was burned the first time. You remember how perfectly it worked. Sepsis overcome in hours; renewal of the nerve fibrils and lymphatics complete in under three days. How is she?"

Fleming got himself a drink. " Not too bad, except for her hands. I must get back. I don't want a dead girl on the premises."

She glanced at him, amused. " So you think of her as a girl now, do you? But you were mad to come here," she repeated. " I don't know exactly what's doing back at the station, but the search is certainly still on."

He glanced at his watch. " Got to be going," he apologised. "And thanks for the stuff. Talking about madness, you're pretty crazy to be doing this for me; I'm an enemy, or didn't you know?"

" No, I didn't," she answered. "As for doing it for you, I'm doing it for her. She's mine too, don't forget. I made her! "

They walked together towards the departure bay when the public address system announced the flight for Skye and Lewis.

"I don't expect I'll be seeing you again," she said. "I've been offered a new job. No point in staying at Thorness now this Andromeda project is over. It should be quite an experience, new faces, new tasks."

"Where?" he asked.

"In the Middle East, one of those places all sand and oil, but little else."

Fleming wasn't particularly interested. "Best of luck," he said vaguely. He impulsively bent down and kissed her on the cheek. She seemed girlishly pleased.

Fleming passed through the doors to the airport apron. There seemed to be only four or five other passengers—all entirely innocent looking.

He was unaware of a middle-aged man, discreet in black homburg and tweed overcoat, who had been standing beside the magazine kiosk, reading the *Times*. He lowered the paper when Fleming handed his ticket to the B.E.A. girl for checking. Once Fleming had passed from the building the man hurried towards the road exit. The chauffeur in the car parked there immediately started the engine . . .

3

GALE WARNING

FLEMING did not get back to the island until late that evening. He had to wait until darkness before he dared launch the boat which he had heaved up on to the shingle in a small inlet of the loch. The rain poured down remorselessly all the way back, but he was in high spirits and drove the little boat full out. The speed wasn't much, but the noise was considerable. He was so excited about getting back that he did not care whether any search vessels were around to hear him and investigate.

He burst into the cottage with a yell of greeting. Preen was sitting talking to Andre. Her appearance alarmed Fleming. Her face, even in the lamplight, was almost putty coloured. But at the sight of him she stood up and stumbled across to him, throwing herself against him, her arms held high to protect her swollen hands.

"Easy, easy," he whispered to her, clasping her gently. "I've got the repair kit. You'll soon be okay." Over her head he grinned at Preen. "Everything in order. Not arrested or even questioned. And I didn't tell anyone about you!"

Preen was visibly relieved. "I'll get you something to eat while you do whatever you can with her hands . . . An ointment, is it?"

"I suppose you could call it that," Fleming agreed, helping Andre to the sofa. "But a special kind. The only good thing I know of that came out of our inter-galactial tuition. But the less you know about that the better, in case your honest soul should ever be taxed by our lords and masters. You can take it from me that your forebodings about a pretty corpse are over."

He took the little box from his pocket. "Enzymes—a glorious little ferment of living cells, all ready and willing to build anew."

Preen shook his head, bewildered. He went to the kitchen

45

and opened yet another tin of soup. Fleming began immediately on the treatment.

The almost transparent jelly-like material spread quickly when it came in contact with Andre's unnaturally hot, mutilated flesh.

She watched him carefully, without any vestige of a memory that it was she who had programmed the computer to produce the formula, or had interpreted the stream of figures on the output recorders.

Fleming removed her shoes and carefully tucked a blanket around her, placing her hands on a folded towel. " Sleep if you can, my pretty," he murmured. " The pain will ease, slowly but steadily. And in the morning. No pain. You'll see! "

She wriggled lower on the sofa and smiled at him like a trusting child. Obediently she closed her eyes.

All the way back to Thorness, Madeleine Dawnay brooded on the offer of a job in Azaran. Essentially a lonely woman, she had always immersed herself in work as an anodyne for the subconscious unhappiness she felt about her lack of sociability and attractiveness. Her synthesis of living cells, culminating in the development of a female organism which vied with, and in some ways surpassed, natural womanhood had been a triumph which she believed justified her life and held out entrancing promise for the future.

Then came the burns she suffered from the computer and the terrible mistake in the compounding of the healing enzyme formula so that the injections destroyed instead of constructed. Not only did this experience show her the dangers of believing that the half-understood equations from the computer were benign and valuable, but the hovering of death had frightened her more than she would have believed possible.

It was wonderful, of course, to discover that the fault in the enzyme had been entirely in human minds, and that the formula was literally the gift of life. But there remained the nagging suspicion that John Fleming was right. The intelligence which actuated the computer was not impersonal and objective. It had its own purposes, and they did not seem to include the welfare of man.

In any case all the work was over. The glittering prospect of building a scientific technocracy for Britain had evaporated in

46

the smoke from the computer building. She even felt relieved that the great binary code which had reached them out of space, and on which it was all built, had gone up too. She would be glad to get away from it all, to return to ordinary research.

Azaran appealed to her idealism and her curiosity. Here was a little country, temporarily and superficially wealthy on its subterranean El Dorado of oil, but poverty-stricken in the basic needs of fertile land and adequate food for its people.

As soon as she got back to Thorness, she asked for leave to visit the Foreign Office and set off at once for London.

The minor official in the Middle East Department was inclined to dismiss Azaran as a comic opera state. He described the President as a man of dying fire. The revolution which had put him in power and ousted the dynastic ruler just after the war had been a bloodless affair of little international consequence. The President had hastily assured the British oil interests that he would maintain all agreements provided some slight adjustment of the royalty arrangement could be made. This was done after the usual haggling. The President had announced that the revenue would be used to improve the lot of his people.

The desert would blossom through irrigation. Schools would be built. Roads would open up trade. Hospitals would stamp out the diseases which killed one child in five and cut the expectation of life to 32 years. The schools, the roads, and the hospitals had gone up. But the desert remained desert, and now the oil was giving out.

" There's water," the official went on; " a French company sank artesian wells. To the north there's a subterranean lake with more water than the oil deposits to the south. Trouble is the surface. Not even sand; mostly stones and rock. You can irrigate it but it won't grow crops."

" The erosion of several thousand years can't be put right with a bit of water," said Dawnay quietly. " There'd be no official objection to my going?"

" None," the official said, " so far as the F.O. is concerned, that is. We're anxious to maintain our friendly relations with these people. They're a small nation, but any friends are valuable nowadays. The terms of your engagement are naturally not officially our pidgin. You'd be interviewed by Colonel Salim, the ambassador here. He's a slippery customer, though probably it's largely Arab love of intrigue. Anyway, he's probably just the go-between for the President."

Dawnay left the interview, her mind made up. She would take the job if the terms were reasonable. A taxi deposited her at the Azaran Embassy fifteen minutes later.

She was ushered into Salim's office without delay. Rather to her surprise, he seemed to know all about her career and he discussed her work with considerable intelligence. More or less as an afterthought he mentioned the salary. It was fantastically large and he heard her slight gasp.

"By British standards the income is high," he smiled, "but this is Azaran, and one commodity we have in plenty at present is money. The Europeans—doctors, engineers and so on—who work for us need some compensation for absence from their homeland and the fact that of necessity the job is not for life. In your case we had in mind a contract for five years, renewable by mutual arrangement.

"But it's the work which would interest you. We are an ancient nation stepping late into the twentieth century, Miss Dawnay. Eighty per cent. of our food has to be imported. We need to have a programme of vision and scientific validity to make our country as fertile as it is rich." He hesitated. "For reasons that will become clear shortly this will become more and more vital for our future, even for our very existence."

Dawnay hardly heard his final words. The old excitement about a problem of nature which challenged the ingenuity of the mind had taken hold of her.

"Colonel Salim," she said quietly, "I'll be proud to help. I am free to go as soon as you wish." She smiled a little ruefully. "As you may know from what seems to be a comprehensive survey of my background, I have no private ties, no relatives, to hold me here. And for reasons I can't go into, my recent work is now completed."

Salim gave her a large, warm smile. "I shall telephone my President immediately," he said. "I know he will be deeply grateful. Meantime, there are the usual international formalities to be seen to—inoculations, vaccination, passport, and so forth. Shall we say the day after tomorrow—about 10 a.m.—to complete the arrangements? I can then discuss the actual time of your departure."

Dawnay agreed. The decision made, she was anxious to be

48

gone. She telephoned Thorness and had her batwoman pack her few belongings and put the cases on the train. Ruefully she told herself that apart from a mass of books in her old room at Edinburgh University she owned nothing else in the world. Nor was there a close friend to whom she had to say goodbye.

She went shopping the following morning, getting a Knightsbridge department store to fit her out with tropical kit. She reduced the salesgirl to despair by approving the first offer of everything she was shown. It was all done in a couple of hours. The store agreed to deliver the purchases, packed in cases, to London Airport when instructed.

Next morning she found a doctor and had her inoculations. They made her a little feverish and she rested in her hotel room that afternoon and evening. Promptly at 10 a.m. on the following day she presented herself at the Azaran Embassy.

Salim greeted her courteously, but he was ill at ease, half listening to a powerful short-wave radio from which, amid considerable static, a stream of Arabic spluttered quietly.

" Splendid, Professor Dawnay," he said eventually, after glancing cursorily at the passport and inoculation certificates. " Here are your visa and air tickets. I have provisionally booked you on the 9.45 flight the day after tomorrow. Will that be suitable?"

Before she could reply he sprang up, rushing to the radio and turning up the volume. He listened attentively for a couple of minutes and then snapped off the switch.

"That was the announcement of our freedom," he said dreamily.

" But you *are* free! " Dawnay looked at him in surprise.

He turned to her. " Political freedom is a matter of paper and ideals. Real freedom is a matter of business. We have at last broken off our ties with your country; we have renounced all our oil and trade agreements." He indicated the radio. " That is what you heard." He smiled at her again. " You can see why we need the right people to help us. I shall be returning to Azaran myself as soon as diplomatic affairs are cleared up here. We want to remain on friendly terms with Britain; with all countries. But we need to be independent in the best sense of the word. So you will help us! "

Dawnay felt slightly disturbed at this sudden turn of events. Throughout her career she had studiously avoided politics, believing that scientists were above party and national factions, their duty being to the welfare of mankind. " I hope I can do something," she murmured politely.

Salim did not appear to be listening. He began frowning over the documents she had handed to him. " No yellow fever inoculation?" he queried. " Surely you were notified that it's necessary?"

" I don't think so," she replied. " But I can have it done today."

He stood up and smiled ingratiatingly. " I can do better than that. It so happens that the embassy doctor is here this morning."

He pressed a switch on his intercom. "Ask Miss Gamboul if she can manage another yellow fever inoculation," he told a secretary.

There was a pause and then a man's voice replied that Miss Gamboul could do so.

Again the sense of misgiving prodded Dawnay's brain. For a moment she could not identify the reason. Then she found it. A woman doctor was not usually described as Miss. She dismissed the suspicion as trivial, putting it down to Salim's incomplete knowledge of English.

While they awaited the doctor's arrival he came round and leaned against the desk, close to Dawnay. " Tell me about a colleague of yours, a Dr. John Fleming. I believe he worked with you at that Scottish research station. Is he still there?"

" I can't say," she answered shortly.

" I heard one report that he was dead."

" I'm afraid I can't tell you anything about him." Her tone was all he needed to tell him that Fleming was alive, but he did not react to it. He looked up instead at the opening door.

"Ah, Miss Gamboul! "

A woman in a white coat had entered without knocking. She was dark-haired and rather attractive and—one could put it no closer than that—somewhere in her thirties. She had a flawless skin, and a good brow above fine dark eyes; but she did not look in the least like a doctor. Even in her white coat she gave an impression of sensuousness and haute couture; Dawnay felt sure that she was more used to being called Mademoiselle than Miss.

And yet there was a surprising degree of professional intelligence and seriousness in her face. Dawnay did not like the hardness in her eyes nor the thin red-pencilled line of her mouth, but most of all Dawnay did not like people to be enigmatic.

She noticed that the nails on the hand which clutched a napkin-covered white dish from which the base of a hypodermic protruded were varnished bright red and the ends were pointed. Dawnay glanced automatically at her own stubby, close-cut nails. Neither doctors nor scientists, she felt, should allow themselves such unhygienic luxuries as long nails and lacquer.

"Now, Professor Dawnay, which arm would you like punctured?" Her voice was business-like; she had a strong French accent, Dawnay realised with satisfaction.

Stifling her instant dislike of the woman, she said she would prefer to be injected in the right arm. She removed her coat and pushed up the sleeve of her blouse.

Mademoiselle Gamboul dabbed her upper arm with a wad of spirit-soaked cotton wool. Dawnay looked away when the needle went in. It was badly done and the clumsy jab made her wince.

Salim had not moved away. He watched the inoculation as if fascinated. He began to talk rapidly. "You'll have every facility for your work when you get to our capital, which is called Baleb. We have recently completed building the laboratories. Anything you need —— "

His voice seemed to thicken, and his swarthy face, looking down at her still bared arm, became hazy.

She tried to fight off the sense of dizziness.

"Can—can I have a glass of water?" she faltered. "I can't be as fit yet as I thought . . ."

Her head slumped forward. She felt the hardness of the rim of a glass pressed against her lips and she drank some water. Her vision cleared a little, and she saw the red fingernails around the glass.

From an immeasurable distance, yet clear and menacing, came Salim's voice again.

"Now, where is Dr. Fleming? If you know, you will tell us every detail. Now, I repeat, where is he?"

As if it were some other woman talking, Dawnay heard herself meticulously describing her meeting at Oban airport. Word for word she repeated her conversation with John as if she were reading from a play script. Her memory was crystal clear. And she could not stop until she had explained every detail of the meeting.

Salim laughed. " So that is how a truth drug works." He looked at Dawnay with interest.

Janine Gamboul nodded. " Sodium amytal. It'll work off in five or ten minutes. She'll remember nothing. Tell her she fainted with the yellow fever injection or whatever it was. And see you get her on that plane."

She took off her white coat, revealing a dress which had indeed come from Paris, and a good deal of herself as well. Although she was no longer a girl, the skin of her throat and the upper curves of her bosom looked as young and smooth as her face. She seemed completely relaxed and at ease. She perched on a corner of the table and looked at Salim with a mixture of malice and amusement as she lit a cigarette and slowly and delicately inhaled and exhaled. Salim watched her with something like admiration until she spoke again. " Repeat what you've heard to our man Kaufman," she told him without any effort at grace. " He is unimaginative but resourceful. Tell him that speed is vital. And this girl Fleming has with him. The one he got the medicament for. Tell Kaufman to bring her too."

" But she is nothing," protested Salim. " The man's mistress, one presumes. What do we need with her? We can supply reliable girls once Fleming's out in Baleb. They'll help to keep him happy."

" Nevertheless," said Gamboul, " we will have her."

Salim obediently lifted the receiver of the telephone. It took some time to locate Kaufman. The hotel where he had reported he was staying said that their guest was out tramping; the receptionist volunteered the information that Mr. Kaufman was a great one for the open air and the rolling hills of Scotland. Salim cut her short and grunted that he would ring again. He had no wish to leave his number.

When eventually he got through and Kaufman's guttural voice answered the extension to his bedroom Salim talked rapidly. " We have reliable news. An island off an island near an island." He stopped, aware of the ridiculousness of his words. "A moment, I have written down the names of these places of which I have never before heard. Ah yes, there is a place called Skye? "

" Of course," grunted Kaufman. " I have been. Our friend was seen taking a plane there. But no information."

"And near this Skye is Soay." Kaufman opened a map and

located the word which he could pronounce no better than the Ambassador.

"Good, you have it," said Salim. "Near this Soay there is perhaps a smaller island? "

"I'll need a more detailed map," came Kaufman's voice. " I know there are several. We had better end this call, I think. You may leave things to me."

"I hope so. I have done my part. Now it is up to you." Salim replaced the phone. Kaufman folded up the map and considered.

First he made his plans for a discreet survey of the off-shore islands around Skye. He put in a couple of calls to Glasgow to enrol some assistants whose co-operation for adequate reward had been tested on some previous matters. Then he moved to Portree. There he hired a powerful little launch on the pretext of photographing sea birds. The well-paid owner did not question Kaufman's statement that he specialised in taking flashlight photos by night of their roosting habits. Bird watchers were all queer—but profitable.

The lonely peace of Preen's island pushed time into the background. Fleming mentally noted the fact that it took two days for Andre's hands to start building new flesh; on the third there was no need for bandages.

Life by then had settled down into a rather pointless round of waking, preparing scratch meals from Preen's store of canned and dehydrated food laid down in quantities literally to outlast a war, arguing over a game of chess, and gently helping Andre's memory to re-discover the threads of life.

There was little opportunity to go out even to check the fish nets Preen had laid down in rocky inlets, but one still, misty day Andromeda went down alone to the small beach and when she came back to the croft she was looking puzzled.

"The mist is going back into the sea," she said in her slow, vacant way.

Fleming did not believe her and she never had an opportunity of proving it, for the weather changed again to an interminable frenzy of storm and gale. There seemed to be no end to the restlessness of the sky and sea. When they listened in on Preen's transistor the forecast invariably included gale warnings, and the weather was so wild throughout the northern hemisphere that it was usually mentioned in the news bulletins. Andre continued to look vacant and confused and began to grow a little clumsy.

But there was a sense of impregnable security within the cottage while the wind howled and battered outside. The tension which Fleming had felt at first whenever the door rattled violently or something banged outside had eased to a pleasant fatalistic calm.

Consequently he was quite unprepared one night when, as he was quietly playing chess with Preen and Andre was half-lying on the sofa staring at nothing, the door cracked loudly and immediately burst open. He sprang to his feet, knocking over the chessboard. Three men were grouped in the doorway. They were thickset, brutal and wild-looking. The water streamed from their oilskins and their tousled heads.

The tallest of them took a step inside, jerking his head to the other two to back him up. He never took his eyes off Fleming, so that he did not see Preen open the chest, grabbing his automatic rifle from inside it.

" Get out! Get out of here! " Preen bleated, prancing from side to side. His anger at this new invasion of his isolation made him oblivious of danger.

Fleming had moved back to protect Andre. She clung close to him, watching wide-eyed. " Better do what the gentleman says," Fleming advised the intruders.

The leading man stepped backwards, bumping into the two behind him. They half-stumbled as they hit the doorposts. Suddenly the leader dug into his oilskin pocket. In a flash he was pointing the snout of a Luger at Preen.

" Look out! " yelled Fleming.

Without taking aim, Preen fired a burst. Five or six explosions of high velocity bullets reverberated round the room. Glass from the window tinkled on the floor. The man with the gun collapsed without a sound, his mouth agape, his eyes still fixed straight ahead. One of the others screamed like a child and staggered drunkenly into the darkness, collapsing outside. The third simply fled, his footsteps crashing along the stony track to the sea.

Preen had dropped the gun at the force of the recoil. But he started to charge after the third intruder, his mouth working

54

in frenzy of anger. " Hold it, Preen," Fleming yelled. " Don't go outside. There may be more."

Preen did not seem to hear. He was still in the light from the open door when a gun barked from the darkness. Preen stopped dead in his tracks, spun round, and fell to his knees, groaning.

" Take this," said Fleming, picking up the rifle and thrusting it into Andre's hands. " If you see anyone, point it at him and pull this." He crooked her finger round the trigger.

Then, crouching low, he ran outside and sprawled beside Preen. He waited for a moment for bullets to come spurting out of the dark at him, but nothing happened. All he could hear was Preen's agonised breathing. "All right," he said, " you're not dead. I'll get you inside and patch you up."

He started dragging him towards the door. He paused while he heaved the body on the path out of the way. The man was quite dead, like the one outside the cottage. He motioned Andre to put down the gun and she helped him to get Preen on to the couch.

Fleming dragged the other body out over the step and then shut the door. The bolt was useless but the catch still held. He paused to get his breath before he examined Preen.

Blood was spreading through his sweater below the armpit. Fleming cut the material away and pulled the shirt aside. The blood was not spurting. But there was a neat hole at the side of the chest and another more ragged one below the shoulder blade where the bullet had come out.

No blood was coming from Preen's mouth, so Fleming felt sure that the lung had not been pierced; the worst was a chipped or broken rib.

" You're not badly hurt, Adrian," he said. " I'll put on a pad to staunch the bleeding; and then we'll use the old magic treatment. Just leave it to your old Professor! "

He made Preen as comfortable as possible, talking optimistically about the enzyme. His optimism seemed to convince the watching, worried Andre, though he himself did not really believe in it. The little which was left after Andre's treatment would doubtless tackle sepsis and re-create the surface skin. It could not deal with splintered or broken bone, nor with any internal injury.

He resigned himself to the fact that in the morning he would have to go over to Skye and get a doctor. And he would have to let the police know that a couple of corpses were lying around.

Meantime there was the puzzle of who the thugs were. When Preen fell asleep and Andre was dozing in the easy chair he cautiously crept outside and looked over the dead men with the aid of a flashlight. They looked even uglier in death than they had in life. Both carried wallets, but the contents were money only; no driving licence, no envelopes or letters. The absence of identifying items was in itself suspicious. His mind went back to the time he and Bridger had been shot at when they had taken a day off from building the computer. Bridger had clearly known what the attack was all about, and badgered by Fleming he had impatiently snapped out the word " Intel ", regretting it as if he had said too much.

It had seemed ridiculous at the time to link a secretive but perfectly legitimate world-wide trading cartel with gunmen lurking on a Scottish moor. But after Bridger's murder the word had always had a sinister flavour in Fleming's mind.

That a commercial enterprise should use strong-arm tactics to obtain secrets of the kind Thorness could provide did not really surprise Fleming once he had accepted the situation. It was in accord with his conception of the rat race of individuals and nations to amass wealth and exert power. That was why he did not find it difficult to accept a theory that Intel was behind this abortive attack, though the motive remained a mystery. If the information they had obtained from Bridger had been even superficially right the brains behind Intel must be aware that the individuals counted for nothing without the machine they served. Not even Andre could provide saleable information.

Not even Andre——. Fleming very rarely displayed fear, but like any intelligent man he often felt it. He felt it now, and Andre was the reason. One of the assailants had got away. He would no doubt be back sometime with reinforcements, and they would come prepared for a shooting battle. He had no wish to die himself; but he dreaded far more the plan Intel might have for the girl. It was another reason why he would get help.

He took Preen's boat for Skye at dawn. He phoned for a doctor from the first house he found with a telephone, explaining that the patient was suffering from a shot wound and adding that there were also two corpses to be picked up. The doctor informed the police before he set out. By then Fleming was well on the way back.

Fleming had the mischievous pleasure of shouting out, " I'll come quietly!" as a boat-load of police arrived at the cottage door later in the day.

It was all very sedate and polite. They treated Andre and him with deference, hardly knowing what it was all about. They let him remain beside Preen until the doctor had made his examination and reported that there was little wrong, but an x-ray would be needed to check for bone injuries. Fleming noted with amusement that the doctor could not get his eyes off the tiny circles of young healthy flesh already growing around the bullet wounds.

"And this happened only last night? " he kept muttering.

They were taken down to a police launch where Preen was laid in the stern, comfortably wrapped in blankets. A constable was left behind to watch over the two bodies, which would be picked up later when the C.I.D. from Inverness had made their usual on-the-spot checks.

Fleming and Andre said goodbye to Preen when they disembarked on Skye. Their involuntary host seemed almost distraught at the parting. "You must come again," he said.

" If we ever get out of the Tower, we certainly will," Fleming grinned.

Expressing soft Highland apologies, the station police sergeant said that he would have to put his prisoners in a cell when they got to Portree.

" It's forbye a murder case, ye'll be understanding," he said. " But it'll be the Inspector to decide on a charge, if there's to be one. I'm going to permit the young lady to be with you. I'll have your word of no trouble, sir? "

" Of course," said Fleming. " We're grateful for your hospitality."

They had to wait in the cells for a couple of hours. The sergeant's wife sent in two steaming plates of mutton stew. Both ate ravenously. It was good to eat a proper meal after Preen's diet of soup and vegetables.

Then Quadring arrived. He was smiling. But not with any touch of triumph. He seemed relieved to see them both alive and well.

" You've given us one hell of a chase, Fleming," he said. "You are all right, my dear? " he added, looking hard at Andre. " Well, as you may imagine, your bosses are very excited at the way you've both turned up, particularly Dr. Geers. I'm afraid I have instructions to take you to London right away. There'll be a Transport Command plane touching down presently."

" I expected that," Fleming replied. " But I hope you'll get your sleuthing powers working on just who the gentlemen were who visited us last night."

"Any ideas? " Quadring asked.

Fleming hesitated. " Nothing definite," he answered.

The failure of Intel's attempt to kidnap Fleming and Andre had caused consternation as much as anger in Kaufman's mind. He had learned to be completely unprincipled in the service of whoever paid him, but he had a distaste for personal violence. He had tried to explain this to a war crimes court back in 1947 when he sat in the dock along with the riff-raff from one of the minor camps. He had vehemently protested that he had never laid a hand on a single Jew or gipsy prisoner; his only connexion with the extermination section had been to supply them with his carefully tabulated lists of outworked and over-age prisoners. The court had been obtuse; they had sentenced him to seven years, reduced by his perfect behaviour to five.

The charming man who had then offered him a confidential post with Intel had been the first person to appreciate the virtues of Herr Kaufman's life. " We like to use men like you," he had said.

And now he had badly let down these considerate and generous employers. Two men shot dead and a third getting out of the country as fast as he could. His frantic report over the phone to Salim had not been an experience he would like repeated. Unkind things had been said; even threats. Salim had appeared to be repeating the words of someone else in the room, judging from the way he constantly paused. Finally Kaufman had been told to be at Oban airport and await a caller. A director of Intel coming from Vienna. Kaufmann had never previously met any executive above district manager.

Nervously he hung around the airport building. An hour passed, then another. Beads of sweat glistened on his close-cropped head despite the coldness of the day. He wanted to run away. But he knew he dared not. For one thing it would be disobedience of orders; for another he was Intel's employee for life; there had been so many things he had done on their behalf which were in the crime dossiers of the police of a dozen countries. . . .

" So you are here. . . ."

It was a woman's voice. Kaufman spun around and saw Janine Gamboul. He grinned with relief. So they were going to use the old trick of feminine allure to get hold of Fleming.

But he had to be cautious. " Excuse? " he said gutturally. " You are . . . ? "

She ignored his question. " You are Kaufman. Where is Fleming? "

" But Colonel Salim said a director from Vienna. . . ." Kaufman mumbled.

She cut him short. " So naturally you imagined a man."

" You are . . . ? " he stuttered. Then he was all deference and politeness. " I am sorry, I did not realise."

" I repeat, where is Dr. Fleming? Or have you frightened him off? "

" He is at the same place. The little island. It was not my fault. Two men were killed. And I am not a gunman."

She walked towards the airport café, not troubling to see whether he followed. He rushed ahead to open the door for her. When they were seated at a table in a quiet corner she lighted a cigarette and drew in a deep lungful of smoke.

" We shall arrange things better this time," she murmured. " We must have Fleming quickly. Nothing is more vital."

" May I ask why? " he muttered.

She gazed at him with impatient contempt. " To help us with some equipment. He has some special knowledge we need." She gave him a cold smile. " It's really the result of your commendable activities on behalf of the company. Stupid you may be, but you are loyal and energetic. I think you should have been told before."

She dropped her voice to a murmur. " When we heard that a message had been received from space you recall that you were told to make contact with Dr. Denis Bridger, Fleming's partner. You did well, Kaufman. From Bridger you got the specification for making a computer to interpret the message."

"Nothing ever came of it," said Kaufman mournfully. "Bridger—er—got himself killed."

"So you think nothing came of it?" she laughed. "We have been building a copy of that computer; in Azaran. Only now we need a little expert advice. Salim has got Professor Dawnay, but she was only indirectly involved. She'll possibly be useful. But Fleming will be essential."

Kaufman felt relieved. Even happy. He ventured to light a cigarello.

"So you see, Herr Kaufman," Janine Gamboul finished, stubbing out her cigarette, "this time there must be no mistake in enrolling Doctor Fleming on our staff."

4

SQUALL LINES

THE attendants in the Palais des Nations at Geneva told one another that there had not been such a smoothly running international conference for years. Russians nodded cheerfully as their interpreters repeated the heart-felt views of an American delegate. Even the French were inviting ideas for co-operative effort. In fact, the whole thing was almost boring.

The reason was that the subject under discussion was the weather. Everyone could agree that it was undeniably bad. As gales blew indiscriminately over East and West, and abnormally heavy rainfall was prevalent throughout the Northern hemisphere, no sensitive nationalist could find an excuse for blaming his neighbour.

A few nations, imaginative enough to realise that weather control was within the realms of possibility, had sent scientists as well as meteorologists to Geneva in the hopes of getting some agreement about methods and policy before haphazard experiments began. Britain was among them. That was why the Ministry of Science had despatched Obsorne as an *ex officio* delegate.

Osborne had gone, disturbed in mind. Despite inter-departmental briefs which had been circulated to draw attention to climatic phenomena for which there was no precedent, this weather conference seemed really of just academic interest— one of those United Nations' activities which kept a lot of people happy and did no one any harm. Osborne wondered whether the trip had been arranged as a preliminary to a transfer to some innocuous department like Met. as the result of the suspicions of his complicity in the Thorness business.

The Minister had been remarkably considerate about the whole thing. Security officers were still interviewing personnel, and Osborne's assistant had become very nervous and timid. Osborne had brightly insisted that if they both stuck to the story that the assistant had accompanied him to Thorness on that momentous night all would be well. It was perfectly normal for a senior official to go around with his P.A. Rather unwillingly the assistant agreed to stick to his story. Osborne suspected that real pressure by the sleuths, or the simpler method of putting the young man on oath, would exact the truth. It was another reason why he would have preferred to remain in Whitehall to watch for a weakening of his assistant's resolution and to give moral support.

Once in Geneva, he decided to make the best of it. Whatever foulness the winter was producing elsewhere, in the Alps it just meant more than the usual amount of snow. Heavy night falls were followed by brilliant sunshine with clockwork regularity. The lake lay ice-blue in the brightness; the famous fountain spurted high in the sky, its spray in rainbow colours. The clean, snow-cleared streets were alive with delegates and their relatives enjoying themselves between sessions.

When he looked through the tall windows of the rooftop café at this pleasant scene he thoroughly regretted the time spent in the close and over-heated conference room. But Professor Neilson's paper had not been without interest. These Americans certainly got down to bedrock when there was a problem to be solved.

Osborne had left before the discussion began—with its inevitable pointless questions which were really statements. He was lazily watching his café filtre drip into the glass when a woman approached his table. She was not young, but looked intelligent and pleasant.

" Mr. Osborne? " Her accent was American.

Osborne stood up. " Yes," he answered. " I don't think I know—."

She smiled. " I'm Professor Neilson's wife." They shook hands and Osborne pulled out the adjoining chair. She sat down.

" I'm afraid you've missed your husband's paper," he began. " He's just finished reading it. Everyone was most impressed. He'll be out soon; the discussion should be almost over."

She did not seem to be heeding what he said. " Mr. Osborne," she said quietly, " I think my husband would like to talk to you. Not about the conference." She glanced towards the door where a crowd of delegates were moving around the foyer. " If you could possibly wait till he comes. I'd rather let him tell you what it's about."

" Of course," Osborne said. " Meantime, may I order you something? "

She nodded. " Some coffee, please."

When Neilson arrived he looked round carefully, then sat down and addressed himself without any preamble to Osborne.

" I suppose my wife has left it to me to tell you. I badly want to talk. I'll come to the point. How much do you know about an outfit called Intel? "

Osborne took time to decide on his answer. " They're a big international trading consortium. Very big."

" Sure," agreed Neilson, " they're big. The thing is: are they reputable? "

" I don't really know," Osborne said cautiously.

" Mr. Osborne," said Mrs. Neilson. " This morning we had a cable from our son. We haven't seen him for two years. All the cable said was ' Will meet you at the café Nicole in Geneva one evening this week, Intel permitting ' It's the first clue that he was even alive we've gotten since the Christmas before last."

" But you knew more or less where he was and what he was doing? " Osborne suggested.

Neilson gave a short laugh. " He went after a job in Vienna two years back. A postcard said he was okay and not to worry. That's all."

" What sort of job? " Osborne asked.

" Well, I guess that as he graduated from the Massachussetts Institute with a Ph.D. in electronics, it'd be a job in that line."

" I believe Intel have an office here, or certainly in Zurich. Have you enquired? "

" Of course," Mrs. Neilson replied. " They said they knew nothing about the staffs at the firm's offices outside Switzerland. That's why I persuaded my husband to ask you for information."

" But why?" Osborne demanded.

" Because you're a friend of a friend of my son's," Neilson said. " John Fleming. Jan brought him home a couple of times when Fleming came to the Institute on an exchange set-up with the Cavendish Laboratory at Cambridge. They were great buddies. And, of course, we know Fleming became a key man in your Ministry's programme."

"I don't think there's anything I can do to help you," said Osborne woodenly. "We've lost touch with Professor Fleming. . . ." He paused, embarrassed, and then went on hurriedly, "but I'm not returning to London till the day after tomorrow. Perhaps I could meet your son? If he says in his cable that he's coming this week it must mean either this evening or tomorrow."

The Neilsons were grateful. They invited him to have dinner with them at the café that evening, and, if Jan didn't turn up then, the following evening as well.

That evening Mrs. Neilson insisted on going to the café by seven. "I'll sit in the front part," she told her husband; "then he'll be sure to see me. We can go into the dining room later."

She ordered a kirsch and was taking the first sip when he materialised out of the dusk and sat down beside her without speaking; a pale, serious young man, very much on edge. She was shocked by the way he had aged and got so lean; and by how nervous he seemed. He kissed her on the cheek, but he pulled his hand away when she tried to clasp it.

"Please don't make us conspicuous, Mom," he muttered. "I'm sorry if that hurts you. But—well, you see, I've good reasons." He stubbed out a half-smoked cigarette.

"Surely, son," his mother said, trying to smile. "I understand. But at least you're here. I can look at you. It's been so long."

The love in her eyes hurt him. "Mom," he began, hunching towards her across the table. "I've got to talk, and I may not have much time. You see, I'm on the run. No," he tried to smile, "I'm not a criminal. The shoe's on the other foot. The crooks are after me."

He paused when a waiter came for his order. He sent the man away for a large Scotch, and then started to talk, hurriedly and a little incoherently, as if time was running out.

Soon Neilson arrived with Osborne. The two men had met just outside the café. Neilson greeted his son with delight, thumping him on the back and grinning happily. "We'll celebrate this with the biggest steak the Swiss can think up. And champagne." He remembered Osborne was standing quietly beside them.

"My apologies, Osborne," he said. "I'd like you to meet my son . . . Jan, Mr. Osborne is a friend of Professor Fleming."

Osborne had just extended his hand when a youth with a flashgun and a cumbersome plate camera came up.

" Professor Neilson," he shouted at them. " Un moment, s'il vous plait. A picture, please. For the American press."

He bustled around, pushing all four into positions he wanted for the photograph. Jan he had standing between his seated mother and father, Osborne well to one side. Satisfied, he backed towards the café entrance, peering into the range-finder.

" Bon! " he exclaimed. The flash momentarily blinded everyone with its burst of white light.

Simultaneously Jan fell sideways against his father, moaning. The photographer disappeared into the street, and a gentleman who had been reading a newspaper at a table beside the door put on his hat, slid something black and shiny into the breast pocket of his overcoat and walked quite unhurriedly after the photographer.

The Neilson's were bent over their son, but Osborne had seen the careful and methodical movements of the man near the door. He had seen what that black thing shoved inside the coat was, noticing the squat round cylinder of a silencer on the muzzle of the gun. He loped through the door—in time to see a Citroen, its number plate covered in frozen slush, pick up photographer and gunman and cruise away along the lakeside road which led to Vevey and the frontier.

He returned to the Neilsons. " It's no good," he said gently. " They got away."

The Neilsons took no notice. They were isolated by their grief as they awkwardly nursed the body of their dead son, one on each side.

Mrs. Neilson looked helplessly at her husband. " He—he told me he feared this," she moaned. " They've been hunting him for months. They kept him prisoner before that, but he escaped. They made him work."

" Who did? " her husband exclaimed. " Where could he have been imprisoned? "

She began caressing Jan's hair, touching his eyelids. " He said it was in a country called Azaran."

In a discreet house on the outskirts of Berne Kaufman was compiling the details of the report he had to send his employers.

The gunman stood at the side of the bureau desk, eyeing the bundle of American dollars which he had earned.

"So the pictureman was late," Kaufman said; "he will be reprimanded in due course. But you are sure you killed the Neilson boy before he could talk?"

"He wouldn't talk much after he was hit," the gunman laughed. "But he talked plenty before. To his mother. And she can talk to her husband—and to some Englishman the old man brought with him. He was introduced to the boy as Osborne."

Kaufman sighed. "Osborne. It would have to be. All this killing. I dislike it. One death—and you have to organise another. So it goes on."

He pushed the money to the corner of the desk. The gunman stuck it inside his coat, a cushion for the revolver which lay there.

"Get out of the country right away," Kaufman told him. "As for me, I shall have to return to England."

Andre and Fleming were flown to the R.A.F. station at Northolt to avoid publicity problems at London Airport. A Government car awaited them on the apron and they were driven straight to the Ministry of Science.

The Minister had decided to handle the interview personally, with Geers sitting in to brief him on the technical side. He had a foreboding about questions in the House some time or other about this business if the secret leaked, and he had no intention of having to admit inefficiency. He was also a just man, which was why he had called a solicitor from the Attorney General's office to sit in and watch over the normal rights of a British citizen. His worried mind found a touch of humour there. Was the girl a British citizen? She had no birth certificate; no parents. So far as Somerset House was concerned she did not exist. It was an interesting point if this affair ever came to a legal trial. He fervently hoped it wouldn't.

The Minister greeted his visitors coldly. But he went out of his way to stress that this was in no sense a trial; it was an informal enquiry.

Fleming, untidy and doing his best to disguise the strain he felt, laughed sardonically. "Very informal," he said. "I noticed the informally dressed plain clothes nark hanging around the

66

door just in case I might make a run for it. Ah, and my dear Geers is here as well."

The Minister ignored him and turned to Andre. " Sit down, my dear," he said gently. " You must be very tired. But this is unfortunately necessary."

He sat at his desk and re-read the brief report of the preliminary questioning Quadring had sent by tele-type.

" I'm informed that you are suffering from amnesia," he began, and motioned to Geers.

Geers rose from his chair to the Minister's right and confronted the girl. "Andromeda," he said harshly. " Surely you haven't forgotten the factors involved in the synthesis of living tissue? Do you really mean to tell us you know nothing about the fact that one of the formulae obtained from the computer on which you worked enabled Professor Dawnay to construct living matter in the laboratory? And that the outcome of that work was you yourself? "

Andre looked back at him, wide-eyed but quite calm, with the placidity of a child. She slowly shook her head.

Geers' face flushed with frustration and anger. " You're not going to insist that you can't remember your work with the computer? "

The solicitor coughed discreetly. " I think that is enough, Dr. Geers," he said mildly. To Andre he murmured, " Don't worry to answer all these questions just now."

" I agree," said the Minister, glaring at Geers. " The girl's unfit and distraught. Perhaps we can have her history properly explained to her in a calmer atmosphere."

Fleming strode forward to the desk. " That's the last thing! " he shouted.

The Minister looked at him coldly. " I beg your pardon."

Hurriedly the solicitor interposed. " I think that my professional advice would be that this lady must testify once she is medically fit and has been properly informed of the past. Her evidence would, of course, have to be before a properly constituted Board of Enquiry."

" I could brief her," Geers said eagerly.

The Minister looked at him with hardly concealed distaste. " I would have preferred Osborne if circumstances had been different. In any case, he cannot be brought back from Geneva until tomorrow." He smiled at Andre. " Perhaps you'll wait in the ante-room while we talk to Dr. Fleming?"

Fleming crossed to the door and opened it. He smiled reassuringly at her as she went out.

" Now, Dr. Fleming, why did you abduct this woman? " The Minister's gentle tone had changed.

" That's beside the point," Fleming retorted truculently.

" Then what is the point? "

" That the message from the Andromeda nebulae, and all that derived from it, was evil." Deliberately he forced himself to speak calmly and quietly. " It was sent by a superior intelligence that would subjugate us, and would have, if necessary, destroyed us."

"And because you thought that, you destroyed the computer." The Minister's tone was grim, though the inflexion suggested he was posing a question rather than making a statement. " Yet you seem to be ready to do anything to protect the girl who worked it. Your contention surely involves her in your condemnation."

" The girl is nothing without the computer. The will, the memory, the knowedge—they were all in the machine. You can see there's something lacking in her now that the computer no longer exists—thank God. Something missing in her character. Ask Geers; he knows what she was like . . ."

The Minister ignored the invitation. He had no intention of getting involved in by-ways of ethics when he believed the issue was far simpler.

" I put it to you, Dr. Fleming, that you destroyed the computer and you abducted the girl because she might have told us what happened."

" I took her because she needed to be protected from the people around her." Fleming looked at Geers.

The Minister picked up a sheet of paper tucked into the bulky file before him. " Perhaps you'd care to comment on the fact that Mr. Osborne's assistant, the man supposed to have accompanied him to Thorness on the night of the fire, admitted when questioned late this afternoon that he did not go there."

" You'll have to ask Osborne who he did take, won't you? " said Fleming.

" We shall," the Minister glowered. " In the meantime, Dr. Fleming, you must consider yourself under surveillance. To avoid the necessity of formal arrest and indictment at Bow Street, with all the unpleasant sensationalism affecting both ourselves and you and the girl, I hope you will co-operate sensibly. I cannot force you to be our guest without a charge. But we can arrange very pleasant accommodation."

" So Magna Carta still operates? " said Fleming sarcastically. " If I insist on being arrested, on what grounds could you cook up a charge? "

" Defence Regulations," murmured the solicitor. " The relevant Acts would be —— "

" Spare me the details," Fleming interrupted. " I'll come quietly. And where is this—er—hotel for unwelcome guests of the Government? "

" Not too far away," said the Minister vaguely. " It will do you good, or at least the girl will benefit. A glimpse of more spacious days of the kind one pays 2s. 6d. on Sundays to inspect. I'm afraid I can't be more specific than that. The army's been using part of it ever since 1942. It would be best, I think, if you went there right away and both got a good night's rest. You may see things more clearly, even sensibly, in the morning."

The car journey took a couple of hours. Even Fleming could find no fault with the accommodation or service. Someone used to this sort of thing had arranged for every comfort—drinks, clean clothes, books, baths, everything. Andre was as lavishly provided. Fleming was, however, not over-enamoured with the solid-looking maidservants who hovered around. Their white overalls did not disguise their regulation hair styles and their khaki nylon stockings and sturdy black shoes. Fleming had never approved of women in the armed services.

But he found the clumsiness of the 6 ft. waiter who served their excellent dinner amusing. There was something about a policeman which could never be disguised, not even when he was a member of the Special Branch.

Otherwise they were left to themselves in the days that followed. They could walk as much as they liked around the vast parkland. Fleming noticed that Andre seemed to be growing increasingly vacant and that she stumbled quite often even on the smooth grass. He also noted that the chain link fence was the usual Government type, precisely like that round Thorness. The old gatehouse at the entrance to the main drive had been visibly transformed into a guard room. The guard carried an automatic rifle.

One afternoon Andre was taken away. Geers had arrived and wanted to talk with her. She spent many hours of the ensuing day with the scientist. He did his work well. Andre emerged thoughtful though still curiously unmoved. She told Fleming that she accepted that all Geers had said was true, but it was like the life outline of some other person. It struck no strong chord in her own memory, although she realised that she had been involved in the destruction of the computer.

" What will they do to us? " she asked when they sat in the lounge, idly watching some inanity on T.V. late that evening.

Fleming was quiet for a time, marvelling that the moronic woman simpering at the camera had just won a spin dryer for confirming that the Amazon was a large river. " I imagine they'll wait until poor old Osborne joins us here," he said eventually. " Then they'll have a trial in camera. He and I will be beheaded at the Tower, Osborne a perfect gentleman to the very end. As for you "—he found he could not go on, and they sat without speaking for a long while in the flickering half-light of the telly.

Suddenly there were footsteps outside, heavy ones, on the parquet flooring.

" Who's that? " Andre asked. Both had grown accustomed to the flannel-footed silence of the minions who watched over them.

" Could be Osborne," Fleming suggested. " It's about time he joined the party. Nice if they let us all spend our last days together."

But it wasn't Osborne. It was Kaufman. He was dressed in an over-long black overcoat. In one hand he held a black homburg, in the other a briefcase. He was momentarily taken aback at the sight of Fleming and Andre.

" Excuse please," he murmured, shutting the door quietly. " I had expected to meet Mr. Osborne . . . ." He nervously licked his lips and then put on a big smile. " I was informed he was due here this evening. Instead I have the honour of greeting Dr. Fleming." He advanced, podgy hand outstretched.

" Mein frend Kaufman," mimicked Fleming, ignoring the handshake. " How did you flannel your way into this place? "

Kaufman drew himself up. " I am representing Mr. Osborne's

lawyer. It is all so difficult, this matter. But now I have the good luck. I meet you."

He peered myopically through his spectacles at Andre, still sitting in her easy chair. "And this is the famous young lady! " He crossed to her, bowed, and took her hand, brushing the back of it with his lips.

" You see, my dear, how charming these Viennese are," said Fleming.

Kaufman scowled. " I do not come from Vienna, but from Dusseldorf, mein liebe Doktor! "

" It's not so long since you were taking pot shots at your liebe doctor," Fleming pointed out. " Not you, of course. You get other people to pull triggers and make uncomfortable trips to small private islands."

Kaufman seemed genuinely embarrassed. " I am not a free agent," he said. " I do not act as I would wish."

" Only as your bosses in Intel wish."

There was something unexpectedly sad and bitter in Kaufman's answer. " Some of us are not lucky enough to do the things we would choose."

Fleming nodded. " Why did they send you after us? "

"You have something my directors want." Kaufman was restless. He tip-toed to the window and pulled aside the heavy chintz curtains. Momentarily light swept over his face from moving lamps. At the same time there was the quiet throb of an idling engine and the faint swish of wheels braking on gravel.

" Your client, Mr. Osborne, maybe," suggested Fleming.

Kaufman shook his head. " Mr. Osborne is supposed to be already in this house. No, Dr. Fleming, this is a van. It will stop round the back, in the stable yard." His voice grew clipped and stern. " Now, please, you will both come with me." He partially drew the curtains and pushed open the long, low window.

"Don't take any notice of what he says," Fleming muttered quietly to Andre. " Just go on sitting there."

" Please," beseeched Kaufman. "Last week I have a young man shot dead. A nice young man. I did not even know him. I do not like such things."

There was some noise outside and a trench-coated figure sprang lightly over the sill. He was a thin, sallow-faced youngster hardly out of his teens. His narrowed eyes darted round the room. The gun in his hand was held rock-steady.

71

"Come on," he ordered in a small morose voice, "it's bloody cold and wet hanging around out there. Let's get going."

Kaufman moved behind the gunman. "We wish to have you alive, Herr Doktor," he said, "but we should be prepared to stretch a point with the young lady." The man in the trench coat pointed the revolver towards Andre. There was a studied movement of his thumb as he spun the bullet chamber. Fleming knew it was a crude theatrical gesture, but a purposeful one. He beckoned to Andre. With her hand in his they crossed to the window.

Kaufman climbed through the window first, turning to help Andre. The gunman brought up the rear, his pistol close to Fleming's back, but suddenly whirled round as he heard the door into the lounge opening. The others were already on the terrace. Fleming stopped dead and looked back.

Osborne was standing in the doorway, gaping at the gunman. Just behind him was a soldier, wearing the scarlet armband of the Military Police.

"What the dickens, Who the devil . . .?" Osborne managed to say as the soldier pushed him roughly out of the way. But it was too late. The gunman fired—once. Osborne crashed back against the door from the impact of the bullet. The gunman leaped to the window and fired again wildly as he clambered through. The bullet missed the soldier, who had started to rush forward, but sent him sprawling for cover.

From where he lay he blew his whistle for aid, while Osborne collapsed slowly to the ground with his left hand clasped to his right shoulder and a frozen look of surprise on his face.

"What a damned ridiculous thing to happen," he said slowly and distinctly, and then slumped forward.

Outside, in the darkness and the gusty rain, unseen hands grabbed Fleming and Andre. They were picked up bodily and pushed into the back of a van. The rear doors were slammed shut, and the engine started. Then with a scream of protesting tyres the van shot away, rocking so violently that it was impossible for Fleming to get to his feet. The vehicle gathered more speed on the long straight drive to the gates. Fleming heard confused shouts as they roared past the guardroom and on to the highway. Time after time they almost overturned as the driver took sharp turns at full speed, the sideways skids forcing

Andre and Fleming to lie flat, bracing their feet against the steel sides.

After a while they settled down to a fast, steady speed. Fleming guessed that they were on a motorway. He cursed the fact that he had no watch, but he estimated that this stretch lasted for half an hour—say forty miles since they had started.

The van slowed, swerved to the right and again there came bursts of speed alternating with abrupt turns. The bumpiness suggested a badly made road or lane.

Gingerly he stood up and with the aid of the futile flame from his cigarette lighter looked quickly round the van. He knew it was just a gesture. The interior was solid metal. The door was secured by the usual lock bars from the outside. There was no aperture beyond a small wire-meshed peep hole at the front near the driver. This was covered.

The van slowed down to a crawl, cruising slowly over uneven ground. It began to bump badly and the tyres made no more noise. They were obviously on grass. Then the van stopped.

There was a pause before the rear doors were opened. Rain was pouring down. Kaufman stood there smiling in the glimmer of a shaded flash light held by someone to the rear. Beside Kaufman stood the gunman.

"Well, Doctor," said Kaufman, "will you be so good as to get out; the young lady as well?"

Taking his time, Fleming jumped down. He lifted Andre out. "Your friend has rubbed out the perfectly harmless Osborne," he told Kaufman. "I wouldn't say that we're harmless, so what's your programme in our case? And where are we?"

"On a disused airfield of our great American allies," Kaufman said. "The runways are enormous and still excellent. We are saving you the unpleasantness of a trial and imprisonment for sabotage. I am sure your Government consider you a traitor." He removed his glasses and cleaned off the globules of rain. "No more time for talking." He seemed almost regretful. "The plane must leave immediately. Come!"

The gunman moved behind Fleming, and Kaufman led the way. Soon Fleming could see the wet, shining surface of an air-craft fuselage.

"Welcome aboard madame—and you, sir," said a woman's voice.

Fleming laughed at the madness of it. The girl at the top of the aircraft's steps was neatly dressed in a dark blue uniform. She was the usual type of air stewardess, trim, neat, and pretty. In the glowing red of the night emergency lights in the cabin Fleming saw that she was oriental. Swiftly she directed her guests to a couple of seats forward, helping them to fasten their safety belts. She completely ignored the man with the gun, who went to the seat across the gangway and sat there, half turned towards them, the gun still in his hands.

Kaufman disappeared through the crew door. The starter motor whirred. First one engine whined, then a second.

"Jets!" muttered Fleming to himself. "Trust Intel to do things properly. No expense spared."

There was no run-up of power. The jets were given full throttle with the brakes on; they sighed down from their crescendo, and then began to whine once more. The aircraft moved smoothly down the runway.

As soon as they were airborne they climbed steeply. The pilot obviously intended to get well clear of the commercial air lanes with their inquisitive radar controls. Soon they were through the clouds and bathed in cold moonlight. Fleming estimated from the stars he could identify that they were heading in a southerly direction.

When Kaufman emerged from the cabin he confirmed this. "We have just crossed the English coast," he beamed. "We are now over international waters. All is well. I suggest you try to get some sleep after the hostess has served refreshments. We shall be landing in about four hours in North Africa."

"Whereabouts in North Africa?" Fleming enquired.

"Of no importance," said the German. "Just for refuelling. The major part of the journey follows. To Azaran."

5

SUNNY AND WARM

DAYLIGHT came long before the aircraft slowly lost height and crossed the Azaran frontier. Fleming, gloomily looking through the aircraft window, found nothing to arouse his interest. The brown-grey land, flat and interminably dreary, stretched towards the horizon where low hills drew an uneven contour. Now and then he saw a blur of dust where a camel train moved along the dark threads which marked the age-old desert tracks. Apart from a few ragged shaped blobs of lighter contours, the pattern of a few miserable houses round a water hole, the place seemed lifeless.

The jet's whine sunk to a hum and the port wing dipped. Below Fleming saw the discs of the top of oil tanks, and not far from them the tracery of derricks. The ground slid closer and a town came into focus, its white buildings brilliant in the morning sun. The aircraft swung the other way, and the horizon dropped past Fleming's window. When the machine levelled off he just had time to note a long grey building, flat roofed and modern. It stood isolated some five miles from the town.

The jet engines picked up power, eased, and faded. They were landing.

A soft heat struck their faces like a muffled blow when they emerged from the cabin. Arab soldiers, in battledress and American-style steel helmets, lounged around with sten guns at the ready. An ancient British limousine, the camouflage paint peeling from its body, drew up beside the aircraft. Kaufman, sweating profusely, hustled Fleming and Andre into the rear seat. He himself sat beside the army driver.

A good concrete road led straight into the town. As soon as they reached the slummy outskirts, where huts roofed with battered corrugated iron clashed obscenely with decrepit but still lovely houses of traditional Arabic architecture the road widened into a badly maintained highway, packed with people. Women, veiled and graceful, led donkeys half hidden under huge panniers. Some men were in Arab costume, but most wore cheap, shabby Western clothes.

The Azaran flag hung from every building. Here and there loud speakers blared Oriental music, the discord heightened by distortion. The driver went full tilt into the mob, his hand continually on the horn ring. Past the huge market place, where hundreds were standing around, aimless yet animated, the car swung through the narrow entrance to a large house. Two sentries looked poker faced at the car's passengers as the driver carefully steered the car into the cool, shady courtyard round which the house was built.

Kaufman alighted and spoke some words to an Arab in a neat Western-style suit. Then he disappeared through a doorless entrance. The Arab came across to the car and in careful English ordered Andre and Fleming to follow him. He took them across the courtyard, up some stone steps and through a beautifully ornamented door.

"Wait here, please," he said. He closed the door behind him.

Fleming strolled round the room. It was small but high ceilinged. A series of narrow slits, fitted with modern glass, allowed panels of sunlight to pattern the stone floor. Persian carpets hung on the walls. There were comfortable modern chairs as well as fragile little oriental tables. On one of the latter stood a brass tray with a silver jug and tiny cups. Fleming picked up the jug. It was hot; the aroma of coffee smelt good. He poured some of the thick, syrupy liquid into the cups and handed one to Andre.

"What is this place?" she asked as she sipped the coffee.

Fleming took off his sports jacket and unbuttoned his shirt. "A very hot country," he grinned. "A place called Azaran which seems to be small but likely to be notorious. This is doubtless some pasha's desirable residence. Unless it's Kaufman's."

"He is not a bad man," said Andre.

Fleming glanced at her with surprise. "You sense that? Basically you're right, I'm sure. The trouble is the hard veneer stuck on that lovely, harmless soul of his."

But Andre's attention had drifted away again.

There was a rustle of the hangings in the far corner of the room. Janine Gamboul came towards them. She was wearing a silk sheath dress and managed to look both cool and eye-catching.

" Doctor Fleming?" she murmured, pausing in front of him, unsmiling.

" Who are you?" Fleming asked rudely.

" My name is Gamboul," she answered, turning from him and studying Andre.

" The lady of the house?" he asked.

She did not take her eyes off Andre. " This is the home of Colonel Salim, a member of the Azaran Government. He could not come himself. He is extremely busy. Today is the anniversary of Azaran's independence, and this year the celebrations have a special meaning because the Government has terminated the oil agreements. In case of interference the frontier has been closed."

"A great day, as you say," Fleming said. "And this Salim had us brought here?"

She turned then and looked him over slowly. " I—that is to say, we—had you brought."

" I see. And you—singular or plural—are the flowers-by-wire service, the great Intel?"

" I represent Intel," she said coldly. She looked once more at Andre. "And you are —"

"A colleague," Fleming said quickly.

Janine Gamboul let the ghost of a smile play round her sensuous lips. " You are ——?" She asked Andre again.

" We are what is popularly known as 'just friends', in the rather old fashioned and more exact sense of the term," Fleming said. " Her name is Andre. Just Andre."

" Please sit down, ma petite," she said pleasantly to Andre. " I hope you're not too tired from your journey; that you were well treated."

" Not particularly," Fleming answered for her.

" I'm sorry," she said formally. " We brought you here because we think we can help each other. You're on the run from the British Government. They won't get you here, this is a closed country. No extradition."

" That's your version of helping us. Now suppose you explain how we're to be forced to help you?"

She was saved from losing her temper by the arrival of Salim.

The late ex-Ambassador was in a perfectly tailored uniform, with two rows of medals on his breast. He clearly found life very good indeed.

"Ah, Dr. Fleming," he exclaimed, flashing his white teeth

and extending his hand. Fleming turned his back on him. Not put out at all, Salim went to Andre. "And you are Miss ——"

"Andre," Janine said.

" Just ——? "

Gamboul shrugged. " Si. So the locquacious Dr. Fleming says."

Salim took Andre's hand in both of his. " I'm charmed," he murmured admiringly.

Andre smiled a little. " How do you do," she said politely.

Salim released her hands and threw himself in a chair, stretching his long legs in their immaculately polished boots. " Well, to explanations. Dr. Fleming, we are now a new country. Except for our oil we are under-developed. Not since two thousand years ago, when we were a province with our own rights under the old Persian Empire of Xerxes, have we been anything but a slave state of other people. We need help now we are independent."

" You go about hiring help in a curious way," said Fleming.

Salim waved his hand expressively. " How else could we have got you? The Intel organisation has sunk a great deal of capital here, in the form of industrial and research developments. As the host government we shall benefit. We have engaged a great many progressive and brilliant people—scientists."

" Collected in the same way? " Fleming enquired.

" In different ways. Once they are here they find it worth while. We treat them well. They don't usually wish to give it up."

" Do they have any option? "

" Let us have a drink," Janine Gamboul interrupted. Salim nodded and pulled a bell cord.

" You're a physicist, Dr. Fleming, and a mathematician specialising in cryrogenics," she went on.

" Sometimes," Fleming agreed.

Salim motioned to the manservant who brought a bottle-laden tray to put it down. " What will you have, Janine?" he asked. " We had another young scientist working here—Neilson .... What would the young lady and you like to drink? Whisky, or something soft?"

" This is very un-Moslem of you," said Fleming with a small smile.

Salim turned to him slowly and seriously. " I am a modern man," he said without affectation and turned away.

" In that case," said Fleming, "Andre would like some fruit juice if it isn't laced. I'll have a Scotch, neat." Fleming regarded his impassive back. " So Jan Neilson was here? I suppose your intelligence service knows that Jan, Denis Bridger and I were at the Massachussetts Institute of Technology for a spell? It all begins to fit . . . ."

Salim handed Andre and Fleming their drinks. He busied himself with two glasses for Gamboul and himself. " We thought a lot of Neilson; he was very brilliant." His voice was detached, as if he were quoting a hand-out.

" But dead?" Fleming asked.

Salim turned again and stared calmly at him. " Neilson did all the real organisation of our main research project. But he failed to complete it. Even if he had stayed I think he was in a blind alley." He looked thoughtfully at the ice bobbing about in his glass. " So, of course, we had to find a better man."

" To do what?" Fleming found his hand was shaking with anger and fear.

Salim came close to him. " You worked on the Thorness computer. We have one."

" What sort?" Fleming asked, dreading the answer.

Gamboul gave a short laugh. " You ought to know, Dr. Fleming. Your late colleague, Denis Bridger, provided the design. Your other late colleague Neilson built it."

Fleming fought to keep calm. " I suppose you don't really know what you've got hold of," he said at last. " I'll give you the best advice I can : blow it up."

"As you blew up the other?" Gamboul's eyes were dancing with amused triumph. " I'm afraid you won't have the same chance here."

" How do you know that we, that I ——"

She waited before she answered, savouring the pleasure of the impact to come. " Professor Dawnay told us."

" Dawnay!" Fleming could only stare at her.

" She came here of her own free will," Salim interposed. " With you and the lady professor we feel we have the needful set-up. The computer Neilson built is to be the basis of all the technology Mam'selle Gamboul's organisation has placed here."

He crossed to the window slit and peered out. The noise of the crowd was an incoherent accompaniment to the still booming public address system. " Those people out there are emerging from a long sleep," he said with sincerity. "You're a liberal-minded man, Fleming. You will help them to awake and take their place in the modern world."

"Where is Madeleine Dawnay?" Fleming demanded.

"At the Intel research station," Salim explained, "where you will be taken. It is very comfortable, up to the best oil company standards. We may be poor, but we are not barbarians." He drew himself up proudly. "But I must nevertheless point out that you are in no position to refuse to co-operate." He looked thoughtfully at Andre, sitting quietly, complete puzzlement on her face, as she glanced from Salim to Fleming and back again. "We will keep the young lady here to ensure your co-operation."

Fleming sprang to his feet. "No!"

Salim hesitated. He looked towards Gamboul, who nodded. "All right," he said. "We'll leave the young lady with you."

Janine Gamboul put down her empty glass. "We have talked long enough. I'll take them to the research station," she told Salim. "My car is waiting."

When Fleming, his hand on Andre's elbow, passed through the swing doors of the computer building which Gamboul held open, he stopped almost as if he had been hit in the stomach.

The hall was uncannily like that at Thorness, except that the khaki-clad armed guard inside had a swarthy face instead of the cheerful ruddiness of the sentries he had got to know so well in Scotland.

The air was the same—the cool lifelessness of air-conditioning. Through the grey painted door to the computer section the similarity was accentuated. Here was the heavy, indefinable smell of electricity, the pervading hum of a myriad active circuits, the inhuman personality of a room built entirely of control panels.

And there, down two steps it stood—the familiar rectangular mass of steel panelling with its control desk and cathode ray screens.

He moved forward slowly, still holding Andre's elbow. Several young Arabs were working on the machine. In an odd, outlandish way they reminded him of the British technicians he had supervised two years back at Thorness. They were even talking to one another in English—as if it were the natural language for science.

Gamboul called one of them.

" This is Abu Zeki," she said. " Dr. Fleming."

Abu Zeki's eyes gleamed with pleasure. He seemed a sensitive and likeable young man, with delicate Arab features and a crew-cut which gave him a curiously beat-generation look. He too was obviously " a modern man ". " How do you do sir? " he said. " I've heard much about you, of course. I am to be your senior assistant. I hope I shall be of use; anyway I can pass on your instructions to the staff." He looked proudly along the control panel of the computer. " We are going to do great things with this."

" You believe that, do you? " Fleming said quietly.

" I'll show you around," Gamboul interrupted, and led them along the endless bays of wiring.

She knew her way remarkably well. She accurately identified every section of the huge machine, though Fleming noted that it was the second-hand knowledge of the layman who was concerned with what things did rather than how they did them. The layout was slightly different from what he had built at Thorness, but the input, the output and the huge memory circuits were basically the same.

They returned to the wide gangway in front of the control unit. " Construction was completed some time back. It was fully programmed. But nothing happened. That is why we need you. It presents no problems to you so far as operation is concerned? "

" Probably not," Fleming admitted. " The layout is super-ficially different. But in essence it is identical." He gave a mirthless laugh. " It should be. It has been built from instructions in the same message. You know what happened to the Thorness job? "

Gamboul shrugged her shoulders. " We're not interested in what went wrong there. We want this one to go right. We want to build up a centre of production unsurpassed in the world and free from interference, political or otherwise. This machine is to be Intel's brain."

Fleming felt mesmerised by the baleful quietness. He dreaded to see once again the ominous section which made this computer unlike any other man-made brain—the heavy brass terminals nestling in their plastic insulation guards.

He turned to Abu, standing deferentially nearby. " Where is your high voltage output? "

81

Janine Gamboul looked at him suspiciously. " Why do you ask? What is its purpose? "

" There are two high tension leads extraneous to your control panel. Or there should be."

Abu nodded. " There were, yes," he agreed. " We led them into the end compartment. We did not understand their purpose." He led them down the passageway and slid the grey panel on its smooth runners. Fleming stared at the harmless looking metal shapes. Hateful memories crowded into his brain. He turned to Andre, but to his relief she seemed quiet and unstirred by interest.

" Dr. Neilson considered they were for sensory communication with the memory circuits," Abu said. " So that the operator could have direct contact with the computer's positive calculator relays. He worked out that it should be done visually through this display." He nodded towards a battery of aluminium-sprayed cathode ray screens which were ranged above the terminals.

" I remember! "

Fleming turned at the sound of Andre's voice.

Her eyes were alight with excitement. Fleming felt suddenly sick. Things seemed to be moving remorselessly and inevitably beyond control.

He moved close to her. " You know what this is? " he whispered. " It's what we were running away from."

She did not turn to him. She seemed transported and her eyes remained on the control panel. " Don't be afraid," she murmured. Fleming could not decide to whom she was talking.

He whipped round on Gamboul. " Just blow the whole thing up. Now."

She looked at Andre, and then at Fleming. She began to smile, not concealing her contempt. " Destroy it? " she exclaimed. " We shall control it." Her tone changed. " Now I will show you to your quarters. They are very comfortable. Your old colleague is most anxious to meet you once more—Professor Dawnay."

She led them from the computer building into the cruel heat outside. A soldier immediately came forward and in obedience to a few words in Arabic from Gamboul, escorted Fleming and Andre to a row of bungalows shaded by a few palm trees. Andre was still dazed and walked without speaking.

Madeleine Dawnay was sitting in a deck chair on a tiny, browned patch of grass. Her face was already tanned though she

82

looked gaunt and thin in her tropical clothes. She greeted them both with unaffected joy.

" My dear," she said taking both of Andre's hands in hers, " I'm so happy to see you. Your maidservant has been told exactly how to look after you." She turned to John. " So you're here."

He did not offer any greeting. " I'm here because I was hijacked," he said quietly. " I shan't try to get out yet awhile because of what I've just been shown. But as for you, Madeleine, I'm damned if I can see how you can voluntarily work for this lot."

Dawnay refused to be offended. " It's no use sticking labels on them, my dear. The circumstances are so different. I must say I was alarmed at first. I suspect Salim drugged me in London. I don't know why."

" To find out where I was. You were the only person I told, and they turned up immediately."

She was deeply upset. " I'm sorry," she said miserably, " I'd no idea."

" How did they get you? " Fleming asked.

" By asking me nicely. They've got a most interesting agricultural problem. They want to be self-supporting with food. They've tried all the usual ways of fertilising barren land. But they realise they need a really new, wholly scientific conception. I hope—I think—I can help."

Her unquestioning faith in the goodness of science had always worried him. Their easy comradeship had been strained when she had seen no risks in the first success with her life-synthesis experiments. She was caught in the same unbalanced enthusiasm now.

" Madeleine," he said gently, " if we can't get away from this place without finishing up abruptly dead then surely I can at least warn ———"

She looked at Andre, sitting quietly near them, dreaming in the comforting dappled shade from the palm trees. " Who can you warn, John? " she asked. " Who'll listen to you now that they know what you did back at Thorness? "

" So we just stay here and do the thing's filthy work?" he asked bitterly.

She frowned. " My work isn't dirty. I'm trying to help ordinary, mortal people, a good many of them starving at this moment. Salim may be ruthless, but his motives are good. He wants to do something for his country.

Fleming reached for a cigarette box which an orderly had silently placed on a table at the side of his chair, along with some iced fruit. The service, as Gamboul had promised, was very good. He lit a cigarette and then thoughtfully watched the smoke spiralling from the glowing end. " There's one possibility," he said at last. " I can probably get the circuitry right pretty easily. Neilson obviously did a fairly good job, and young Abu Zeki knows his stuff. The computer will work, but it'll depend partially on the information we feed into it. If I make it think I'm for it . . . ."

He paused to sip his drink. " That was my mistake last time. I attacked it, and I couldn't really win. But if I inform its memory circuits that they—Intel and Co.—are really against it, its logical processes will come up with something to defeat them."

" Perhaps by destroying them—and the whole country? " Dawnay suggested.

Fleming nodded. " That would be better than the alternative. Which would be that it would lay down the law wholesale through Gamboul, Salim and the rest of the crooks they're working for."

Dawnay looked thoughtfully across at Andre, who had relaxed in a day-dreaming half sleep. She looked very lovely and feminine.

"And the girl? " she asked.

' I've stopped thinking of her as anyone from, well, outside this planet. She's a virtually normal piece of human chemistry. The danger is when the machine gets her and uses her. I want to stop that whatever else I do or don't do. I've grown rather fond of her."

" Don't sound so sad about it! " Dawnay laughed.

He glanced to make sure that Andre was not trying to listen. " There's more to it than that. Her co-ordination's going. She spends too much time like she is now. And when she moves around it's jerky, like a mild spastic case. I thought at first it was shock or the after effects of her experience, physical after effects of her injuries. But it's getting worse. There's something wrong with the way she was made."

" You mean I made a mistake . . . ."

" Not necessarily you," he reassured her. " Something wrong with the programming for the calculations."

He stopped talking. Andre opened her eyes, stretched lazily, and sat up. " What gorgeous sunshine," she said smiling.

She walked, rather jerkily, out of the shade and began to look around. Fleming and Dawnay saw her move near the doors to the computer building. The sentry, lolling against the wall, stepped forward, thought better of it, and let her pass inside.

Fleming jumped up out of his chair. " Why don't they stop her? "

He started to move away, but Dawnay put out a hand to stop him.

" She'll be all right."

" With *that*? " Fleming asked her. " You're mad."

" I'm not mad. Leave her there."

Reluctantly Fleming stayed. They waited tense and alert as the minutes ticked by.

Abruptly the vague vibrationary hum which came all the time from the building grew louder, and there was a rhythmic clicking.

What the hell's that? " shouted Fleming, jumping to his feet.

Dawnay's exclamation, " It's the computer, it's working," was needless. Both of them rushed across to the swing doors and down the corridor.

Abu Zeki came running towards them.

" What's happened? " Fleming asked.

" I can't say, Dr. Fleming," Abu replied. " The young woman came in, stood looking around, and then sat down before the control panel in the sensory bay."

Fleming pushed past him. The master screen was quivering with wavy bands of light; crazy geometrical patterns shifted across, faded, and changed their shapes.

Seated in the chair at the panel was Andre.

"Andre," Fleming called, pausing in the face of some force which he did not understand but which seemed to paralyse his legs. She did not turn. "Andromeda," he yelled.

Very slowly she turned her head. Her pale face was glowing with joy.

" It speaks to me! " she cried. " It speaks! "

" Oh my God," Fleming groaned.

Abu coughed. " I must go and inform Mam'selle Gamboul of what has happened," he said.

6

CYCLONE

FLEMING watched with misgiving the transformation which came over Andre. The lethargy and almost childlike innocence disappeared. She was alert and avid for activity; yet she seemed unexcited. Fleming knew that the change was due to the computer, yet this was a different Andre from the robot of Thorness —the changes were indefinable but nevertheless they were there.

He was a little comforted by the frankness and trust which she showed towards him. He thought about it all night, alternately lying on his narrow, comfortable bed and then pacing about the small, neat, air-conditioned room which had been allotted him. By the morning he had made a decision. If he was to cancel out the evil which he felt in the machine he must somehow trick it into working in the way he wanted. This he had already decided to do—it was his only possible ally against his hosts. But he could not trick it if it was working through Andre; he could not trick her. He had to gamble on making an ally of her too. In the morning he told her all he felt about it.

When he had finished she laughed almost gaily. " It is very easy," she insisted. " We must tell it what to do."

He did not share her confidence. " I can't see how it's a practical policy."

She became thoughtful. " I think the facts are these. All the real complexity is in the calculating and memory sections. The memory is enormous. But when a calculation has been made it has to be presented for assessment in a very simple form."

" You mean like a company's brief balance sheet summarises all the complex activities of a year's trading? "

She nodded. " I expect so. But if the balance is weighted ——"

" I get it! " he interrupted. " The decision circuits act like the shareholders reading that balance sheet. On the basis of what they read into it they decide future company policy." He

86

frowned. " But I'm dead sure that our balance sheet, produced by the computer's memory section, is nicely tricked up via the programme formulated by the original message, the stuff from Andromeda. So the decision circuits will execute its orders, not ours."

" Unless we change them."

He got up and paced around the room. " Our changes would just be deletions. The result would be a glorified adding machine. Neither enemy or ally. There'd be no sense of purpose."

" But it could be given our purpose," she said urgently. " One that we communicated to it. Or at least, one I communicated. I can do it, John."

" I suspect you can. That's why I've tried to keep you away from it."

" You can't," she said quietly. " It is the reason why—I'm here." She stretched her hand and brushed it against his. " If you want to use the computer you'll have to trust me."

He turned to look at her, his eyes searching into hers. " I think I'll go for a stroll around the compound," he said abruptly. " You get some rest. You aren't fit yet. And don't think too much about all this."

He went past the sentry and paced up and down the sandy waste ground which lay around the buildings. Then he made for Dawnay's quarters.

Madeleine was surrounded by maps of the country, making notes of the geological factors. She seemed glad to abandon her work and gossip.

He told her of Andre's confidence and how he believed that she was just deceiving herself; the computer would dominate her as before.

She regarded him thoughtfully. " I don't think so, John," she said. "At least, not unless you drive her back under its spell. If you're hostile and suspicious you'll alienate her. You've built up ties between the two of you—ordinary human emotional ties. Those are strong influences."

He looked away. " What I want to know, Madeleine, is what's happening to her—physically? "

" What you've seen for yourself. Some sort of deterioration of muscle control. I'll have her examined if you like. But if, as I suspect, it's some motor deficiency in her nervous system there's nothing we can do about it."

87

"Oh my God," he said harshly. "The poor kid." He was silent for a moment. "It may be part of the programme which planned her: to chuck her aside when her job's over."

"There's the possibility that it's my fault," Dawnay said. "I made her—seemingly with built-in deterioration." She controlled herself and smiled. "Really you have no choice, John. You'll have to trust her as she has trusted you over these past weeks Let her alter the computer in the way she plans and let her work with it." She hurriedly bent over her maps so he could not see her uncharacteristic tears. "From what I've seen of her muscular movements it won't be for very long. Let her final days be happy and useful. She may even get you out of here."

Fleming went to see Andre in her quarters—another small, neat air-conditioned room like his. She was sitting eating a meal off a tray. He was as appalled by the way she talked about her work as by the difficulty she found in conveying food to her mouth; but he was relieved that her speech had not so far become disjointed. The deterioration was not affecting her vocal muscles nor, thank God, her brain.

When she had eaten he took her arm and they walked the short distance to the computer building. Despite the fact that they were on a smooth path she stumbled once or twice.

Once before the computer console she seemed to regain all her powers. Automatically she took control and the computer immediately came to life, the clicking of relays providing an accompaniment to the ceaseless sullen hum. Oscillographs were soon pulsating and the main screen portraying a coherent pattern.

Fleming stood in the background with Abu Zeki, watching Andre seated at the console, her head tilted to watch the screen above her. At last, satisfied, she swivelled round on her chair and smiled triumphantly.

"It is done," she said. "The computer is fully operational."

Abu turned to Fleming incredulously. "This girl, Dr. Fleming. She has done this? Just in a matter of minutes?"

Fleming took him back to the duty office. He sat down at the desk. "I'm going to ask you to accept that what I'm telling you now are facts," he began. "The girl can communicate with the computer, picking up the electro-magnetic waves and interpreting them, re-transmitting her orders in the same way." He paused. "You don't believe me, of course?"

88

"Perhaps I must believe; but I do not understand," Abu confessed. Fleming liked the young Arab scientist. There was honesty, inherent decency, about him. He believed that the man could be an ally. He told him that Andre was a man-fabricated being, constructed in order to forge a link with the computer, even if that had not been the intention of her human mentors.

Abu listened attentively, but he politely protested that the method of communication between her and the machine was still inexplicable.

"Look," Fleming said, "we have eyes and ears and noses because they're the best instruments for picking up information in our sort of world. But they're not the only ones even ordinary humans like you and I have. There are senses we haven't developed and senses we've let atrophy. The girl has another sense we haven't—and that's what she is using. To give information to the machine and to receive it."

"How will she use it?" Abu asked.

Fleming shrugged. "God knows, Abu Zeki, God alone knows."

Both men started at a slight sound by the door. They had not noticed that Andre had come quietly into the office.

'How do you want me to use it?" she demanded.

She did not wait for their answer. With hesitant steps, growing quicker as she progressed, she returned to the sensory console.

Abu, when he had time to digest the information Fleming had given him, was immediately anxious to use it. A young man like thousands of others in Azaran, he had been more fortunate than most in that his father had worked on the oil plant. The company had provided educational facilities for the workers' children. Abu had grabbed the opportunity. An imaginative English teacher had realised the boy's potentialities, helping him with spare time tuition.

When Abu was sixteen the new regime had emerged and the idealistic President had announced a state scholarship programme. Abu Zeki had been among the first twenty youths selected. He had emerged the only real success of the scheme.

Naturally Abu was grateful. He was also patriotic. The chance to work on the construction of a computer which surpassed any in the world had thrilled him. The presence of Europeans to direct his activities had not seemed anything but reasonable. He had been told that Intel was sponsoring the enterprise. What Intel was he neither knew nor cared. The basic fact was that this was an Azaranian project to better the country. Abu believed that not only was his own career rosy with promise but that he was working to ensure that life for his baby son would be even more wonderful.

He had been in despair when the computer failed to work, feeling that he was somehow to blame since Neilson had disappeared. Now, all that was in the past. In co-operation with this cynical yet likeable Englishman and his girl friend, the product of some weird and wonderful scientific gimmickry, he could repay the trust his President had put in him.

From the files in the records office Abu took several sheets of calculations. They had been passed over to him by Dawnay for processing by the computer. There had been nothing to do but file them until it was operational.

He mentioned what they were to Fleming.

" Give them to the girl," Fleming said wearily. " Let her feed the data in her own way."

Abu gave Andre the sheets of figures and busied himself in the office. He went through blue prints and circuit diagrams. His brain did not register any detail. He was forcing himself to do something while he listened anxiously to the rapid clicking of the machine.

It was twenty minutes before the output printer motor whirred and the circuit light glowed red. From the slot the print began to emerge, jerking slowly to the left and then abruptly to the right as line after line of equations was typed.

Abu stood mesmerised, reading the figures on the jerking paper. The motor sighed to silence and the circuit light went out. The calculations were complete. He tore off the paper and rushed to Fleming in the record office.

" Some of Professor Dawnay's calculations," Abu said. " This is the result of handing the project to Miss Andre. It's quite extraordinary! "

He crossed to another filing cabinet, a locked one. He withdrew a bulky file of papers, sorted through them, and went off to talk to Andre. By the time he returned the output printer was beginning to work again.

Fleming, still lounging at the desk, occupied with his thoughts, looked up lazily. " More stuff," he said. " What is it? "

Abu kept his back to Fleming. " I'm afraid I'm not allowed to tell you, Dr. Fleming."

" Look! " Fleming paused, trying to curb his anger. " What am I supposed to be here? In charge, or what? "

" I'm sorry," Abu said with sincerity. " But I have my orders."

Fleming looked at him levelly. " What have you given it? " he asked again. But Abu stared back at him with gentle obstinacy.

" It is work which Mam'selle Gamboul wishes done. I am not at liberty to discuss it."

' Then I'll stop it.'

" I'm afraid you won't, Dr. Fleming."

Abu nodded towards the nearest sentry, who was watching them with a sour, bored interest. Fleming turned on his heel and stalked out.

Outside the office another sentry was leaning against the pillar, shading himself from the glaring sun. The soldier abruptly stepped forward and snapped to attention.

Fleming glanced across the compound and saw Janine Gamboul walking beside an elderly bearded man and talking quickly and brightly. Abu came out and stood beside him.

" Who's that with the glamorous Gamboul? " Fleming asked.

" That is our President." Abu's eyes were alight with pride. " He must have been visiting Professor Dawnay's laboratory. Her assistant told me that she's working on something quite new: a protective membrane to prevent water evaporating from the soil, but letting the oxygen and nitrogen molecules through so the land could breathe. It's a marvellous idea. It will make the desert blossom."

"And no doubt about to take a leap forward." Fleming nodded to the record sheets from the computer which Abu still held.

" I wonder if the President will be coming here," said Abu hopefully.

But the President did not visit them. He glanced across to the computer. Gamboul said something. He nodded and disappeared into the headquarters building.

The afternoon siesta had put the town to sleep when Gamboul drove to Salim's residence. She found him taking his ease on the stone balcony, looking out over the quiet square and the acres of shabby roofs with a few minarets which made a dun-coloured pattern into the shimmering haze. He was in uniform, as he liked to be.

She threw down her wide-brimmed hat and crossed to the table where bottles and a bowl of ice stood.

Salim did not trouble to get up. " Been doing your duty? " he murmured.

" I've taken the old fool round the establishment," she answered, busy mixing her drink. " That will keep him quiet for a bit. He was most impressed with the Dawnay woman. Naturally,"—she gave a brittle laugh—" I didn't take him into the computer building, though he asked what was happening there." She sipped her drink, frowning as Salim made no effort to offer her a chair. " I'm going inside; it's cooler, and there may be somewhere to sit."

He heaved himself to his feet and followed her through the bead screen to the spacious room he used as an office. Across one wall was a detailed map of Azaran. Little flags of various colours were pinned here and there. Gamboul glanced at it with lazy curiosity and then stretched himself on a sofa. She was growing tired of Salim.

He came close, looking at her body in its thin and too tight dress. " Who's this girl you had brought over with Fleming? " he demanded.

Gamboul hunched her shoulders. " I don't know. Abu says she is highly intelligent. Kaufman's report merely says she was connected with the Thorness computer. They used quite a number of females up there. Dawnay for example. Kaufman thinks the girl was connected with the destruction of the machine and Fleming's shielding her. Presumably they're lovers."

Salim was disturbed. " Have her watched closely," he ordered. " We don't want to risk sabotage. And you'd better get out of Fleming who she is. I'm sure you could manage that."

She smiled at him, running her hand down her hip and thigh. " I don't think I fancy Dr. Fleming." As if the subject bored her she got up and crossed to the map.

" What is all this playing around with little flags? "

Salim stuck his thumbs in his belt and stood solid and sure in front of the map. " The flags mark troops I can rely on. Roughly, an infantry battalion here, in Baleb, and a squadron

92

of armoured cars. Some motorised units on the frontiers and the main army barracks at Quattara. Also the majority of the air force units."

" To do what? " she asked.

" To support me. Us." He corrected himself. " The computer must be safe. It belongs to Intel, and Intel holds the concession from the President. And I am not yet the President."

Gamboul studied his face. " Is that what you want? " she asked.

Salim returned to the balcony to look over the city. His eyes lifted to the lovely old palace which stood on a slight eminence to the right. " The President is a soft man," he murmured. "A tired man. He fought for independence, but now he thinks he can rest. He could be influenced—by any liberal-minded bumbler."

Gamboul was close beside him, her body touching his. " Like the Dawnay woman? " she suggested.

" Dawnay? " The idea seemed new to him and of no consequence. " Anyone could persuade him to interfere with your work, and then you and I would lose control. We must prepare for that eventuality. Why do you think I came back? "

" You're planning a coup d'etat! " she said, surprise and admiration in her expression. "And I didn't know."

He turned and put his hands on her shoulders. " You're with me, aren't you, Janine? "

She leaned forward until her body was pressed hard against him. " I thought you knew," she whispered. " When will it be? "

He looked out across her shoulder to the rooftops. " For Arabs time is a servant. When the time is right I shall act. Perhaps two days; a week. Not more."

At Fleming's insistent request Madeline Dawnay asked for a doctor to come and see Andre. The efficient and smooth-running staff organisation of Intel said that they would have a neurologist in the compound within twenty-four hours.

He arrived the following morning. He was an Arab, who diffidently mentioned to Dawnay that he held a degree in neuro-surgery from the Radcliffe Infirmary at Oxford and had continued his studies at Johns Hopkins.

His examination of Andre was long and thorough and Dawnay was impressed.

93

She answered the knock on the door of the neat little sick bay and found Fleming outside. " You can't see her yet," she said, coming out to join him on the verandah. " The doctor's still busy. Taking a lumbar puncture for a spinal fluid check. But his preliminary diagnosis is much the same as ours. Her muscular system's going more and more wrong. Maybe some gland has packed up, or her nerve set-up is different from ours, needing a blood nutrient that was there when she was built but is now depleted."

" You mean it wasn't in the blueprint? " he suggested.

Dawnay shrugged. " It isn't being made now," she said shortly.

" Could we synthesise it? "

" I wouldn't know where to start. Back home I might get advice and help. . . ."

" So what happens? " he asked harshly.

" She'll lose the use of her muscles progressively. It'll show in her limbs most obviously, but one day it'll be the pectoral muscles and then the heart." She turned to look at the closed door. " That's what the doctor is explaining to her now. I asked him to." Her calmness broke quite suddenly. " I made her! I made her to suffer this! "

He gripped her arm. " Madeleine. You didn't do it deliberately. And what about me? Who started it all with the design of the computer? Who prevented her dying more or less peacefully in that cave? "

Dawnay did not respond. She went on staring at the closed door. Presently the doctor came out. He looked across at the two of them, and then away as he crossed to the visitors' block.

" She ought to be properly nursed; sent away," Fleming said.

Dawnay gave a mirthless laugh. " You can see them allowing her to leave here. She's produced my crop formula. They know how useful that will be. There will be other things for her to do for them."

" There is another thing, already," said Fleming, remembering what Abu Zeki had told him at the computer.

" What? "

" I don't know exactly," he said thoughtfully. " I only hope what I think it is is wrong."

As if to contradict him, six jet fighters abruptly screamed across the sky, climbing fast from the airfield. They watched the machines become dots in the blueness of the shimmering canopy of sky. Dawnay wiped her face. I'd better talk to the doctor, John. You have a word with Andre. Be gentle with her."

He knocked softly on Andre's door, waiting for an answer, almost dreading to go in. A pretty little Arab nurse came and opened the door, silently standing aside to permit him to enter.

Andre was sitting beside the austere iron bedstead, wearing a housecoat. The brightly coloured flowers of the pattern accentuated her extreme pallor. She was leaning back with her head turned sideways so that her long fair hair hung across her cheek. Fleming guessed that she had been crying.

The nurse brought a small, hard chair, and Fleming sat down.

"Andre; Andromeda," he murmured. "There may be some answer." He saw the hair move as she gave a slight shake of the head. "We've done so much together," he insisted.

He put his fingers gently on her chin and pulled her face round. She reacted weakly, jerking away and covering her face with her hands. "Don't!" she begged. "Do you think I want to die? That it's nice to know I'm doing what you want? To end existence just like you ended the existence of the other computer?"

The words hurt him badly. "It's not what I want," he said, trying to keep his voice under control. "I'm frightened for you. And sorry for what I've done. I want to get you away from here, and all it means."

"Away?" she repeated, wonderingly. "But why? I've done what Dawnay asked; she has her data. And I've done what you asked; I've changed the computer's decision circuits . . ."

Her voice tailed away. Fleming felt a stab of real alarm; he knew that she had been on the point of saying more.

He went closer to her. "What else have you done, Andre? What else? At least be honest with me."

Her manner changed. She moved her head, pushed the hair from her face. She tried to smile at him. "I have seen what is the purpose of the message frrom out there."

He fought down the feeling of primitive terror that was sending the blood pounding in his temples. "You've what?" he whispered.

"It's hard to explain," she said uneasily. "I'm a bad translator. But I know it's all right. We must put ourselves in the hands of the people who will protect us."

95

He let the words sink in, grappling with the fact that once again he had lost a battle. In his over-confidence he had believed he had persuaded Andre to do as he believed right, to make the computer her slave. But she was quietly stating that she wanted to serve " people who would protect us ". People, she called them—this intelligence across the time-space of the universe—as if they were her brothers.

Before he could find words she sat up, smiling and confident despite the difficulty of the physical movement.

" Now I have seen the message I understand," she said. " You are frightened because you know only that the computer can have power over us; not why it has."

" You are what I'm frightened of," he said. " Now the computer's been doctored, the only way the message can enforce its will is through you. That's why I want you to get away from it! Live while you can, peacefully!"

She shook her head. " You think it's evil," she protested. " It isn't. It's giving us a solution, a power. If you are to survive you need that power. All that is happening in the country is only a symptom of what's happening all over the world. It's unimportant. We can take it all out of their hands and use as we want! "

He marvelled at her faith and feared her assurance; it was as if she pitied his limited imagination.

Abruptly she fell back on the sofa. The enthusiasm was spent; all it left was a frail, rather timorous young girl. " It drains me," she whispered. " It takes all my strength. It will kill me even quicker than you thought."

" Then leave it alone! "

She passed her forearm wearily over her head and gripped the back of the head rest. " I can't," she said. " I've something to do before I die. But I can't do it alone." Her lower lip trembled and she began to cry.

He crouched down and put his arm protectively around her waist. " If I'm to help; if I'm to trust you, you must tell me. In words—simple words—what is the real core of the message? "

For a time she lay with her eyes closed. Fleming did not interrupt her reverie. Then she gave a slight shudder and tried to move. He helped her sit up.

" You must take me to the console," she said. " I don't think I can explain in words. But I can show you."

He helped her to stand and held her by the arm as she walked with jerky, staggering steps the short distance to the computer building. Once inside, she seemed as usual to draw on hidden strength. She needed no assistance to sit before the sensory panel. Almost instantly the machine began operating, the master screen producing the familiar pattern of wave forms which the output printer translated into figures.

Fleming stood behind her as she gazed enthralled at the interminable pattern. " It's the high speed information between the equation groups which contains the real message," she said. " It tells about the planet from which the data came."

Fleming watched the screen. He could identify the wave forms which were the electronic versions of figures, but the occasional surges of angular blobs of light which intervened were meaningless to him. He had always imagined them to be the normal pick-up by the sensitive selenium cells of stray currents in the machine's framework.

" What does all this gibberish tell you? " he asked.

Andre's eyes never left the screen while she began to explain. " That it has been through all this. It knows what must happen, what has happened in other planets where intelligences have only developed as far as yours. You endlessly repeat a pattern until it wipes itself out."

" Or the world gets too hot and does the job for us?" he suggested.

Andre nodded. " Life of a biological creature begins very simply." She talked slowly as if paraphrasing a complicated mass of information. " But after a few thousand centuries it all becomes so complicated that the human animal can no longer cope. One crack—a war perhaps—and the whole fabric crashes down. Millions are killed or die off. Very few survive."

" Who start again," he finished for her.

She swung round to look straight at him. " In about one hundred and thirty years from now there will be a war. Your civilisation will be destroyed. It's all exactly predictable. So can the period before recovery be calculated. Just over a thousand years. The cycle will then repeat itself. Unless something better happens."

"As has happened on some planet in Andromeda? "

" Yes," she replied. " The species changed, adapted itself in time. Now it can intervene for earth people."

He had to take his eyes off her; off the dazzling, ever-faster moving patterns on the screen. He felt sick at the way she talked about " earth people " as if she was some alien creature.

He walked down the aisle, the whole length of the computer, and back again. Its cloying warmth reached out to him despite the air conditioning. Then he made his decision.

"All right," he said firmly. " Let's try to learn from it. Let's discover what we can and then tell people so they can decide what they think best."

She made a gesture of impatience. " That's not enough," she said. " We've got to take power. That's how we're meant to use the message to help us. Not to destroy the people here but to help them, and in the end they will hand the power over to us. It's all been calculated."

The simple directness of her faith exasperated him because he knew it was an emotion too strong for him to destroy. Nevertheless, he determined to fight it.

" Every dictator in history has argued like that—to force people into actions for their own good," he said. "And I'm supposed to think that it will be all right if we help impose the will coming from somewhere in Andromeda through Intel or these people in Azaran or any other dirty little power-drunk agency you choose. It's ridiculous! "

" That's only the means," she said. " What's important is the end."

He crashed his fist on the console desk, making her flinch. " No," he shouted. " I fought it before at Thorness, and I fought you at first—because the world must be free to make its own mistakes or save itself." He looked at her with a mixture of remorse and fury. " That's why I trusted you to handle this."

" I only did what was logical."

" I should have left you—left you to die," he whispered.

She turned back to the console. The screen had darkened, its aluminium coating grey and lifeless. " I shall die very soon anyway," she said.

All his fears for her returned and he could only stand in silence with his hand on her shoulder. Neither of them moved. Then he heard the printer in the output bay tapping rapidly once more.

He strode across and read the figures appearing on the steadily emerging roll. The equations were terribly familiar,

98

taking him back to an afternoon at Thorness more than two years before.

Mesmerised, he read the stream of figures which continued to emerge. He sensed that Andre had come across and was standing beside him.

" What is this? " he demanded.

" Basic calculations for a missile interceptor," she said in a matter-of-fact voice. " Surely you remember the Thorness project? There are a few minor modifications in this one."

He whirled on her. " Why have you programmed the machine for this? "

"Abu Zeki wanted the calculations," she said. " They need means of defence. It's all part of the plan."

He ripped the paper from the ejector and crumpled it in his hand. " For God's sake, stop," he begged her. " I didn't save you to work for them, to obey every filthy order they give you. You still have freedom to choose what you'll do."

She made some reply, but the roar of jet engines screaming at high speed over the building drowned her words.

' What? " he said when the racket had died away.

" I said it's too late," she repeated. " I have chosen. It's already started."

Fleming turned away from her and walked quickly down the corridor to the main doors. The pallid heat struck him in the face as he ran into the open space clear of the buildings.

The compound gates were closed. A light tank stood in front of them. On the main road a convoy of army lorries was roaring at high speed towards Baleb.

Slowly he returned to the residential area, hoping to find Dawnay. He badly needed some kind of normality among all this madness.

Dawnay wasn't in her room, and he went to her laboratory. A white-overalled Arab girl assistant was bending over a microscope.

" Professor Dawnay? " she said in answer to his enquiry. " She is not here. She went to see the President half an hour ago," she added calmly. " Now there is revolution."

7

STORM CENTRE

MADELEINE DAWNAY'S visit to the President was an impulsive action, resulting from an argument with Kaufman. The German was constantly roaming around the establishment, keeping himself informed of any tit-bit of information which might help to ingratiate himself with his superiors. Although all senior staff were in theory employees of the Azaranian Government, in practice it was Intel which made the decisions. Consequently Kaufman, as the senior Intel representative regularly available, was regarded as a liaison officer by the directors.

Dawnay's bio-chemical experiments had progressed far enough for field-testing. Study of the terrain suggested that a coastal area near the Persian Gulf would be a good one. But she wanted to analyse the tidal strip to ascertain what effect wind and sea had had on the soil. On one of Kaufman's visits to her laboratory she asked for him to arrange transport for her to make a series of trips, imagining it would be a routine matter.

The German immediately became suspicious. He demanded to know the reason, and her natural retort that he would not understand seemed to anger him.

But Dawnay could be very obstinate when she chose. She insisted that if she was to carry out her work the arrangements must be made. Kaufman muttered that he would have to get a government permit.

"Fine," Dawnay said. "You can jump in your car and get it right away, can't you?"

He frowned. "At this moment, almost impossible."

This was more than Dawnay was inclined to take. She removed her overall and picked up her sun hat. "If you enjoy putting up ridiculous obstacles then I'll see the President myself."

"I wouldn't count too much on the President," he said, "but by all means go if you want." He went to the reception desk to call her a staff car. When it came he opened the door for her with a studied flourish.

On the short journey to the Presidential palace Dawnay's anger seethed and she reminded herself of Fleming's pessimistic views on the whole set-up. She determined to discuss more than a trip to the coast with the President. After all, she told herself, he was head of State and if a challenge came Intel could no more win than mammoth oil companies in half a dozen little states had been able to do.

The streets seemed very empty, although this did not particularly arouse her interest. She had visited the capital so rarely that she had no means of comparison.

The car slowed at the palace gates until it was waved on by a lounging sentry. The man showed no interest in it. Dawnay alighted and passed through the doorless portico.

A bearded Arab in native costume bowed and put his hands to his forehead in greeting. The palace was beautiful and very old, unspoiled by any attempt to repair the crescent arches or the filigree stonework with plaster.

A little incongruously, the old Arab picked up a house telephone fixed to the wall behind a pillar. After some murmured words he returned to Dawnay and said in halting English that his master would see her.

A little negro boy tripped down the stairs, greeted her with a dazzling smile and in his soft soprano voice asked her to follow him. They went to the first floor and along a labyrinth of passages, silent with age-long peace. The boy knocked on big double doors and threw them open.

The President advanced towards Dawnay, his hand extended. His creased face, she thought, was that of a very old man—older than she knew he actually was. But his eyes were bright and intelligent, and he was meticulously neat and tidy, his beard trimmed short, and his large sensitive fingers soft and gentle when they shook hands. The jarring note was his Western dress —an old-fashioned though well-cut tweed jacket and breeches of the kind English aristocrats wore on week-ends fifty years before. Dawnay envisaged some London tailor carefully repeating a bespoke order originally given in the spacious age of pre-1914.

His courtesy was as genteely old-fashioned as his appearance. Delighted to be entertaining an English lady, he explained that he had been looking through his film slides and hoped she would be interested in seeing some of them.

" Photography is my hobby," he said. "A way to have mementoes of my country—its people, its valuable archaeological and historical features, and of course the improvements which, with Allah's help, I have been able to make."

The negro boy was already standing beside the projector. At a nod from his master he switched off the ceiling lights and began the screening. Dawnay hid her impatience and made polite and appropriate remarks as her host carefully explained each picture. The show ended at last. The boy switched on the lights and was told to leave.

The President took a chair facing her and folded his arms in his lap. "And now, why did you want to see me? " he asked.

Urgently Dawnay recited the words she had been rehearsing to herself as she watched the slides. She hoped she was cogent, objective, and fair. She told him of the origin of the computer design, of the bio-chemical experiments which culminated in the creation of the girl, and finally of the reasons why Fleming had contrived the destruction of the machine in Scotland.

The President was quiet for some moments when she had finished. " I have only your word for all this," he said quietly. " It is, as you will understand, somewhat difficult to accept, or, perhaps I should say, understand."

' I'm sorry it can't be made more clear, your excellency. We don't understand a great deal of it ourselves. Dr. Fleming has always suspected its purpose."

"And do you? "

She pondered on her reply. " I think there are right ways and wrong ways of using it," she eventually said.

He darted a glance at her. "And we are using it in the wrong way? "

" Not you, but Intel."

" We are in their hands," he sighed, like a weary old man. " This is a difficult time."

He stood up and crossed to the window, pulling the heavy draperies aside and letting an almost blinding shaft of sunlight into the dim room. For a time he looked out on the city which dropped away below the palace. " When one is in my position, a government has to show results or it does not survive. Intel gives results."

He returned to the middle of the room but remained standing. "I am a moderate," he smiled. "There are factions here which are fiery, youthful, impatient. They are also powerful. I need all the help I can get to retain the people's loyalty."

The door had opened, and the little negro boy had appeared. In his hand he held a telephone. He plugged it into a wall jack and then stood before the President, holding the instrument free of the cradle. The President took the phone and listened. He said a few words in Arabic and then gave the phone back to the boy.

He walked across the room and stood once more before the window. A soft thud, a long way off, sent a tiny vibration through the old building. It was followed by the harsh reverberation of automatic fire. The President pulled the curtain back across the window and looked at his guest.

"I do not think, Professor, that I shall be in a position to help you. The telephone call was from Colonel Salim, an efficient and ambitious officer." He paused to listen to the distant rumble of heavy engines and the racket of caterpillar tracks which rapidly grew in volume on the roadway below the palace. "That, I imagine, is the proof of what he told me."

Only half understanding, Dawnay stood up and hesitantly moved to the door, thanking him for his patience in listening. She remembered too late that she had not asked for a permit to visit the coast.

"Goodbye, Professor," the old man said. He did not look at her. He had sat down, very erect, very still, in an old-fashioned high backed chair. Dawnay had the impression of a king who had only his dignity left to sustain him.

The negro boy was standing in the passage outside. His eyes were big with fear or perhaps excitement. He almost ran in his anxiety to escort her to the courtyard.

The car she had come in had gone. Instead, two soldiers came across and stood on either side of her. They motioned with their guns that she was to wait near the doorway. Presently an army scout car came to a halt beyond the portico. The soldiers jerked their heads to show she was to enter it.

A young officer saluted her. "We take you back, Miss," he said in halting English.

The driver had frequently to pull out of the way as mobile columns roared towards Baleb. There were a few half-tracks and some light tanks. Their crews were in war kit but they were standing in their vehicles. They obviously did not expect serious shooting.

The gates to the Intel compound were open but an armoured car was stationed outside, and there were groups of helmeted troops everywhere. Dawnay was driven straight to her quarters, where more guards were patrolling. The young officer who had accompanied her indicated courteously but firmly that she was to remain in her room until further orders.

The military coup organised by Salim had been based on three actions—to close all frontier roads and ports, take over control of the capital, and to secure the Intel establishment. The Intel action, was, of course, a formality, thanks to Janine Gamboul.

The first clue Fleming had as to what was happening came from Abu Zeki. The two men had quarrelled for the second time. Abu had proudly told Fleming that the destruction of the missile equation sheets had been futile because the punched master tape was intact. He had gone on to boast of the power and might his country would have with the defence devices the computer could design.

"Already we are grasping that power. Even now Colonel Salim's troops are taking over our protection."

" From the President? " Fleming asked.

" The President's a tired, senile old man. He's finished."

"And Intel? "

" They're taking over with Intel," Abu Zeki replied. He saw Fleming glance towards the empty sensory bay. " If you're looking for the girl she's not in the building. She is in our custody."

Fleming hurried from the building and ran across to the residential area. Two armed guards stood before the door of Andre's quarters. He tried to push between them but they did not budge.

" They'll not let you in; I'm afraid they no longer trust you, Dr. Fleming," said a familiar voice.

He wheeled round. Kaufman was walking slowly towards him, grinning. "Anyway, the girl is not here," the German went on. " She is being cared for. Meanwhile Mademoiselle Gamboul wishes to see you."

" Where? " Fleming grunted. "And when? "

Kaufman's smile disappeared. " Now," he said. " You will come with me." He led the way to his car.

They drove to Salim's house. There were no soldiers there and no servants met them as they went upstairs. Kaufman opened a door and motioned to Fleming to enter. The door closed and he was left alone.

He walked round the familiar room where he had first met Salim, and then wandered out on the balcony. It was a few moments before he moved to the far end where some cane furniture stood around a table. On the table were bottles of whisky and glasses. He felt he needed a drink.

His approach to the table took him past a sun screen and alongside a chaise-longue. He let out an involuntary shocked gasp.

Janine Gamboul was sprawled on her side, her head drooped over the edge and her arm hanging limply to the floor. Her face looked pale as wax, except for the red line of her lipstick and the dark pencilling of her eyebrows, and her eyes were half open and glazed.

Fleming's immediate reaction was that she was dead. He bent down and put his hand under her head, lifting it back on to the chaise-longue. She moaned.

Then, as he pulled her arm against her body he saw the glass on the floor. He sniffed it: it smelt of whisky.

He was just about to leave her when she opened her eyes fully and laughed. She hauled herself up with difficulty into a half-sitting position and waved clumsily at him.

" You thought I was dead? " she giggled. " I'm not, as you see. I told Kaufman to ask you here. I wanted to talk." With studied effort she put her feet on the ground and stood unsteadily. " Lemme get you a drink." She staggered the few paces to the table.

She slopped some whisky into two glasses and then gaped around. " No syphon," she muttered thickly. " Been drinking it neat, but you like soda—yes? Salim must have it in his room." She managed to pick up the two glasses and waveringly started for the door from the balcony. Fleming stood motionless, watching her.

She stopped and half turned. " What are you looking at me like that for? " she said thickly. Then, with an arch smile, " it's no use getting ideas about me; not till I've learned more about the other woman, your woman . . . ."

She started off once more, putting the two glasses down on a heavy sideboard while she swayed over the cupboard beneath.

There were two syphons there but apparently it was too great an effort to lift one out. Instead she bent down with the glasses in turn and squirted in the soda. Fleming, who had moved no nearer than the doorway, did not see how deliberately and accurately she half-filled one glass from each.

She was humming a little French love song as she swayed towards him. She gave him one glass, and fell into an easy chair with the other.

" Tell me all about your girl friend," she murmured, looking at him over her drink.

" Hasn't Abu Zeki told you all you need to know? " he said sullenly.

She giggled. " Oh, something quite fantastic. So absurd that of course I believe it—and want to know more. A votre santé! " She raised her glass.

Fleming hesitated and then sipped his drink. The bite of the whisky on his palate made him feel better. He decided to play along for a little while. She was still acting drunkenly, her speech slurred and her body limp. It made her more attractive than usual.

" What have you against us? " she asked. " The smell of commerce? The dirt that's supposed to stick to money? "

" Partly," he grunted.

" We haven't such a bad record in this country," she continued. " There was nothing here till we came. Now that Salim's taken over we can progress still more." Her eyes were bright with excitement. " Perhaps we shall become fabulous and great, like medieval Venice or the East India Company. Anyway soon no one will be able to compete with us. The whole world will be at our feet."

" Or at hers," he observed, sipping again from his glass.

She leaned forward. " Hers? " she repeated. " Why don't you tell me about her? There is something she alone knows? Something she will do? "

Her eyes were fixed on him, unblinking, malevolent. He had a ridiculous feeling that she was mesmerising him. To break it he looked away and gulped the rest of the whisky. As he put the glass down he knew the drink had been drugged. His legs felt weak and he couldn't stop his mind wandering purposelessly into vagaries about the past. He groped for a chair he couldn't properly see and slumped in it.

106

Immediately Gamboul was across and standing over him.

" Now you'll tell me," she ordered.

He talked hesitantly at first, sentences unfinished, subjects trivial and unconnected; but by the end of half an hour she had learned the whole story.

She sat looking at the half-conscious Fleming sprawled awkwardly in his chair for a long time after the questioning. She wondered if this enigmatic but highly desirable Englishman had somehow outwitted her and faked his reaction to the truth drug. She dismissed the idea as absurd; she knew all there was to know about its effects.

She picked up the house phone on Salim's cleared desk and gave an order for Fleming to be taken back to his quarters. For herself she called for a car to be brought round.

Twenty minutes later she arrived at Andre's quarters. The door was open and only one guard was near. She asked him in Arabic where the white girl was, and the man answered that she had come out and gone to the building opposite. Frightened, he added that they had not been ordered to use force to prevent her moving within the station.

Gamboul went to the computer building. Abu Zeki was not there; only two guards walked ceaselessly up and down the main corridor. She saw Andre sitting quietly before the sensory screen in the communication section.

" What are you doing here? " Gamboul asked suspiciously.

Andre smiled at her. " I am waiting," she said tonelessly. " For you. You are the logical choice." She looked intently at the darkened screen. " What have you forced Dr. Fleming to tell you? "

" You—you know about that? " Gamboul exclaimed.

Andre nodded. " It is all predictable. No doubt you could not believe all he said. But I will show you. Sit beside me. Do not be frightened. There is no need."

Gamboul pulled across a chair. Andre gave her a reassuring nod and then placed her hands on the sensory controls. The screen produced a dot of light which expanded and faded. Then came a vague, misty imagery in half-tones.

" What is that? " Gamboul whispered.

Andre's voice was flat and mechanical. " Watch," she said. " I will explain. It is where the message comes from. Soon you will know what has been calculated for you to do."

107

Far into the night the two women sat before the screen, the frail, slight figure of Andre taut and somehow proud; Gamboul, motionless, transfixed, as her eyes tried to assimilate the strange figurations which hovered, cleared and grew misty on the screen, while her brain absorbed the low murmur of Andre's interpretation.

Abu Zeki was the only person, apart from the uninterested guards, who saw them there. Recognising Gamboul, he turned away. The woman intimidated him, and he disliked her. In any event, he had heard of her intimacy with Colonel Salim. It would not be wise to get involved with the new dictator's mistress.

He went to his quarters and lay on his bed. He knew he would not be able to sleep properly, the time was too momentous. He thought happily about the brave new world that had been born at the moment the state radio announced the change of government. Yet there was a niggling premonition of disaster at the back of his mind. He recognised that this was the result of his talk with Fleming. He liked Fleming; liked the way he saw through the trappings of a problem to the heart of it. Abu wanted to learn to be like that.

Deliberately he forced his mind to shift to pleasanter things —his wife, his baby son. But it was no good. The low hum of the computer seemed to permeate the very air. He dozed off . . . .

The hum. So it was still operating. He sat up and looked at his watch. The luminous hands showed 3.30. If the women were still there they had been working for at least eight hours.

He got up. Already the eastern sky had a pinkish tinge. He ran across the compound to the computer block. A guard, asleep on his feet, started with fright. Abu identified himself and the man lolled back against the wall.

Inside the block the lights were bright, and the air was heavy and warm after the sharpness of the night air from the desert. Abu crept forward slowly. The two women were still there, staring at the screen. Andre's voice was so low that he could not make out what she was saying even when he stopped a few feet behind them.

" Mm'selle Gamboul," he said. " What is happening? Miss Andre, it is I—Abu Zeki."

For all the notice they took he might have been a voiceless ghost. He felt a prickle of fear and crept quietly away.

Outside he stopped and breathed deeply the fresh, lovely air.

He felt better and it cleared his mind. He realised what he must do next.

He ran to Fleming's quarters. A guard outside, wide awake, barred his way. The soldier called over his shoulder and the door opened. Kaufman came out.

" I must see Dr. Fleming," Abu said.

Kaufman grunted that he could come in. Fleming was sprawled, fully clothed, on his bed. A couple of chairs facing each other showed where Kaufman had been resting while watching him.

Abu shook Fleming roughly by the shoulder. " Doctor Fleming," he begged, " you must come right away! "

Fleming groaned, opened his eyes, and screwed up his face. " What time is it? " he mumbled.

" Nearly four."

Fleming sat up with a start. He fought off a bout of dizziness.

"The doctor has had a little drug," Kaufman explained. " He will be all right presently."

Fleming got gingerly to his feet. " What's the matter, Abu? " he asked, ignoring the German.

" I do not understand what is happening," Abu said: " Mm'selle Gamboul came to the computer yesterday evening. She was with the girl. I went to bed. They are still there—in the communication unit. I spoke to them, but they took no notice. They did not seem to know I was with them. They were watching the display tube."

Fleming ran his fingers through his hair. " Oh my God! I should have guessed." He crossed to the door. Kaufman moved in front of it, his plump hand round the handle.

" I have orders," he said uneasily.

Fleming braced himself for a show-down. Hastily Abu intervened. " He must come," he shouted at Kaufman; " he is needed for the computer."

Kaufman looked doubtfully from one to the other. He was bewildered. The computer was everything. His job was above all else to serve it.

" If he must, he must," he grumbled. " But I will escort you," he said to Fleming. " My orders are to watch you."

" Hold my bloody hand if you want," snarled Fleming; " but for God's sake let's go." He turned to Abu. " Go and wake Professor Dawnay," he ordered. " Tell her to come over to the computer block right away."

The air and the short walk did him good. The fuzziness in his brain cleared and he soon felt he had proper control of his limbs. He slammed through the swing doors and loped towards the computer section. Immediately a guard pointed his automatic rifle at him. Kaufman took a step to one side.

Fleming stopped, the muzzle against his chest. Down the lighted corridor he could see Gamboul rising from her chair. A different Gamboul. She was meekly listening to something Andre was saying. Then she nodded and came towards them.

Kaufman moved behind Fleming and gripped his arms, pinioning them against his body. Gamboul passed them all as if they did not exist. Her head was tilted back and there was a vague smile on her lips.

Fleming struggled to free himself. " Stop her," he yelled. " For God's sake don't let her get out of here."

He struggled violently, but Kaufman held him. " You will stay with me! "

Gamboul had passed through the entrance hall and there was the sound of her car moving off before Madeleine Dawnay came hurrying in.

Kaufman released his grip on Fleming and nodded to the guard. " They may pass."

Fleming ran to the console and bent over Andre. She glanced at him and then leaned back, lost in reverie. Dawnay came up. She was alarmed at the death-like pallor of the girl.

" What is it, John? " she asked. " What's happened? "

Fleming grasped the back of the swivel chair and pulled Andre round so that she could not avoid his gaze.

" What have you done? " he whispered.

She smiled serenely. " What had to be done," she murmured. " Mademoiselle Gamboul knows what to do." Her lip curled almost contemptuously. " She was not afraid when I showed her the meaning."

Suddenly her strength and assurance left her and she crumpled up like a sick, helpless child.

Dawnay bent over her. " She's desperately ill, John," she said gently. " Let's get her to the sick bay."

Fleming snapped an order to Kaufman. Frightened and ser-vile, the German came forward, lifting Andre by the shoulders

110

while Fleming took her feet. They carried her to the sick bay, where Dawnay ordered them outside while she and the nurse got the girl to bed.

Kaufman tried to talk to Fleming, anxious for reassurance; he sensed that he was somehow involved in a disaster and would be blamed for it. Fleming ignored him and the German walked away disconsolately.

When Dawnay came out she drew Fleming away from the door. "She's weak, terribly weak," she whispered, "as if she'd been making some enormous effort. But she's falling asleep. The nurse will tell us if there's any change. Come across to my room and I'll make some coffee."

While the percolator was heating Dawnay asked if there was any news from outside. "Colonel Salim's taken over completely, I suppose?"

"I don't know much," said Fleming wearily. "I was drugged last night—by the Gamboul woman. Made me tell her about Andre. Probably the same drug as they used on you in London. Afterwards she must have come straight here to the computer and found Andre waiting for her."

"But why?" Dawnay demanded.

Fleming sighed. "The computer has selected Gamboul as the boss. I thought it would choose Salim, but this is cleverer. Through her the machine will take power."

"How?"

"I don't know. Somehow the machine communicated to her what Andre couldn't put into words for me. I suppose it managed to give Gamboul the sort of appalling, momentary flash of revelation saints and prophets are said to have. It's all so damnably logical and inevitable. Like Andre's always saying, the whole thing's predictable."

The coffee was bubbling. Dawnay poured out two cups and handed one to Fleming. "I've never had quite this feeling before," she said. "Of everything closing in."

He laughed shortly. "You know I have. And I also proved that appealing to someone, Osborne for instance, or taking destructive action, didn't really help." He stirred his coffee violently, splashing it in the saucer. "Now the computer's won. the whole thing's out of our hands—for good. We're finished."

Appropriately, as if for effect, a gust of wind moaned across the compound and scratched grittily against the outside walls.

111

Dawnay went to shut the door while sand spattered against the window.

She stopped, seeing Abu Zeki running across to them. He stood panting when he arrived, getting his breath. " Dr. Fleming," he got out at last. " Colonel Salim is dead."

Fleming nodded, as if he felt no surprise. "And all his army stooges? "

Abu licked his lips. " I don't know," he said. " I don't really understand. The army guards have gone from here. There are just the Intel wardens and orderlies. But they are now armed. I cannot understand."

Fleming stood up and stared out of the door. " I'll tell you what's happened," he said. " Gamboul's taken control. She either had Salim murdered or did it herself. She is perfectly capable of killing, even if an exterior force didn't tell her to. There can't be hitches in this plan, so if Salim's coup has failed it isn't a mishap but a stage in the general scheme. What about the old man? "

" The President, you mean? " Abu asked. " He is still in his palace. The message announcing Colonel Salim's death came from him, personally."

Another gust of wind swept through the compound. Fleming bent his head as sand stung his eyes. He turned and shut the door. " The President will be the lady's front man. She'll pull the strings and he'll twitch. We'll all be her puppets soon."

Dawnay slowly drained the last of her coffee. " John," she said thoughtfully, " it's very strange."

" Strange? What's strange about it? Gamboul's doing just what she's compelled to do. Part of the programme."

She shook her head impatiently. " I don't mean the political thing. But the wind. Here it doesn't normally blow like this, not at this time of the year."

" Doesn't it? " he answered absent-mindedly. "A nice reminder of Thorness. The weather was hell when Andre and I were hiding up on that island."

" Yes," she agreed. " Conditions were abnormal there as well. I think I'll do some work in the lab." She looked already pre-occupied, as if she were working. " I wish I could get those sea samples I wanted."

" Lucky to have something to do," Fleming said. " I don't feel anxious to report as an obedient serf to that electronic dictator across the way." He looked at Abu. " But someone had better be there, Abu. Go over and hang around for instructions. I've no doubt Gamboul will be sending her Teutonic stooge with some orders."

Fleming wandered back to his own quarters. The wind still blew, sweeping momentarily stinging gusts of sand and then subsiding as quickly as it had come.

He glanced at his watch. It was early, just after 6.30. He switched on his short-wave radio, tuned to the B.B.C. Middle East service. He wondered how long they'd be left with even this one-way link with anywhere else.

The static was bad, the voice from London fading and distorting so that it was sometimes inaudible.

". . . . No further news has come in about the situation in Azaran. The frontiers remain closed, and during the night the government station at Baleb has merely continued to re-transmit the President's announcement that a military junta has been set up . . ."

The spluttering drowned the bulletin for a few minutes. When it eased the newsreader was saying ". . . . similar conditions are reported from all over Western Europe and from countries bordering the Mediterranean. Gales of unusual force are being recorded as far afield as the East coast of Africa, in the vicinity of Aden, and from weather stations in Iceland and Newfoundland."

Fleming switched off the set. He found it almost natural that the world's weather should have gone mad at a time when the world itself was moving irrevocably to a crisis.

8

FORECAST

ON the following day Janine Gamboul summoned Kaufman to her office. Instead of one of her usual chic frocks she was wearing a plain tailored suit, but he noticed at once that there was something else different about her; she had a dedicated and, at the same time, unnaturally exalted air.

She did not look up from her desk when Kaufman entered, and he stood stiffly at attention a little distance away from her.

When she had finished writing, she glanced up at him coldly, not inviting him to sit down.

" The situation is perfectly quiet," she said in decisive tones. " I suggest you inform your department of this fact, together with a report of what happened. Explain that we are in control and will remain so."

"And Colonel Salim," he asked diffidently, " what shall I say about him? He was well regarded by the Vienna office."

She shrugged. " Tell them the facts. That I—that he was shot because he was in the way. He was a petty nationalist and if he had got power he would have used the computer for his own stupid little ends. You can explain that? "

She dismissed the matter and picked up the sheet of paper on which she had been writing. " This morning the President is giving audience to his Council. Poor little man. He's very bewildered, and frightened. But he realises that he must co-operate. He is perfectly amenable, particularly since Salim was dealt with. He will ensure the loyalty of all these old men of the government. You will attend the meeting to represent Intel. I have outlined proposals so far as we are involved." She handed him a document.

Kaufman took it and read it slowly. Occasionally he nodded,

114

as if pleased. " I have always done my best," he murmured. " You may rely on me in the future."

" Good," she said, with a gesture of dismissal. " Now go to the palace and instruct the President's secretary."

The councillors were seated around the Presidential dais: a dozen proud, elderly Arabs in traditional dress. True to their race they concealed whatever emotions they felt as the President, with a kind of tired dignity, gave them a carefully doctored version of what had happened and told them that he himself was taking personal control. The traitor Salim, the way of his death unexplained, was to be buried without military honours; all officers who had taken part in the revolt were already suspended and would be court-martialled. The troops and all civil branches of the Government would be answerable only to the President's personal edict. In due course there would be elections, but in the meantime the existing Parliament would not be called into session.

At a nod from the President these edicts were translated by his secretary into English, out of courtesy to Kaufman.

One Councillor half rose to his feet. "And who will the President be responsible to? " he demanded, deliberately speaking in English and glaring at Kaufman.

" To himself," Kaufman answered sharply.

The President remained impassive, and the Councillor sat down, muttering into his beard.

" Gentlemen," said Kaufman, rising proudly to his feet. " The President, and therefore the country, can rely on a continuance of help on an increasing scale by the mercantile consortium, Intel, which I represent. To further the welfare of Azaran without interference, it is the wish of my superiors that the country should not renew diplomatic relations with other nations."

The words were translated and caused a low hubbub of conversation.

" You should say more about the kind of help you are to give," said the President uneasily.

Kaufman beamed. " The Consortium is producing new instruments of defence and technical value. It will shortly be making available a new process, perfected in our laboratories here, to turn the desert into fertile agricultural land."

He waited while the secretary translated, and a wizened old Arab whispered urgently to the secretary.

"The Sheik Azi ben Ardu wishes to know what the process is."

"It is a spray," said Kaufman shortly. "In a short while it will be demonstrated."

The Councillor who had asked the question about Presidential responsibility glowered at Kaufman. "And the wind that has come out of season and blows our soil away, what can your laboratories do for that?"

Kaufman had no prepared answer. He looked to the President for help.

"What can they do?" the President replied mildly. "The wind is the servant of Allah. We must not question it."

Fleming had never been under any illusion about his situation. He knew that he was virtually a prisoner, but only on this first morning of the new regime did he feel the reality of it. There was no work he wanted to do, or could be persuaded to do, knowing what it would be. There was no one to talk to; even Abu had disappeared into the executive building, in answer to a summons from Gamboul. Guards were patrolling everywhere. Before breakfast they had forbidden Fleming to approach the sick quarters where Andre lay. The best he had managed was to insist on seeing the nurse who had come out and reported that her patient was a little worse, but was sleeping.

He sat a long time over a late breakfast, ignoring the coarse brown bread, fruit and olives they always served, and drinking cup after cup of sweet, thick coffee.

Then he strolled across to Dawnay's laboratory. The guards eyed him suspiciously but did not prevent him from entering the building.

Dawnay was busy at a laboratory bench. She greeted him absent-mindedly and did not react very much to his worried talk about Andre.

"There's nothing we can do for her," she muttered. She paused and then picked up one of a row of large test tubes.

"I'd like you to look at these, John," she said.

He glanced at the one in her hand. It was full of a semi-transparent, greyish fluid which clung to the glass when she shook it. The other tubes seemed to be identical.

"What are they?" he asked.

"Sea water samples they got for me." She gave a short laugh. "I must admit that Intel are efficient. They wouldn't let me go

116

and take my own specimens, but they did much more than I asked. Not only are these from the Persian Gulf, which I wanted, but they've had samples flown in from the Mediterranean and Indian Ocean and even the Western Atlantic. So that there should be samples from other areas for comparison, I suppose."

"And is there anything to compare? " he asked.

She shook the tube vigorously. The fluid inside went completely opaque.

" See? " she said. " Now, normal sea water should be like this one. You'll see it's clear." She handed him another test tube.

Fleming picked up some of the other tubes. They all went opaque when he shook them. " Sure Kaufman didn't fool you and get them all from the same place? " he grinned.

She shook her head. " Not he. He got his orders from Intel, not from me. You know what he's like. If they told him to fetch water from the Antarctic he'd get it. But I want you to watch what happens when this milky sea water mixes with the clear sample."

She took a clean test tube, poured in some of the clear water and then added two minute drops of the opaque fluid. The milky droplets dissolved and disappeared. Dawnay clamped the tube in a holder with a light reflector behind it.

" Now watch," she said.

Slowly the water clouded near the bottom of the tube; the cloudiness spread upwards until the water was as opaque as the others.

" I wonder how the fish like it," murmured Fleming. "Any idea what it is? "

"A bacterium," she said. " Come over here."

He followed her to the table where she switched on a light and focused a microscope. " Look at this slide," she told him.

Fleming peered into the microscope, adjusted the focus, and gave a low whistle. A globular organism was palpitating; as he watched, it divided and swelled. Thirty seconds later the division was repeated. He straightened up from the microscope. " Know where it comes from? "

Dawnay made no reply. She picked up a slide from a small cabinet and slid it into a second microscope. " This one's dead. It conforms to no bacterium group I've heard of. It's a very simple organism, as you'll see if you look at this one which I've stained. It doesn't appear to have more than one remarkable

117

property—the ability to reproduce fantastically. If it wasn't shut in the test tubes ——." She hesitated. "If it had the whole ocean in which to breed . . . ." Again she stopped.

Fleming walked back to the bench, thoughtfully looking at the neatly labelled test tubes. "The areas marked on these specimens," he said, "rather coincide with those I keep hearing in the B.B.C. shipping forecasts and weather reports—storms, gales, and so forth."

"Yes," she agreed, "and one of them we know quite well. A very rich mixture."

She lifted a test tube labelled "Minch" gingerly, as if she were half afraid of it. "The channel between Scotland and the Hebrides."

"With Thorness on the east side," he finished for her. "So what?"

"It must have all started somewhere," she said. "In the originating area it would have a higher density of bacteria than the more newly infected zones."

He stared at her. "You've no proof for saying that this one from the Minch . . . ."

She shook her head. "No. All these samples were populated to capacity when I got them. There's no telling the percentage of bacteria when they were drawn from the sea. To make a proper check I'd have to get accurate and localised storm centre reports and then make on-the-spot checks of sea water samples in the same zones. There just might emerge a correlation between these little beasts and the weather."

"Or again you might not," he said with a rather badly-contrived heartiness. "Look here, Madeleine, we don't want to get too imaginative or maudlin about all this. Collate the data, sift out the facts, draw the inferences—that's the routine. And incarcerated here we haven't got a chance of doing much, though I guess you can do a break-up on the bacterial structure.

"But it's pretty obvious, the smart way they got you all this ocean, that Intel have some notions along your lines—that the weather is more than naturally upset. My guess is that you can put in a chit for samples from here to Timbuktu, or at least wherever there's a bit of sea, and the resourceful Kaufman will send off his minions with their little buckets and bottles to get them for you. All you can do to inject some sense and order into the sources you need is for us to glue our ears to the B.B.C. bulletins."

They agreed that one or other of them should try to listen in to every bulletin and weather report, making notes of the areas mentioned.

There was no dearth of information. The midday bulletin gave priority to weather news. The first hurricanes ever recorded in Britain had caused death and destruction on a major scale from Penzance to Wick. The electric grid had broken down because of smashed pylons. Huge areas of Lancashire and East Anglia were flooded. The Air Ministry could hold out no hope of improvement. The barometric pressure remained the lowest ever known outside tropical areas.

Fleming and Dawnay heard that bulletin together. Neither had any need to write down the details, and neither felt inclined to talk about it. But when a boisterous gust of wind abruptly surged in from the desert, whirling up little spirals of sand and making a clatter as open doors banged and windows crashed, they both felt the burden of something sinister with more force than the distant wavering voice from London had caused. The wind was hot and dry, but Dawnay shivered as it buffeted her.

Fleming moved the tuning dial on the short-wave set, searching for more news. Words, music, and more words flicked in and faded—meaningless to occidental ears. Then he found what he was looking for: the Voice of America.

A beat record clamoured abruptly to its close and the announcer came on with his station identification. The news which followed had no political significance. As in London, ideologies and flag-waving had been shelved. The news was solely of the weather.

" The United States Weather Bureau," said the newsreader, " today gave warning of further gales approaching the Eastern seaboard of the United States. They are expected to be on a similar scale to those which swept across Western Europe during the night. American scientists are speaking of a shift of world weather patterns comparable to those at the beginning of the Ice Age . . . ."

Fleming snapped off the switch. Dawnay got up. " I'll be in the lab if you have any ideas," she said.

More or less deliberately they avoided one another in the next couple of days. They both felt completely helpless, but they listened meticulously to every bulletin, noting down the areas where the storms were worst.

The wind scale figures were the best guide. On the third morning, after the early morning bulletin had reported more havoc in Britain, the Netherlands, France and Spain, Fleming went back to Dawnay's lab. He was impressed by what she had been doing. One end of the laboratory had been cleared. A huge map of the Northern hemisphere had been pinned up on the wall. Coloured pins were dotted about it, thickest in a strip from Gibraltar to the Orkneys, with a big cluster east of the Hebrides.

" Hello, John," she greeted him. " You see, a pattern's emerging all right. And that's not all." She beckoned him across to a long bench against the wall on which several dozen test tubes stood in a long row.

" Kaufman hasn't had time to get all the samples I asked for, of course, but ten more arrived late last night. From off-shore spots in Britain. I told him that all samples were to be boiled as soon as possible after they were taken. This bug is killed at 100 degrees Fahrenheit; that way there wasn't any chance of a bacterial increase during transit."

She stubbed a finger on one test tube. " That's the thickest. It comes from the coast of Obanshire. The evidence is circumstantial of course, but I think we must accept it. I've arranged for Andre to be brought here this morning."

Fleming started. " But she's sick," he protested. " She can't help."

" She is sick, and getting sicker," Dawnay answered. " That's why we must see her quickly. Please, John, you know I'm not callous—but she must help if she can and I believe it's possible."

Fleming sighed. " You're the boss. But I don't like it."

A nurse pushed Andre to the laboratory in a wheel chair. Fleming managed a welcoming smile as he clasped her hands. It was not easy; she looked desperately fragile and her eyes stared out of her drawn, pale face.

He was appalled by how much she had deteriorated since he had last been allowed to see her.

The nurse made her comfortable and then Dawnay explained the situation, showing her the test tubes and pointing out that the most opaque sample came from the Minch.

" What is the Minch? " Andre asked.

120

" The channel off Thorness, where all this started," Dawnay said harshly.

" It is impossible. It does not make sense. It has nothing to do with the message." She looked from Dawnay to Fleming, bewildered and wary. " The message has a different plan."

Dawnay snorted. " There won't be any different plan if this engulfs us. Think, girl; think! "

" There is nothing about it in the computer," Andre insisted.

Fleming took a step forward. " Not now, maybe," he said thoughtfully. " But there's something vaguely familiar about this bug. I'm sure there is. How far have you got with your analysis, Madeleine? "

Dawnay said nothing, but went to her desk and picked up a file. "As far as I've got has been coded in binary. Is that of any help? " she asked.

He took the file, walked to the window, and sat on the sill while he studied the figures. He laid the file aside. " It confirms my hunch, memory, or whatever it is. It reads terribly like something I already know."

" Then it's something you started," Andre interrupted.

He looked round in surprise. " That I started? "

"At Thorness. That's why this machine has no memory of it." She paused and lay back, as if trying to summon up some strength. " How many times did you try to destroy the other computer before you succeeded? " she asked.

" Several."

"After one of those times the computer decided to hit back. With this bacterium." Her eyes became cold and hostile, giving Fleming an empty feeling of despair. " You have a great force sent to help you and you turn it against you. You won't listen to me. You won't listen to anyone. You condemn your whole race because you won't accept. There is nothing you can do now. It will engulf you! "

There was a sort of inhuman resignation in her tone. Fleming turned away, making for the door. He felt sick to his soul.

For a day or so afterwards he avoided everyone. Intel had provided its internees with a first class library and subscriptions had been taken out for the world's technical journals. He read in a desultory sort of way, his brain hardly registering the information. The journals were all back numbers; interference with communications since the storm cycle had increased had

121

cut off all but essential supplies, although some Intel transports still plied between Azaran and Europe.

He heard the hum from the computer and guessed that the thing had drawn Andre to it, no doubt on orders from Gamboul. He could imagine what the machine was working on—rocket interceptors of the kind that had been its first official triumph at Thorness. There was a ghastly this-is-where-I-came-in flavour about the whole thing. He wondered a little how the formulae were being handled once the output printer had produced the equations. Without proper interpretation they were just gibberish even for skilled electronic engineers. But, of course, there was Abu Zeki. Fleming readily accepted that the young man was as good as any highly-paid boffin in his particular line of country; it wasn't surprising really. The Arabs had invented the whole basis of mathematics as modern civilisation knew it.

Fleming pondered a lot on Abu, not just Abu the first-rate product of a technological age, but Abu the man. He was innately decent, kindly and blessed with imagination. His patriotism was fiery and nationalistic, but he did not let his emotions completely stifle his reasoning.

Fleming swung off the bed where he had been sprawling, his mind made up, and picked up his room telephone. In a losing battle one ally was better than none at all. He would ask Abu to fix some time when they could talk without interruption.

The operator told him Dr. Abu Zeki was in the computer block. Fleming had no wish to go there and see Andre slowly dying as the machine sucked the last use out of her. He asked to be put through, not caring that the call would probably be monitored.

" Hello, Abu. Fleming. I wondered, with the week-end coming up, whether we could have a chat? Maybe I could meet your family? I'm afraid my tame guard would probably have to come too."

" Why yes, Dr. Fleming, I'd be honoured to be your host." Abu sounded guarded. " It will be good for you to meet the ordinary people of Azaran. My home is very simple, I'm afraid, but you will be welcome. Please stay overnight."

They fixed a time to leave on Saturday at midday, when Abu was off duty till Monday morning. Deliberately Fleming phoned through to Kaufman's office to request permission for a social visit. The German was out but a secretary took the details. The pass was brought to Fleming's quarters that evening. No one queried the reason.

Abu was the proud possesser of a little Italian car, and his home was only twenty-five miles from the Intel station. But, as he explained while they sped along the highway past the airport, his contract demanded that he live on the site except at weekends.

" My wife doesn't like that, but she has her mother with her," Abu went on " With the baby to look after, Saturday soon comes round."

It was as though he were talking about Surbiton, Surrey, or White Plains, New York. But the similarity soon ended.

The road petered out into a wide track of rolled stones and then to a little more than a sandy track. Abu dropped his speed when the little car laboured with its unaccustomed load of three men. The guard, sitting in the occasional seat at the back, cursed in Arabic about the bumps, but he seemed glad to be away from the compound, even though the wind sent sand whirling grittily into the car.

The track began to wind with a gradual gradient. The terrain became more stony. Ahead the low range of mountains, rocky hills really, grew more defined despite the sporadic sandstorm. Fleming had often looked at them because of their fascinating, ever-changing colours at different times of the day. In early morning they were pink, changing to white when the sun climbed higher. By midday they were always blurred by heat haze; in the evening they towered black and vast.

Abu pointed to a small collection of rectangular, flat-roofed dwellings lying on a tiny plateau immediately below a fault in the range.

" That is my village," he said, " or at least the one where I have made my home. People have lived here since long before your Christ. Look! "

Fleming followed the direction of Abu's glance. The rock face bore traces of enormous bas-reliefs—formalised animals and serried ranks of bearded warriors. None was perfect, rock falls jagging into the sculpture.

" Persian," Abu explained. " English archaeologists were here many years ago; more recently the Americans. All have gone now, of course. What they were really interested in was the temple. You'll see it round the next bend."

Dwarfed by the rock face, the temple was just a ruin, a few pillars still standing amid a mass of rubble. Abu said that the pillars were Roman, but the site had yielded remains of several civilisations and religions—Assyrian, Persian, and a few tablets of Egyptian origin. "As you know, Azaran has been a vassal of many empires," Abu said. " Now of none! "

He bumped off the track and down what was little more than a donkey path. His wife was standing outside the tiny house, a pretty woman, little more than a girl. Although she wore Arab costume she was unveiled.

She lowered her eyes when Abu introduced Fleming, but her welcome was warm, and in perfect English. " Lemka was at Cairo University, among the first girl students under Colonel Nasser's new scheme," Abu said proudly.

" You are hot," Lemka said to Fleming. " Please come inside out of the terrible wind. It is cooler. Perhaps you will have some of our wine." She glanced towards the car and saw the soldier leaning against the shady side of the vehicle.

" What is the man doing? " she asked, clutching her husband's arm. " You are now under guard? "

" He is an escort for Dr. Fleming," Abu told her, but she was not completely satisfied.

" There is much trouble in the city? " she asked. " On the radio they say so little. Just that the coup is over and all is peace again. Is it so? "

" Yes," Abu said. " Everything is normal. Now get us something to drink and then see about a meal. I have told my friend he will have to take what the English call pot luck."

Lemka passed through the curtained opening to the tiny kitchen at the rear.

' My wife is Christian," Abu said; " that is why she is not so effacing as most Arab wives."

" But you are Moslem? " Fleming asked. " Yours is a Moslem name."

' I'm a scientist," he retorted. "And I am also for my country."

Fleming eased himself down on the low backless settee. "And I'm for the whole human race—more or less. Look, Abu, you didn't believe me about the computer, did you? Well, now believe me about the girl."

Lemka returned with a jug of wine and some glasses. She

124

poured some out and handed a glass to Fleming. The wine was sweet and thin, but refreshing.

" It's a pretty simple set-up," Fleming began, not caring that Lemka was listening. " Intel built the computer and employed you to help operate it. As you know, after Neilson got away it wouldn't work, so they hi-jacked me and I brought the girl. Intel's aim was to get a technical edge on all their competitors and a well-protected base from which to operate. Hence the missile designs you've been working on. Your President was agreeable to the arrangements. This suited the intelligence behind the computer. But it didn't suit Salim. He was an intelligent and ambitious man. He wanted to have absolute control of the whole set-up."

" He was a patriot," said Abu defiantly.

Fleming shrugged. " He certainly wasn't a man to play second fiddle to another influence. Andromeda knew it, or at least she learned it from the computer which could calculate such an eventuality. So Andre made the decision: to put the power into the hands of Intel, in fact. Our handsome boss was shown the message, or part of it, and had the meaning of it explained to her by Andre the night they were together in the computer."

"And that could influence her? " Abu was doubtful.

" Influence her? " Fleming retorted. " Obsess her completely. She had Salim killed or probably shot him herself. She's a convert who suddenly saw a vision. It made her fanatical."

" Like St. Paul? "

Both men started. They had forgotten Lemka. " But how could a vision be put into words? " she asked.

" St. Paul managed it," Fleming suggested.

" He only described it in your Bible," Abu said. " He couldn't pass it on as he really knew it."

" You're right," Fleming agreed. " You can't pass such things on, but you can impose them. That was the intention of the computer, then of Andromeda, and now of Gamboul. You can also describe the inferences. I myself have had a glimpse of that description."

Abu thoughtfully examined his empty glass. " You believe what you say? How would you describe this vision? "

" It says that mankind goes round by a long road, and it

125

may be too long. We may destroy ourselves before we take the next step."

"But if we can have the help of a higher intelligence and avoid that mistake," Abu protested.

"It's the handshake of death. The friend who knows better than you what's good for you." Fleming pointed towards the tiny window, at the vista of desert they had crossed in the car.

"You've heard of the Pax Romana," he said, "the calm of desolation the Roman legions left after they had forced their idea of right on the barbarians. That's the sort of peace you're working for, Abu my friend. Personally I'd rather we muddled our way along."

"And destroy ourselves?"

"No!" Fleming shouted. "If anything destroys us it will be something sent from outside. Via the computer."

"You have no proof," said Abu obstinately.

Lemka looked from one man to the other. "You should know when a man is right," she told her husband. "And help him."

Abu glared at her but she held his gaze, and slowly he smiled. Awkwardly he slid his hand into hers. "I will try," he said quietly. He turned to Fleming. "On Monday, Doctor, I will seek an interview with M'mselle Gamboul."

Fleming thanked him, doubting whether this futile little manoeuvre would make any difference. With an effort he stirred himself "Fine," he said. "We'll work out the sort of thing to say, to appeal to her conscience, if any. But all this is unfair on your wife. It's the week-end."

The friendship between the two men grew warmer in the few hours away from the strain of the Intel establishment. Abu took Fleming exploring among the temple ruins on the Sunday morning. They had to cut the visit short because the wind was much stronger than on the previous day, bringing small but dangerous cascades of stones and rocks from the precipitous heights behind the temple. Fleming explained Dawnay's and his theory about the origin of the abnormal weather. Abu could accept this because he had seen some of the results of the computer's calculations on the sea water bacteria. He promised to try to explain it to Gamboul.

The two men and the guard drove back to the station at dawn on Monday, choosing an early start because they had

126

already learned that sunrise and sunset brought a short period of calm. As they zig-zagged down the mountainside towards the plain they heard a roaring in the distance and saw a sudden rush of flame up into the sky.

Abu applied for an interview with Gamboul as soon as he went on duty. He was told to report to the executive suite at 11.

She greeted him almost effusively. " Well, Dr. Zeki," she said. " You'll be the first here to know that this morning we tested the missile prototype. It was a complete success. We are now as good as Britain in that field." She smiled expectantly. "And you have other good things on the way for us? "

" Yes, Mm'selle," he said. " But I wish to ask your permission to speak on another matter."

" What is it you want? " she asked, her friendliness vanished, quickly replaced by suspicion.

" I come on behalf of Dr. Fleming. He thinks that the weather conditions in Europe and America, and even here, arise in some way from the computer. From the message." He stopped, momentarily intimidated by her look of implacable hostility. " Dr. Fleming would like permission for Professor Dawnay to contact the International Weather Bureau."

" No! " she banged her fist on the desk like a man. " What he says is nonsense."

" But if the message. . . ."

" I know the message! What it tells us to do is perfectly clear. And the weather is not part of the mission the message has given to us."

Abu shifted a little. " If you would just see Dr. Fleming ——" he began.

She half shouted her answer at him. " He doesn't interest me. He has nothing to say which interests me. Do you understand? "

Abu backed to the door. " Thank you, Mm'selle," he muttered.

When the door closed Gamboul bent over the inter-com microphone on her desk. The red switch was already depressed.

" Herr Kaufman," she called quietly. " You heard what Doctor Abu Zeki had to say? Good! You will have him watched now, all the time."

9

DEPRESSION

OSBORNE stared out of the carriage window at the sprawl of South London. His left arm was still in a sling to take the strain off the pectoral muscle which Kaufman's gunman had shot through. Otherwise he was very little hurt, and the wound itself was healing rapidly.

If he had had a miraculous escape, so had London. Damage from the previous night's hurricane was not as great as he had feared, so far as he could see from the slowly moving train. T.V. aerials were bent grotesquely and a lot of roofs had gaping holes where chimney stacks had toppled. He was jammed against the glass by the pressure of the other standing passengers. The journey from his home at Orpington had taken more than two hours already. He could not complain the train was late; it was unscheduled. With the power lines out of action only diesel trains from the coast were getting through. His train eased forward in stops and starts, passed from section to section by manual signalling.

Being a cautious man, he had started out early, knowing that after a night like the past one travel would be difficult. But he was beginning to worry. The Ministry meeting was scheduled for 10.30. The others, living around Whitehall, would doubtless be there on time.

The train stopped for ten minutes south of the river. Osborne saw Battersea power station, as vast and solid as ever, the usual plume of white smoke from the stack whipped away by the still boisterous wind. Almost imperceptibly they started again, and kept going. The electric signalling system was working here and they swung over the points and cruised gently into Charing Cross. Hastily scrawled notices gave warnings about falling glass from the roof; they were ignored by the rush of exasperated commuters making for the exits.

Out in the Strand life seemed fairly normal. A hoarding had blown down, but traffic was moving, though slowly. The centre of Trafalgar Square was roped off. Nelson still looked across London from his column, but presumably the authorities were taking precautions.

Osborne turned into Whitehall. A barricade or two where windows had been blown out, nothing more. Big Ben stood unharmed, its clock proclaiming that it was 10.21. Osborne quickened his steps. He would be just in time after all.

The Minister was already in his office when he arrived. He grunted a perfunctory greeting and returned to his reading. " Neilson sent a message he'd be on time," he said without looking up.

The American arrived a moment later. Osborne cut short his attempt at a cheerful greeting at the sight of the black band on Neilson's arm. The man looked older; the death of his son had hit him hard.

Without preliminaries the Minister opened the meeting. " No time or reason for formalities," he said. " Professor Neilson wants your help, Osborne." He paused and gave a quizzical look. "As Neilson's in the picture as regards your position over the Thorness debacle, you won't mind my referring to it. To put your mind at rest, the enquiry's shelved. It's pretty pointless with the two main witnesses, Fleming and the girl, missing. So put that business out of your mind for the time being. This is what you might call a national emergency. An international commission's being set up under Professor Neilson, and we want someone to run the secretariat."

" Preferably you," said Neilson. The words were unnaturally hoarse and loud.

Osborne turned to him. " You're feeling it too, are you? " he asked. " The breathing? "

Neilson nodded. " It's pretty general, and worse in the hills."

" They're evacuating the Highlands," said the Minister. " We haven't announced it yet, but it's all part of a general pattern. The air at any altitude is getting too thin to be able to breathe."

Neilson got up and walked to a table where a weather map had been spread out, held in position by drawing pins. " The Alps and the Pyrenees are now depopulated," he said. " Would you just come over here, Minister, and you, Osborne? I can show you what we've so far ascertained."

129

The two men stood on either side of the American. "The atmospheric pressure's falling rapidly all around here"—he swept his hand in a wide curve from the Shetlands to Brittany—" as well as in all spots where we have weather ships or Navy vessels able to make careful checks. In other words, the pressure's lowest over the sea in the Northern Atlantic and into the Mediterranean. The indications are slighter in the Indian Ocean and the Pacific, but they are there. Naturally, air rushes from the land masses to compensate, and so you have your storms and this thin atmosphere."

"What do you want me to do?" Osborne asked.

"If you're fit enough?" interposed the Minister. "Not getting any trouble from your injury?"

"I'm all right, Minister."

"Good," said Neilson. "Now, as you can imagine, the data I've been able to collect is too vague, too sporadic. We want all the news we can get, properly collated, and then rationalised. That takes some organising."

The Minister moved to Osborne and put his hand on his shoulder. "With this regrettable sabotage business hanging over you, the security people are rather agin your continuing to have access to—well, you understand, old boy? But we can second you to this weather job and faces are saved all round. Specious but practical."

Osborne gave a wry smile. Before he could say anything, Neilson began explaining what he wanted. "We've got to work back through the weather records for the past month or six weeks. Your Air Ministry has got out some preliminary data. There's no doubt in my mind that this abnormally low pressure began in one area."

The Minister returned to the map. "And I expect you can guess where that was, Osborne," he said. "It was here." He stabbed with his index finger into a cluster of spirals. Beside his finger point the dotted lines of the prohibited maritime area fanned westwards—the Thorness rocket testing range. Osborne felt no surprise. There was a sort of inevitability about the whole thing.

"So now you have some idea of the channels into which your work may lead," said the Minister resignedly. "But I would impress on you that you must remain objective. For a good while your work must be organising a reporting system from all

130

countries. The U.N. people in New York have pushed through a general agreement for co-operation with the committee. You'll get no niet's or non's."

A mass of wind surged against the building, the modern steel windows protesting but not rattling. It died away as suddenly as it had come. Somewhere in the street glass was tinkling. " The great thing is speed," said the Minister.

For the rest of the day Osborne and Neilson worked on setting up an organisation. Largely it was a matter of instructing clerical staff and setting up communications. The Meteorological people at Bracknell would service the information. They installed a radio link. Land lines were no longer reliable.

Before the spring night had fallen the wind began to increase again. There was every sign of a far worse storm even than during the previous night. Osborne gave up all idea of going home.

Neilson went off to his hotel to get some dinner and Osborne was left alone. He took time off to relax and think. The way every nation, large and small, had signified its eagerness to co-operate had been encouraging and stimulating. One tiny blank appeared in the long list of countries listed as willing to help. Osborne felt it peculiar that in the face of such danger from a natural phenomenon internal politics should be so jealously regarded in Azaran.

He picked up the phone and asked for the communications duty officer in the Middle East Section at the Foreign Office. The phone was answered immediately, but it was difficult to hear. The air had chosen that moment to whirl itself into a frenzy. Osborne had to shout his request, the effort making him gasp for breath.

Equally laboured came the reply: " We'll try, sir, but things are difficult. Line communications have gone to hell, and radio is no more reliable. We'll be lucky to get any message out of this building tonight, let alone overseas. And as you know, sir, there's been an upheaval there. Azaran's officially sealed itself off." A crash drowned out the rest of the words. " Window's just blown in," came the voice. " God, what a night! "

It was mid-afternoon when Fleming heaved himself off his bed and went to his shower. Lethargy was insidiously enveloping him, making it possible to lie for hours doing nothing, sometimes hardly thinking. He had not really imagined that Abu would

131

have any success in getting him an interview with Gamboul, any more than he had a definite idea of what he could say to her if he got the chance. Yet, in the frustration of his existence, he had played a sort of game ever since Abu had gone, pretending that the next ten minutes, or the ten minutes after those, would bring a summons.

It hadn't come, of course. Showered and refreshed in body, if not in mind, he made his way to the computer building. Andre was seated at the console, Kaufman close by. She looked desperately ill. Fleming hesitated beside her, but she took no notice of him and he moved away along the corridor.

The output printer was working and Abu was studying the figures emerging.

" I could do nothing," murmured the Arab, without looking up. " I'm suspected now."

Fleming bent down as if to read the figures. "I don't think there's anything any of us can do—except warn people."

Abu tore off the newly completed sheet and stood up. " Go to my home this evening," he whispered. " Give the guards a slip. I can't come. I'm being watched. Lemka will tell you."

Before Fleming could question him further Abu had walked quickly away to the filing office. Fleming watched his retreating back thoughtfully.

Dawnay came from the other end of the corridor. " I saw Abu Zeki all conspiratorial with you through the glass doors," she said, " so I held back. What was it all about? "

" I don't know," Fleming admitted. "A trap perhaps; he had a session with La Gamboul this morning. Or it may be a wild goose chase. But we may as well go down fighting. And what happy tidings have you got? "

" I know what the little beast is."

" What is it? "

"An artificially synthesised bacterium. If we knew how it acts we'd have an idea of what we're up against."

" Can Andre . . .? " He hesitated.

Dawnay gave a rueful smile. " I tried. She says the computer can't help. It knows nothing about the bacterium."

They walked towards the door, to get away from a guard who had paused near them. " I'm reduced to straw-clutching," he continued. " So I'll try walking into our friend Abu's trap if that's what it is."

She clutched at his arm. " Be careful, John," she begged. " With you gone ———."

" I always turn up," he grinned.

Getting away from the compound wasn't easy. Fleming had to wait until nightfall, and he was not too certain of the place where Abu said he had left his car. But he was helped by the weather. The wind, after sporadic bursts of boisterousness throughout the day, was developing into a major gale. The guards had all sought shelter against pillars and walls from the stinging sand.

His eyes adjusted to the moonless darkness after he had walked from the main compound into the service area. Abu's car was parked among several others. The ignition key was in position as Abu had promised. He drove away, not too fast, in case the speed aroused some hidden sentry.

Following the route was tricky. He wished he had taken more careful note of landmarks on the week-end trip. Twice he ran off the track during a particularly violent gust of wind when dense clouds of sand hit him, but the rear-engined Italian car was ideal for the terrain. He got to Abu's house in a couple of hours.

The door opened an inch when he knocked. He identified himself and Lemka told him to come in quickly.

An old woman in Arab costume was sitting in one corner. She pulled her veil over the lower part of her face but her eyes were friendly. On her lap she nursed a baby.

Fleming looked at the child. " Your son? " he asked Lemka.

" Yes; Jan," she said proudly. " Dr. Neilson was his god-father. You have children? "

" No." He felt awkward with this very direct young woman.

" You would like some coffee? " Lemka said. She spoke to her mother in Arabic. The woman laid the child down in its cot and went to the kitchen.

" What's all this about? " Fleming asked when they had both sat down, Lemka beside the cot which she gently rocked. "Abu couldn't tell me anything."

" I made him ask you to come," Lemka said quietly. " You see, I have a cousin who is radio navigator of Intel's air trans-ports. He's on the Europe run."

" They're still flying there? "

She nodded. " It's difficult, but they get through. It would help if you could get in touch with English scientists? My cousin is not allowed to carry messages. All crews are searched before take-off. But he has promised me he will try."

Fleming became thoughtful. It all seemed like a trap. " Why should he? " he asked.

Lemka's mother came in with the coffee, poured out two cups and stole silently away, squatting on the floor in the far corner. Lemka glanced at her, then at the baby. " He'd do it for me, for his family; for our little Jan."

It was something simple, human—the sort of human value which shone out in this nightmare world. Fleming believed her.

" He's going to London; fine. What could he take? A letter? "

She nodded. " It is dangerous, you understand. People are locked up for such things. Even shot."

" Thank you " was all Fleming could find to say. " I will ask Professor Dawnay what the message could usefully include." He stood up to go.

Lemka came beside him. " What is going to happen? " she whispered.

He drew the curtain back from the tiny window. Sheltered by the precipitous hill, the air was clear of sand and the stars sprinkled the black vault of the sky with a myriad pinpoints of light.

" There are two things," he said half to himself. " First, the intelligence out there in Andromeda that sent the message wanted to make contact with whatever forms of life it could find anywhere in the galaxy—in a sort of evangelical way." He looked down at Lemka and smiled. " Remember how we mentioned St. Paul? "

Lemka nodded.

" The intelligence is a sort of missionary in space," he continued. " When it finds life which responds, it converts it; takes it over. It's tried before, maybe, over several million years on different worlds—maybe with success—and now it's tried here, through the girl Andromeda, for what she calls our own good. That's one thing."

"And the other? "

" Where it finds an intellect hostile to it, it destroys it and possibly substitutes something else. That's what's happening now, because we fought. Or rather, because I fought. And lost." His voice faltered. " That's why, Lemka, you might say that I've condemned the whole human race."

" Not yet," she whispered.

" No," he agreed, " not quite yet. There's just a chance that Professor Dawnay will have something for your cousin."

It was early morning when Fleming got back to the compound. He simply drove openly through the main gates under the flood lamps, waving cheerfully to the sentry. The man grinned back. It was clear that so far as the Western people were concerned the guards were instructed to stop them getting out, not to prevent them coming in.

Fleming waited till the working day had begun before he went to see Dawnay. Whatever they put in the message it had to be terse, factual and conveying something more than an appeal for help.

Abu Zeki was in the laboratory with Dawnay. He looked relieved to see Fleming but said nothing.

Dawnay was bending over a big tank she had had installed below the low long window. The glass top was screwed down. Several rubber tubes and wires passed through seals in the top. They were connected to recording instruments, one of which Fleming recognised as a barograph. In the bottom were two or three inches of an opaque fluid.

She greeted him perfunctorily. " No luck with Andre," she said, busy with notes on the instrument recordings. " She was trying to be helpful, I think, but she hasn't the will to do much. Still, I got some of the data I wanted, thanks to Abu."

" Found anything? " Fleming asked.

" Not much. I now know what it does." She removed a test tube clamped vertically with its mouth over one of the tubes from the tank. " It absorbs nitrogen. You'd find less than 3 per cent. in this sample from the air just above the water surface. It also takes up some oxygen, not much—but see for yourself."

She turned to a filing cabinet and withdrew an untidy sheaf of papers. " Just glance over those formulae, will you, John? Tell me if you've seen anything like them before."

He studied the data in silence. " I said it looked familiar. It still does." He handed the papers back.

" It's another synthesis," she murmured.

He was really alarmed. " Not another one starting? " he exclaimed.

" No," she reassured him. " We worked back to this a long way. Yesterday evening I was on familiar stuff. It came out of

135

the computer at Thorness—oh, it must have been more than a year ago, when I began the D.N.A. synthesis."

" It's part of that? " he asked in a low voice. " Part of the programme which constructed the girl? "

" No. It came up quite separately," Dawnay was firm about it. " I based an experiment on it; one had to at that stage when we were still groping in the dark, really." She moved to the tank and looked with despair down at the opaque, sullen fluid at the bottom.

" I actually made some of these bacteria."

" What happened to them? "

She answered with an obvious effort. " They seemed harmless, pointless. Another failure. I kept them in a whole range of cultures for a week. They did not die, but they did not develop. Just multiplied. So the tubes were washed out and sterilised."

He started towards her. " Don't you realise . . .? "

" Of course I do," she said sharply. " The bacteria went down the sink, into the drain, from the drain to the sewer, and into the sea."

" Which is precisely what that bloody machine intended should happen! But an ounce or so is the most it can have been. It can't have spread the way it has."

" Not impossible," she said. " I've tried to fix the date more or less exactly when I abandoned that line of research. It's an academic point really. But I'm certain it is a year ago at least. With this tank fixed up I have been able to calculate the rate of growth. It's fantastic. No virus or bacteria so far known has a rate even comparable to it. And now the build-up's greater. You can envisage the sort of progression now that it's invaded all the main oceans."

" How long," he asked, " will it take . . .? "

She looked up at him. " Possibly another year. Probably less. All sea water will then reach maximum saturation."

Fleming studied the wall-graph which recorded hour by hour the nitrogen content in the air of the tank. " It does nothing but absorb nitrogen and some oxygen? " he asked.

" Not so far as I've discovered," she replied. " But the sea normally absorbs nitrogen very, very slowly. Plankton and so on. Any artificial fertiliser manufacturing plant takes out in a week as much as the sea absorbs in a year. It hasn't mattered.

136

There's plenty. But this bacteria could easily absorb all the nitrogen in the world's atmosphere. That's what's happening now. It's bringing down air pressure. In the end there'll be no nitrogen and therefore no plants. When the pressure really drops off the scale there won't be any way for us to absorb oxygen, and then there'll be no more animals."

" Unless ——," Fleming began.

" There's no unless."

Fleming glanced at Abu Zeki, standing quiet and expectant in the background. " Madeleine," he said, " thanks to Abu there's a chance of us getting a letter to London."

She showed little interest. " To say what? " she demanded.

" What it is."

" There's no point." She shrugged. " But all right, if you wish. It will be a gesture, though it's too late." She bent once more over the tank, staring down into the fluid. " The girl was right," she muttered. " The computer made life. This time it's made death. So far as we're concerned that's Finis—down in that water."

" We'll write, all the same," Fleming insisted. " Lemka's cousin is ready to take the risk. Keep it short but put in every fact you know." His voice was decisive. It stirred Dawnay a little out of her despair.

"All right, John," she agreed.

Abu smiled. " I'll wait till the note is ready, Professor," he told Dawnay. " I'll go into town for a meal. It's my normal practice. My cousin goes to the same café."

Fleming moved to the door. " Good luck, both of you," he said with forced cheerfulness. " Maybe we can all meet back here later this evening? "

He strode out into the hot wind, making for his own quarters. He was glad to be by himself. It was difficult for him to play the role of optimist. And he wanted time to think. He always thought best by himself, with a bottle of Scotch by his side.

He sent an orderly to the commissariat for a new bottle. The boy returned in five minutes. Intel did not stint the creature comforts, the mental and spiritual dope, for its prisoners.

He skipped dinner and so he was a little drunk when he returned to the laboratory. The wind was as wild as ever, and it was already dark. There had not even been the usual brief twilight. Abu was already there with Dawnay. " I saw my cousin," he told Fleming. " He took the note. I don't know, of course, how he got on at the airport, but I heard the transport take off on schedule. Just on an hour back."

Fleming thanked him. " It may not get through; it may be ignored at the other end, and even if it isn't we don't know what they can do if they study it and accept the truth of it. It would take a lot of swallowing." He flexed his arms. " So we're still really on our own. Which means we need the girl. Go across to sick quarters, Abu, and tell the nurse to bring her over."

" Now? " Abu asked doubtfully.

" Now," Fleming repeated. " Kaufman has her dragged out whenever they want a computing job done. The nurse has to obey, poor lass."

" What do you propose to do with her? " Dawnay asked disapprovingly.

" Use her as an ally."

" She won't play. Anyway, she's too weak."

" She'll have to try, won't she? She's the only thing we've got. If the computer at Thorness made a bacterium there must be an anti-bacterium. I'm not expert in your line, Madeleine, but surely that's a basic fact of biology? "

" Do you happen to know of this bug which will conveniently act in the opposite direction? " she asked.

" The computer must." He waved away her sarcasm. " I realise it's not the same computer, but it managed to reconstruct the formula for the original one, or at least we and Andre made it work. We can do it again, for an antidote."

Before Dawnay could reply Abu returned. He held the door open while the nurse brought Andre inside in her wheelchair. Fleming was accustomed to see the girl a little weaker, a little more wraithlike, every time he saw her. But he had not got used to the way she now glared at him, her eyes smouldering with resentment.

"All right, nurse," he said without looking at Andre, " leave her. We'll call you when it's time to take her back."

The girl stood her ground. " She should not be here, sir; I had just got her to sleep."

Abu interposed. " Please be sure it's all right."

The nurse patted the rug round Andre's legs and reluctantly left. When the door had closed Andre asked what they wanted

138

her for; she did little more than whisper, even that was jerky and hard to understand.

"We need another formula from the computer," Fleming explained. "Another bacterium or perhaps a virus. It's got to kill the first one and then work the other way round. It would have to release nitrogen held in the water."

"And it would have to breed faster than the first one," Dawnay added. "It would be another tricky piece of bio-synthesis, another life-creating process. For that I need a formula."

Andre had listened with almost horrifying intensity, looking from one to the other, hanging on every word.

"But why?" she protested.

Fleming lost his temper. "For God's sake!" he shouted. Dawnay uttered a word of warning and with difficulty he calmed down. Then, crouching beside Andre, he slowly and patiently explained how the existing bacteria were changing the world's weather and making it impossible to breathe, the preliminary to complete destruction of all life. "So we need just one small bug to start breeding on an even greater scale to counteract it," he finished.

Once more she shook her head. "It is not possible," she whispered.

"Look," he said urgently, "if you can come up with one sort you can come up with another—and save us all."

Her big eyes looked back into his. Imperceptibly they softened, the hostility lessening. "Save you?" she managed to say aloud. "What about me?" She tried to move her hands over her breasts and touch her face. The effort was too much and she lay back.

"If you had the strength—you'd try." It was Dawnay who was begging her now.

"I don't know." She shook her head weakly. "It would take too long."

Fleming looked over Andre's head at Dawnay. "Would it?" he muttered.

Involuntarily Dawnay glanced at the girl. "I don't know," she said. "She's . . . . ." She got a grip on herself. "If you mean would I take too long with the actual lab work, that's another matter. There are still twenty-four hours in however many days we've got left, and I don't like sleeping much."

Both of them looked at Andre again. They were two people

139

willing her to obey, to do the seemingly impossible. The ghost of a smile flickered over her mouth, and she nodded.

Fleming turned to Abu. "Get the nurse to take her back," he said. "She's the only ally we've got, poor kid. Tell the nurse to have her ready for duty at the computer at 9 tomorrow morning. Try to explain that we're not sadists. Tell her how necessary it is. Frighten her a bit if you like by hinting how she'll also die if she fails us."

Abu's persuasion—or intimidation—worked. The nurse obediently wheeled Andre into the computer block shortly after nine the next morning. The girl said her patient was too weak to move, and she would have to use the wheelchair to work while interpreting the screen.

Only Fleming was present. Dawnay felt too little hope to be able to bear to watch, and Abu remained in the main office so that he could report any approach by Kaufman or the mysteriously silent Gamboul. One of the things which would have been disquieting, if Fleming had not been so preoccupied with a greater problem, was the way Intel seemed to be leaving them to their own devices.

Andre put her hands unsteadily on the sensory controls. The computer had hummed to activity as soon as she entered the building. But the screen brightened very slowly. Its imagery was blurred, and even when Fleming pulled the curtains over the windows across the hall the pattern was almost indistinguishable. He watched Andre raise her head to the screen; he saw how she seemed to be gripping the controls as if they yielded some supply of strength. Her effort to concentrate was pathetic. Presently she relaxed her hold. Her body slumped and her head bowed to her breast. She began to talk thickly, sobs shaking her shoulders.

Fleming bent over her. "I can't follow them," he heard her say. "Take me away from it." And then she added, as if to herself, "I don't want to die."

The nurse came forward, pushing Fleming away. "She has done enough; too much, you must not ask . . . ." Abruptly she grasped the chair and wheeled Andre away from the screen.

Fleming refused to move out of the way. "Andre," he said quietly, "none of us wants to die, but we all will, unless some miracle starts sucking the air back out of the sea."

She raised her head with an effort. "You will die together.

140

I'll die alone." He put out his hand to comfort her, touching hers. She moved her arm away. " Don't touch me," she whispered. " I must seem horrible to you."

" No! " he said urgently. " You have always seemed beautiful to me. Ever since . . . . ever since we ran away from Thorness. But try to think, please! Only you can help us now. I don't even know what this is doing. Is the power still with Gamboul? "

He indicated the mass of the computer ranged all around him and she nodded her head. " Then why does she never come here? " he demanded.

Andre remained quiet, gathering her strength. " There is no need. She has seen the message. The computer has set her on a path. She will not turn back. Nor will she come here. She needs no more. I could not show her anything. I can hardly see it any more." Her eyes looked askance towards the blank screen. " I will come back when I have rested."

Without asking permission, the nurse started to push the chair away. Fleming did not stop her this time. He watched them disappear through the exit doors and for a full minute he remained where he was, in the heavy silence of the deserted building.

Suddenly he jumped. The output printer was working. It clicked rapidly, then stopped. Once more it started. This time the keys moved slowly but they kept on. He went to the section and took hold of the short length of paper already typed.

" Pretty ropey," he decided as he looked through it, " but some sort of biological data, all right."

He went to tell Dawnay. It was a triviality in itself—this preliminary analysis. But in its inference it was tremendous. It showed that after all Andre would help, and maybe Dawnay could still achieve a miracle—if they had time.

As he stepped out of doors the fury of the wind swept over him, making him stagger. He began panting, and there was no help in the gulps of air he took. With head down and body leaning into a dry, suffocating gale, he plodded through the swirling sand to the laboratory doors. His zest and optimism had gone. Time was something they couldn't buy.

Three thousand miles away dawn was breaking over London —a London stricken with disaster. A few tin-hatted policemen stood in the middle of the wider streets well away from the

141

buildings. The jangle of an ambulance bell occasionally penetrated the howling of the wind. Lights burned weakly on the first floor of the Ministry of Science building from the few windows which had not been blown out and boarded.

The grey light of early morning accentuated the weariness of the four men sitting around the littered table. For several hours they had not contributed a constructive idea. Discussion had really become argument, the futile criticism of over-exhausted men.

Neilson, normally reticent and co-operative, had given way to exasperation when Osborne and the Prime Minister's secretary launched into an interminable argument about departmental responsibility and finance for the expanded activity agreed upon the previous evening.

"You have a wonderful talent here," observed Neilson, "for plodding through routine while the heavens are falling."

"We're tired, Professor Neilson," said the Minister sharply. "We can only do what we feel is best."

"I'm sorry," Neilson said.

The Prime Minister's secretary reached for a cigarette, found the packet empty, and hurled it into a corner. "There's no power over half the country, and the rest is under water, or snowed up or blown down. People are dying faster than the army can bury them. If you could only give us some sort of forecast how long it's going on . . . ."

Neilson was on the point of answering when a secretary came in, tip-toeing to Osborne.

"Something urgent for you, sir," he said. "Brought by a despatch rider from London airport."

Osborne took the buff-coloured envelope and slit it open. With deliberate slowness he unfolded the flimsy paper, and read it.

At last he looked up. "It's from Azaran," he said, "from Madeleine Dawnay." He handed it to the Minister.

"You two had better see this together," the Minister said to Neilson and the Prime Minister's secretary. "It will save time. The Cabinet must be informed right away, of course." He waited impatiently while the two men read the note. "Any proposals, Neilson?" he asked.

Neilson nodded. "Can you get me to Azaran—today?" he demanded.

10

VORTEX

THE four-engined aircraft cruised to the apron, slewed round and stopped. Electric trolleys moved forward to unload the cargo. The crew, tired from a non-stop flight from London during which they had never topped 6,000 feet and had been buffeted for seven hours without respite, clambered down the ladder and made their way to the flight office. A uniformed Arab and a bullet-headed European greeted them perfunctorily as the Captain handed over the aircraft papers. The European flicked through them and passed them to the Arab, and then extended his pudgy hand for the crew's personal documents. He let the Captain go through immediately, but when he looked up at the next two men standing before him he referred again to the papers in his hand.

" Who is this? " he asked in German. The two air crew members looked blankly at him. He repeated his question in halting Arabic.

Yusel, Lemka's cousin, the younger of the two, smiled ingratiatingly. " My second navigator. He not understand Arabic or the language you use first."

The Intel man scowled. " I've not been notified of any change in crew plans. Why are you carrying a second navigator? "

Yusel explained. " For route familiarisation. We have to fly so low; no air pressure up top."

Not really satisfied, the Intel man re-read the documents. When he could find no fault in them, he threw them across the desk. Yusel picked them up and led his companion into the crew room where they got out of their flying kit. His companion was Neilson.

" That's the worst over," Yusel told him. " Now I'll take you to my cousin's house. It'll be quite safe. Her husband, Doctor Abu Zeki, will contact you as soon as he can."

Neilson nodded. " The sooner the better."

143

Yusel drove him to Abu's home and then returned to Baleb. It was late afternoon when he got to the café, and he had to wait an hour before his cousin arrived. When he did come Abu Zeki had the furtive air of a man who knows he is watched. Quietly, over two bottles of locally-made Azarani Cola, Yusel told him about Neilson's arrival.

" He wants to see Doctor Fleming and Professor Dawnay," he finished.

Abu Zeki glanced anxiously around the bare little café.

" I don't know if they can both get away," he said. " But I will tell them."

As soon as he heard that Neilson senior was safely in the country, Fleming decided to throw caution to the winds and go and see him. He told Dawnay to be ready to leave as soon as it was dark, if she was willing to take the risk.

The weather helped them. A violent storm broke with night-fall, sheet lightning illuminating the sky and short bursts of rain lashing the buildings and swirling sand. The guards crept, frightened and shivering, into any shelter they could find. Fleming and Dawnay plodded through the cascades of rain with-out once being challenged.

The drive was appalling, Abu's little car slithering in the thick scum of mud on the desert sand. But the rain had been local. After forty minutes they were driving on dry terrain, the storm providing an accompaniment of reverberating thunder and almost continuous flashes of lightning.

Fleming felt a sense of quite unreasonable relief when Lemka opened the door and he saw Neilson standing behind her. The American's wordless greeting, the way he gripped his hand, was absurdly reassuring.

To Dawnay, Neilson was someone who signified a gleam of hope that she had refused to admit existed, but she was still not sure why he had come. They both sat quietly, suppressing their excitement, while the big calm man ate his way methodically through a bunch of grapes and told them what had been happen-ing in London. They learnt for the first time how Osborne had survived the shooting at their country-house prison, how Neilson had been called in to " head a probe into this weather thing," as he put it, and how they also had put two and two together and traced the source to Thorness. And how they had then come to a dead stop until they had received the message from Dawnay.

144

" Is there really any hope? " he asked her.

"About as much as a grain of sand in a desert."

She pushed aside the little tray on which Lemka had set Neilson's supper and spread out the bundle of papers she had crammed into the waistband of her skirt.

She impatiently flattened out the creases. " These are most of the figures for the D.N.A. helix," she began. " The computer has worked out what I think you'll agree is a feasible analysis. So far as I can judge, it's a potential bacterium. But the molecular structure is one thing. Getting the components and synthesising them another, but it might, possibly, produce the anti-bacterium we need."

Neilson studied the figures. "And this is the work of the machine Jan built? "

She nodded.

" I can't help wondering . . ." A tremor made his words tail off.

Fleming was sitting beside the cot, absent-mindedly revolving a toy suspended for the child's amusement. " What would have happened if your son had stayed," he finished.

Neilson turned to him. " They shot him in cold blood," he said. " In front of our eyes. If I could find the man . . . ."

" I can't tell you who pulled the trigger," Fleming said. " But I know who told him to. A man named Kaufman, who is ' looking after ' us here."

" I should like to meet him," said Neilson.

" Maybe you will."

Dawnay began gathering the papers together. "At least your son's death was quick," she said with compassion. " Which is more than ours will be. Unless these work." She stuffed the papers back in her skirt band. " There's a lot more to come if only the girl can get it for us."

" How is she? " Neilson asked.

Dawnay looked down at the baby; the child was wide awake, smiling at the sight of so many faces around him. " She was an artificial sort of life," she muttered. " Not like . . . ." She turned abruptly away from the baby. " There's some constituent lacking in her blood; something I didn't know about and something the computer didn't allow for."

" Can't she get some help from the machine for herself? " Neilson asked.

" No time," Fleming replied. " She might have done, I suppose, but there was this anti-bacterium job. She elected to work on it . . . ."

Neilson eyed Fleming speculatively. "That was a hard decision," he said.

Fleming paused to light a cigarette. He inhaled deeply. " Yes," he said at last. " It was a hard thing, as you say."

Fleming rose and turned away from the others. He crossed to the window and stared out into the night Hastily, to ease the tension, Dawnay began asking if Neilson wanted copies of the computer data. Neilson shook his head. He explained that the only practical thing would be a test tube of the anti-bacterium. " If the girl can complete the analysis," he started, but Fleming interrupted.

" Shush! " They stared at him. " Lemka's coming."

Lemka, who had been keeping watch on the road, came running across the courtyard to the house. They could hear her sandals on the rough paving.

" We're watched all the time," Dawnay said. " We thought we'd given them the slip tonight."

Lemka burst into the room, her eyes large and round with excitement. " They're coming," she exclaimed. " Soldiers. A whole truck load! "

All of them stood motionless for a few seconds. Then Dawnay took the papers she had put in her waistband. " Hide these," she said, thrusting them into Lemka's hand. " Your husband can pick them up later and give them back."

Lemka took them and turned to Neilson. " My mother's room," she said firmly. " They won't go in there."

" I hope you're right," he smiled as he followed her.

There was a knock on the door, not violent or very loud. Lemka emerged from the rear room and opened the door. A corporal saluted and spoke in Arabic; two soldiers stood beside him. Their guns were still slung on their shoulders.

" He says they have come to fetch you and Dr. Fleming," Lemka interpreted, addressing Dawnay.

" Tell them we'll come right away," Dawnay said, with what she hoped was a bright but casual smile. " We'll be all right, so don't worry. But you'll have to find a safer place for Dr. Neilson. We'll keep in touch somehow."

Lemka extended her hand and clasped Dawnay's affectionately. " My cousin will think of something. We had better not talk more, or the soldiers will suspect us."

One soldier insisted on coming in the car, and the corporal made signs to Fleming to drive close behind the army truck. The weather had cleared a little, the wind blowing strongly but steadily.

Back in the compound the computer block was a blaze of light. Two soldiers took over from the escort and led Fleming and Dawnay into the building. Kaufman was sitting at a desk in the office, his face a mask of suppressed anger. Abu was standing uneasily to one side.

" Now what's all this about? " the German barked at them as they entered. " Why were you outside without permission? "

" Permission from whom? " Dawnay demanded. "And why permission to visit friends; the family of a colleague? "

Kaufman tried to meet her look and failed. " You know you are not supposed to be without an escort," he blustered.

Fleming stepped forward, his fists clenched. " Now look here, you Teutonic gauleiter . . . ." he began, but Abu Zeki stepped in front of him. " They sent for you because it was urgent. The girl collapsed while she was working in the sensory bay."

"Andre? " Fleming was already at the door. " I'll go to her," he called over his shoulder.

" How bad is she? " Dawnay asked Abu.

" She is very weak," he replied. " But there was a little more data from the printer before she collapsed." He picked up a sheaf of record sheets from the desk and gave them to Dawnay.

Kaufman cleared his throat. " You will be more carefully watched in future," he warned, but he seemed uncertain and worried. " How important is the girl to us? "

"About as important as your survival. You won't go on living for long if she doesn't finish this." Dawnay could hardly bear to speak to him, but when she saw the fear come into his eyes she realised for the first time that he was not invulnerable; that he might be able to be worked upon. " So for God's sake—and your own—try not to interfere more than you have to."

He looked at her doubtfully and went away without speaking.

Andre's corner of the sick bay was in darkness. The nurse, sitting beside a screened light, stood up when Fleming tip-toed in. She protested at the intrusion.

" It's all right," he told her. " I just want to see her. I shan't wake her."

The girl gave an annoyed sigh and walked across to the bed with him. As his eyes adjusted to the gloom he could make out the shape of Andre's emaciated body underneath the thin coverlet. Her head and hair were a vague shape in the centre of the white pillow. He bent down closer and saw that her eyes were open, watching him.

" I should have been here," he whispered, gently touching her hair. His fingers brushed her forehead. It was damp and cold.

Very faintly her voice came to him, slow and hesitant. " I have done what you wanted. Professor Dawnay has all she will need now."

His mind hardly registered what she had said. " I ought to have been with you," he said again.

He found her hand. It lay lifeless and unnaturally flexed on the coverlet. His thumb and forefinger felt for the pulse in her wrist. He could detect nothing.

" I am finished," she whispered, guessing what he was doing.

He withdrew his hand. " No, you're not," he said loudly. " We've a trick or two left. Neilson is here. The father of the man who built this computer. He made me realise what I ought to be doing. What *we* ought to be doing. We need some help from it for you as well as us."

He stood up. " Put yourself in my hands," he ordered. " You did before. Tonight you will sleep. Tomorrow I shall come for you. I will take you to the computer. Yes, I know," he exclaimed when he saw her attempt to protest. " You're weak. You collapsed this evening. But this time I'll be beside you, helping you."

He had very little belief that he could really do anything, but he hoped that some fresh strength had passed from him to her. She moved a little, as if relaxing and getting more comfortable. Her eyelids fluttered and closed. Her face took on the serenity of natural sleep.

Fleming went to the door, beckoning the nurse to follow. Outside he talked quietly to her, telling her that she was not to be frightened, and not to talk. " We're all in danger," he explained to her. " Your patient is trying to save us. It's up to us to save *her*. Trust me and we shall do it."

Half-heartedly the girl nodded that she understood. Fleming wished he could convince himself as easily.

He slept little that night, but lay trying to make a new plan of action for the little time they had left. With the light of morning he deliberately followed his usual routine of a shower, shave and breakfast to give Andre every precious minute to recuperate from her collapse the night before. Even then he was early. Sleepy guards, resigned to another couple of hours before the day reliefs took over, eyed him warily when, accompanied by the nurse, he pushed Andre in her wheelchair to the computer building.

After the boisterous, still stormy, weather outside the air inside the building seemed heavy and lifeless. Despite the air conditioning the familiar aroma of Kaufman's cigarellos hung around. Fleming half expected the man to come bustling up, demanding to know what was happening. But the offices were empty. Presumably the German had hung around for hours, thinking. Fleming hoped that whatever conscience he might still have had been at work.

Andre had said nothing when he had fetched her. Beyond a smile in answer to his greeting she might have been in a trance. After he had dismissed the nurse and had Andre sitting in front of the screen he resigned himself to the fact that he would just have to hope to instil his ideas in her mind, without getting a sign of reaction.

And so it was. He talked of what Dawnay believed was wrong with her, how guilty they both felt because of it. He painted a picture unreally optimistic, of what her life could be if she could help Dawnay to help her. In the end he simulated something very near anger, challenging her to prove her power.

She sat with her head drooped, her hands folded listlessly in her lap. Only the occasional fluttering of her eyelids showed that she was awake and listening. He stopped talking after a while, not knowing what else to say. He saw her try to brace herself. One hand was lifted with agonising slowness to the sensory control. The machine began to hum. A pin-point of light glowed in the centre of the screen; it dulled and expanded. Fleming stepped away, not taking his eyes off her, until he was against the wall. There he stood, tense, motionless, watching. The impossible was happening.

After a time he felt a pull on his sleeve. Abu was standing beside him looking puzzled and expectant. Fleming jerked his head towards the office and they walked quietly to it.

" What? " Abu began. " Is she . . .? "

" I think so," Fleming replied, not really knowing what Abu was asking. He tugged his thoughts unwillingly away from Andre. " What's the news from you? "

" I went home after midnight," he said. " I had to pass through the guard room. But the officer seemed to think it was okay for me to go unescorted. My cousin Yusel got home just before me. We've fixed up Professor Neilson where he'll be safe enough. A cave high above the temple, where that rock fault is. He'll be comfortable enough there as he hasn't to move around much. It was hard going for him; the air is thinning here just as Yusel says it is even at sea level in England."

" He's got food and water? "

Abu nodded. " Lemka will visit him regularly, or her mother."

Fleming nodded, satisfied. " It's good of you all," he muttered.

" Young Doctor Neilson was kind to me," Abu said. " We liked him very much."

Both men stopped abruptly. The output printer had started to work. Fleming's thoughts raced back to Andre. " Get the nurse to take her back to bed," he ordered. He walked across to her and put his arm around her shoulders. " Good! " he said. " Now rest—and hang on."

He grabbed the paper coming from the printer, running down the short lines of figures. The details meant little to him, but the general purport was clear enough. It concerned the constituents in plasma. For ten minutes he stood watching the figures emerge. At last the motor died and the computer sank into silence.

Dawnay was working at her laboratory bench in her usual bewildering and seemingly haphazard array of apparatus. Fleming thrust the sheets of paper before her.

" What are those? " she asked, continuing to watch some fluid drip through a filter. " More bacterial formulae? "

" No," said Fleming. " Formulae for Andromeda."

She stopped her work and looked at him wonderingly. " Who programmed it? "

" She did. I more or less forced her. So far as I can judge it's a progression of figures that stands for the missing chemical constituents in her blood. Get it into chemical terms, and we can use it on her."

She took the paper and slumped in a chair. " It would take weeks of work," she muttered, running her eye over the data. "And I have this bigger job." She waved her hand almost helplessly at the jumble of retorts and test tubes on the bench.

" Which Andre got for us," he reminded her.

She was exasperated at the implied reproof. " Let's get this straight, John," she began in level tones. " First you were against me creating her. Then you wanted me to kill her when she was first made. Next you demanded that she was kept away from the computer. Now —"

" I want her to live."

"And the rest of us? " she asked him. " Do you want us to live? How much can I take on, do you imagine? My energy's limited. There's only one of me and I'm dead tired. Sometimes I think my brain is softening." She pulled herself together and smiled at him. " Do you think I wouldn't try to save her if I could? But there are millions of us, John, and our lives are in the balance. I don't even know if this is going to work. Still less that, even if it does, I'll have it made in quantity in time."

She leaned forward and held out the sheets of paper to him. He kept his hands deep in his trouser pockets, refusing to accept them. She let them fall to the floor.

He bent to pick them up and put them carefully on a clear corner of the bench. " You'll have to talk to Gamboul," he said quietly. " She won't see me and doesn't trust Abu Zeki any more. But she might listen to you. If you could persuade her to give us more freedom and more outside help . . . ."

Dawnay was lost in her own thoughts. " I don't know, I just don't know," she murmured.

Without warning there was a tremendous crack of thunder. It shook the building, making the apparatus on the bench shake and jangle. Immediately the noise died away there came the scream of wind.

" Even Gamboul must know that this weather thing isn't something she can handle, that it wasn't part of her damned programme," Fleming said when the racket died down.

"All right," Dawnay agreed; " I'll try to explain to her."

An interview was not granted until the following morning. Gamboul sent an order for Dawnay to come to her private residence, the house which Salim had owned. From all accounts,

Gamboul rarely visited the Presidential Palace any more, not even to go through the formalities of reporting the country's day-to-day activities. The President was kept a virtual prisoner. He did not seem greatly to mind; he was sick. The comparatively slight thinning of the atmosphere over Azaran was already affecting the older people. The President was suffering from bronchitis.

The Salim residence looked shabby and dilapidated. There had been some minor storm damage. No one had troubled to sweep up the rubble. The palm trees which had grown in the courtyard for more than fifty years had been broken by the wind.

An armed guard escorted Dawnay to Gamboul's office. She could see at once how the other woman had changed. The sensuality seemed to have drained out of Gamboul. Her face had become more beautiful in a haggard, almost aesthetic way, and there was something fanatical about her bright dark eyes. Something terrifyingly self-possessed and dedicated.

She was surprisingly friendly, asking what she could do " You have everything you need for our work? " she enquired.

" For yours; not for mine," Dawnay corrected her. Then, without preamble she gave a factual and restrained report on the reasons for the state of the weather.

Gamboul listened quietly, without interrupting. She walked to the window and looked out across the city to the towering masses of cumulus beyond it over the desert.

She was quiet for a time after Dawnay had finished. " How shall we die? " she murmured, walking back to her desk and sitting down. Dawnay explained.

Gamboul waved an expressive hand. " That wasn't the meaning in the message," she protested. " It wasn't meant to happen. Everything was clear and logical. What I saw was—desolation, but not like this. And there was power too."

" What did you learn you had to do? " Dawnay prompted.

Gamboul's mind was far away, reviving that night in front of the computer screen. " Govern," she muttered. " Everyone knows that it has to be, but nobody will make the real effort. A few have tried . . . ."

" Hitler? Napoleon? " Dawnay suggested.

Gamboul was not insulted. " Yes," she agreed. " But they were not brilliant enough, or rather they did not have the help of the brain from out there. It will be necessary to sacrifice almost everything. But not like this! Not now! We're not ready! "

152

" How much power have you? " Dawnay asked.

" Enough here. But this was to be only a beginning."

" It still could be," said Dawnay. She could see now a way of appealing to the other woman's greed and fear.

Gamboul turned sharply to her. " What do you mean? " she demanded.

" It's possible," Dawnay explained, " that we may be able to find a way to save the atmosphere. Not probable, but just a chance. We're getting some help from the computer with a formula that looks like an anti-bacterium. We may be able to synthesise it. But I shall need help and equipment. If we succeed we shall have to mass produce it and then pump it in to the sea all over the world."

Gamboul gave her a look of suspicion. " How can you produce so much? "

Carefully Dawnay explained that with organisation the serum, once made, would increase naturally, possibly at a rate faster than the bacteria already in the sea. " Once we've bred bulk supplies we should have to send batches to all countries, where their own installations could all handle it simultaneously."

Gamboul began laughing. It was not a pleasant sound for there was no joy in it, only overweening exultation. " We will do it," she said, " but we shall not allow other governments to co-operate. Intel will build all the plant you need. Intel will offer the serum at its own price. This will give us the power I was told about. It is part of the message after all. I didn't understand. Now the world will be ours, held to ransom."

Dawnay rose, staring at her. " It's not for you! " She found herself shouting, too deeply shocked to care what risk she ran. " You're mad! It isn't part of the plan! "

But Gamboul seemed not to notice; only stared back at her with glazed eyes and spoke as if to a minion receiving orders.

" Indent for all the equipment you need, Professor. I assure you that there will be no restrictions about that."

A portable projector had been rigged up in the Cabinet Room at 10, Downing Street. The Prime Minister, a few of his senior colleagues including the Minister of Science, and Osborne were sitting at one end of the table watching the screen.

The Prime Minister raised his hand. " That's enough," he said wearily. " Put the lights on, will you? " The scene of a

153

waste of water over what had once been Holland's most fertile farmland faded.

"The point is, sir, do we release it to the T.V. nets? " The Home Secretary enquired.

"Why not? " asked the Premier. "People who can do so, might as well see. Perhaps there'll be some sort of wry comfort in knowing that Europe's even worse off than we are. Anyway, not many will see them. I doubt whether a tenth of the country now has any electricity.

He fingered his pipe, then laid it down; smoking was almost impossible with breathing so difficult. "Any news from Neilson? " he enquired.

"Not yet, sir," Osborne replied. "Another report from Professor Dawnay brought on an Intel transport. It's a technical message the Director of Research is studying. But briefly, she claims that the bacterium is a bio-chemical thing put out by the Thorness computer."

"Is she doing anything? "

"She says she's working on it, sir. We're hoping she will give Neilson a lead and he can help her."

"Couldn't this Arab aviator or whatever he is smuggle Neilson back once there are some facts to work on? "

Osborne coughed deferentially. "I'm afraid the calculations would have to be done there, sir; they have the computer."

The Prime Minister gave Osborne a keen glance. "Thankyou for reminding me of that," he snapped with uncharacteristic sharpness. "And what about the computer's minions, the fellow Fleming and the girl? "

"They're both there," the Minister of Science told him. "They're under guard."

The Prime Minister got up and walked to the head of the great table. "Perhaps it's time we moved in," he said quietly. "This isn't a Suez. We would have support from other quarters."

The Minister of Science shifted uneasily. "My experts have made an appreciation of that eventuality, sir. They advise against it. You will understand, sir, that the computer . . . ."

". . . . Has built them the sort of defence set-up it built us," the Prime Minister finished for him. "So we'll have to try appealing to their better nature, won't we? "

"Yes, sir," muttered the Minister of Science.

154

" Not a very profitable policy, I suspect," said the Premier. " But I doubt whether we or the Opposition can think up any other. I'll get the C.O.I. to draft something for the B.B.C. I suppose there's still some transmitter or other which can pump it out? "

" Daventry is still on the air, sir," the Minister of Science said. " The army's there with a group of mobile power units. We can reach Azaran on short-wave all right."

The special bulletin was broadcast in English and Arabic at hourly intervals throughout the night. Most of the first transmission got through to Azaran. After that, on Gamboul's personal orders, it was jammed.

She summoned Kaufman to her office to hear a tape transcription. The German sat impassively while the tape was played.

" This is London calling the government and people of Azaran," came the far-off, static-distorted voice. " We need your help. The continent of Europe has been devastated. The whole world is threatened by a series of climatic disturbances which have already begun to reach your own country. The air we breathe is being sucked into the sea. Within the next few weeks millions will die unless by some enormous effort it can be arrested. Tens of thousands are dying now. This country has been badly hit. Three quarters of Holland are inundated. Venice has been largely destroyed by a tidal wave. The cities of Rouen, Hamburg, and Dusseldorf no longer exist."

" Dusseldorf." Kaufman repeated the one word and the muscles of his face tightened.

Gamboul ignored him, listening to the tape. "At this moment great storms are raging over the Atlantic, sweeping towards Europe. We need your help to check the course of events."

The voice was drowned in a welter of noise. Gamboul switched off the recorder. " That's where we began jamming," she explained.

" What I want to hear from you, Kaufman, is how they know that we are concerned with it."

Kaufman looked blankly at her. " Dusseldorf," he repeated. " It was my home. My old father . . . . ."

" We are supposed to have a good security service," snapped Gamboul. "And you are in charge of security, Herr Kaufman."

He roused himself as if from a dream. "We have done our best," he said stubbornly.

Gamboul shrugged. "It's no matter now. As soon as Dawnay has the new strain of bacteria we will make ourselves safe here. After that we will make it available to others—on our own terms."

"And meanwhile," said the German slowly, "the rest of the world must wait and die? You do not care? You think other people are not caring?"

She failed to notice the hatred in his eyes. "The world must wait," she agreed. "I know what has to be done. Others don't."

Kaufman was still looking fixedly at her. At long last she felt a little uneasy under his gaze.

"Remember, Herr Kaufman," she said. "You and I are not other people."

11

TORNADO

T R U E to her word, Janine Gamboul arranged priority for any order Dawnay gave. The resources of Intel were such that even in the chaotic conditions of Europe the materials were located, purchased and brought to Azaran by air. Even more remarkable was the speed with which young and brilliant chemists were found, specialists in bacteriology or the molecular construction of nucleic acids. Two were newly graduated students from Zurich, one a girl chemist from the research department of Germany's biggest drug firm. Questioning by Dawnay showed that they had come quite voluntarily, tempted not merely by the lavish salary but for the chance of doing what they had been told was an exciting new channel of research, in what they hoped was a less tempestuous part of the world. They had no idea of the true purposes of Intel, or of the potential nightmare that lay behind the weather disaster. The public everywhere still hoped that the worst would soon blow over.

Dawnay told her helpers the facts of the situation as it was; but she omitted the theories about the origin of the bacteria.

She worked them to the limit of endurance. They caught the sense of urgency and became her devoted servants. She was at work when they turned up in the morning, and was still there when they wearily went to their rest in the evening. Results began to show sooner than Dawnay had dared hope. Precisely ten days after they had begun in earnest the first droplet of synthetic bacterium was sprayed on a minute copper screen and placed in the electronic microscope. It was a dramatic moment as Dawnay adjusted the magnification, her assistants standing around her. Up to 500,000; then to a million. One and a quarter million. It was there: a many-sided formation, spiked, symmetrical. And it wasn't an inert crystal. It lived.

Silently she motioned to her staff to look. One after the other they shared in the triumph. Life, infinitely tiny, had been created.

Almost diffidently Dawnay had to bring herself and her assistants back to reality. This was really no more than a scientific curiosity. The real test lay ahead. The bacterium had to be bred in its billions—enough to fill a test tube. And then it had to be sent into battle against the organism which was its pre-destined enemy.

The precious and all too few droplets were sprayed into a dozen different culture soups. For six long hours there was nothing to do but wait. Tests showed dead bacteria in nine of the tubes; the other three had reached maximum saturation.

From these three, larger cultures were started. They all flourished. It was past midnight when Dawnay decided the real test could begin.

Dawnay drew a test tube of opaque bacteria-sodden sea water from the tank. It was sealed with a sterile rubber stopper. An assistant filled a hypodermic from the culture and handed it to Dawnay. The needle pierced the rubber stopper and the fluid produced a tiny swirl as it flowed into the opacity.

"Now another wait," said Dawnay. Only a slight tremor in her voice indicated the tension she felt. "So let's have some coffee."

She had not told anyone outside the laboratory how close she believed she was to success, dreading the risk of anti-climax. But Abu Zeki, drawn by the blaze of light from the laboratory windows, came over when the waiting period was almost over.

"Come in," Dawnay said, "you're in time to share in a success or help us find excuses for a failure."

"It's working?" he asked hopefully.

Dawnay laughed uncertainly. "In theory, yes. In practice—well, we'll know in a moment."

She crossed to the bench where the test tube had been clamped inside a sterile cabinet. Gingerly she withdrew it and held it to the light as the others grouped around her. Two-thirds of the water was clear and sparkling. She kept it aloft, staring, and even as they watched a few tiny heads of freed gas rose jauntily to the top of the tube.

Dawnay shook herself, bringing herself back to reality. "It's been in the tube for precisely 63 minutes," she murmured. "Now we will test it in the tank."

No need for sterility precautions or niceties of measurement now. Two tubes of culture were poured into the tank, and they all gathered round again to watch. Gradually little pools of clear water appeared, while fat, lazy bubbles appeared on the surface, burst, and were replaced by new bubbles.

"That's the nitrogen being released," Dawnay said. "The air pressure's altering."

It was true. The barograph needle was moving up slowly but steadily.

"You haf done it!" exclaimed the girl from Zurich.

"*We've* done it," Dawnay corrected. "The rest is simply mechanics. Producing on a large enough scale. We must get an hour or so's rest and then check growth rates, the effects of temperature and salinity." She turned to Abu. "They'd better start planning mass production. Go and see Gamboul or Kaufman. Tell them I must have an interview as soon as possible tomorrow—I mean—this morning."

She had no need to go into Baleb to see Gamboul. The Intel chief came to her, arriving at Dawnay's quarters while she was snatching a hurried breakfast. Gamboul asked merely for instructions, as if she were a secretary.

The result was that an hour later the Intel short-wave radio system was transmitting a long stream of orders to the cartel's headquarters in Vienna. Bulk chemical supplies of phosphates, proteins, and amino acids were to be sent by plane and ship irrespective of cost or country of origin. Engineers were to be recruited to work on the Azaran oil installations, clearing the tanks of petroleum and making them ready as breeding tanks. Old pipelines were to be adapted, and new ones laid, to pump the anti-bacteria straight into the Persian Gulf.

The message was merely acknowledged. There were no queries, no promises nor excuses. That night the first squadron of transports flew to Baleb with engineers and cargoes of chemicals. Two of them had crashed in a violent air storm over the eastern Mediterranean and a third blew up when a miniature whirlwind caught it just as it was touching down. The rest got through.

The air lift went on the next day without respite, and the first ocean freighter, hurriedly loaded at Capetown, radioed her estimated time of arrival.

A week after the original test the first bulk supplies of anti-bacteria were poured into the sea at ten points on the Azaran coast, carefully selected after a study of tidal currents. The effect was noticeable within twelve hours.

Fleming, who had been allowed to go with Dawnay to the coast, stood at the edge of the water, where the desert sloped down to make long golden beaches, and watched fascinated as the great nitrogen bubbles came bursting to the surface of the waves. Even the storminess of the sea could not hide them, and in his lungs he could feel a tingling freshness of regenerated air.

He and Dawnay drove back on the third day. " Now we must try to smuggle out some of the stuff with Neilson," she said. " This is all very fine, but it's merely local, and as you see, the weather remains quite unaffected by such a minor activity."

" No hope of Intel sending it?" Fleming peered through a windscreen opaque from a sudden downpour of hail and storm rain.

" Not a chance," Dawnay replied. " They won't release it to anyone except on their own terms. And what those terms are they haven't yet said. But I can imagine." Her words were drowned in a scream of wind which made the car shudder. " The weather's worse," she said, and there was a streak of alarm in her voice. " I wonder if we're doing right, after all. You see what's happening, John? "

He nodded, leaning forward to see the blurred image of the road. " We're treating the sea around here and nowhere else. Millions of cubic feet of nitrogen are being released. It's building up a cone of high pressure in a localised zone; everywhere else the pressure's dam' nigh a vacuum, and the original bacteria will be sucking in the nitrogen as fast as we can pump it out. We'll never win this way, all we'll do is breed hurricanes."

" God, how futile and helpless it all makes one feel," muttered Dawnay.

For an hour Fleming drove on in silence, concentrating on keeping the car going in a land which was just a kaleidoscope of rain, mud and wind.

Some ten miles from Baleb the wind dropped, though the rain continued. The air was abnormally clear, giving an illusion that objects were nearer than in fact they were.

" Look at that! " Fleming jerked his head towards the mountains along the horizon.

160

They stood out sharp and clear, lighter in colour than the purplish black clouds swirling above the crests. And right above them rose an immense spiral of greyish cloud, the top mushrooming and changing shape all the time.

" Tornado centre," said Dawnay. " We're in the calm area around it. Let's hope to God it doesn't move this way."

" That funnel is right over Abu's village, I think," muttered Fleming. " His family must be getting it badly, unless they saw the clouds building up and got to the caves where Neilson is."

But only Lemka had reached the cave when the tornado struck. She had clambered up the mountain with her daily basket of food for Neilson. He refused to let her go back when he noticed the abnormal calm and saw the clouds racing together towards the south.

At first Lemka protested. Her mother and the baby would be terrified by the storm. Besides, Yusel had promised to come with information about getting Neilson out with some contraband bacteria. But when the full fury of the tornado drove them into the recesses of the cave she subsided into frightened silence.

" He'll be all right, and your family," Neilson insisted with a cheerfulness he did not feel.

But things were not all right with any of them. Yusel had arrived at Abu's house shortly after Lemka had left with the food for Neilson. He had intended to set out earlier, hoping to accompany his sister because he had some good news for the American: he could smuggle a message to London the next day.

In his excitement he had not been very careful about his trip. He had not seen, through the rain and sandstorms, a car following a mile behind his.

Consequently he was absolutely unprepared when the door of Abu's house burst open and Kaufman pushed in with a couple of soldiers. Without orders, the soldiers pinioned Yusel and soon had him gagged and trussed in a chair, his arms and legs tied to it with rope.

While Lemka's mother cringed against the wall, holding the baby, Kaufman began methodically slapping Yusel's face with the back of his hand. The blows were not unduly severe, but they were relentlessly repeated, first on one side of the head, then on the other. Yusel grew dizzy, then half-conscious.

161

Kaufman stepped back, breathing heavily. The look on the old woman's eyes above her veil made him uneasy. There had been people many years before who had looked like that—people who had perhaps cringed a little but whose spirit had still defied him. "Take the old woman and the child out of here," he growled.

As soon as a soldier had pushed the woman and baby into the kitchen Kaufman ungagged Yusel. "Now for some sense from you," he said, giving him another slap across the face to restore his senses. "I'm a reasonable man and I do not like to use force, but you must realise the unpleasant things which could happen. They won't if you answer a simple question. Who have you brought into the country?"

Yusel looked up at him with glazed eyes. He gulped and hesitated; Kaufman hit him again. Yusel's brain reeled. His head slumped forward and he began to lose consciousness. One of the guards revived him with a small, painful jab with a bayonet and Kaufman repeated his question.

"Professor Neilson," Yusel muttered.

Kaufman drew in his breath sharply. "Neilson!"

"The father," mumbled Yusel. "The father of the young scientist. . . ."

Kaufman closed his eyes in relief. For a split second he had had a vision of a ghost. "Why have you brought him?" he snarled. "Where is he?"

Yusel sat silent. He watched Kaufman's hands clench into fists and slowly rise to shoulder height. He bent his head in shame and fear. "He's in a cave above the temple," he whispered.

"More," ordered Kaufman.

Once he started talking, Yusel found it easy to go on. When he faltered Kaufman hit him again or a soldier prodded him with his bayonet, until they had the whole story.

Kaufman grunted with satisfaction and turned to the soldiers. "One of you take him down to the car. Keep him tied up. And you"—he turned to the second guard—"come with me. We'll get this American."

He walked outside, accompanied by the soldier. It was still calm, but there was a weird humming sound to the right, its note dropping steadily into a roar of wind. Eager to get to his quarry, Kaufman did no more than glance towards the spiralling

162

mass of blackness sweeping along the distant mountain crests at the far end of the range.

The tornado hit them when they were within sight of the temple. Half drowned by an avalanche of water, unable to stand erect in the wind, they slithered forwards to the slight shelter the great fallen marble columns provided. And there they both lay shivering and in mortal fear, until the storm passed as abruptly as it had started.

"We'll get back," panted Kaufman, "before another storm. See if your comrade and the prisoner are still all right. I will go and see what's happened to the old woman and the child."

He had some vague idea of holding them as hostages, but when he got back to the village the house no longer existed. The flat stone roof had shifted in the wind and brought the walls down. Kaufman looked through the gaping hole where the window had been. He turned away abruptly: the crushed body of a woman was not a pleasant sight. . . .

He found the soldiers tinkering with the car. Water had got on the ignition leads and it was half an hour before they got the engine started. Yusel lay gagged and bound at the back. Kaufman spent the time standing around, looking up at the temple, then at the ruined house which was the tomb of the old woman and presumably the child. His mind was filled with fear and, though he would not let himself admit it, something like remorse.

The engine of the car coughed to life and began to run smoothly. Kaufman got in beside the driver. "As fast as you can go," he ordered, "before another storm catches us out in the desert. And drive straight to the residence of Mm'selle Gamboul. I'll take our prisoner. Mm'selle Gamboul will want to question him herself."

They made it just as the sky again darkened to the blackness of night. As he alighted he could hear the scream of a second tornado approaching from the far side of the city. He ran for the shelter of the house, leaving Yusel in the car.

Gamboul was seated at her desk as usual. Her face was a blur in the gloom. The electricity had failed, and the heavy curtains had been torn away from the windows where the little intricately shaped panes had been blown out.

She looked up as Kaufman came close to the desk. "Ah, there you are," she said impatiently. "I want you to get out

163

to the compound as soon as the storm eases and phone Vienna. Tell them that we're in charge now and they must take orders from us."

He showed no surprise. " I shall not phone Vienna," he said slowly and deliberately. " There are some things you can't make a deal in, and this is one of them. I have been out in it. And I've important news."

She stood up and approached the window, moving to the side in case more glass was blown out. " You're afraid, you too, are you? " she sneered. " Everyone is afraid of responsibility, of taking risks. This afternoon I visited the girl. She is dying, that one. And raving as she dies. She told me that the computer was wrong, that the message did not tell me this. But I know, Herr Kaufman, I know! The power and the knowledge are all in my hands. No one else's."

Kaufman crossed the room and stood beside her. Somewhere in the town a fire had started. Despite the rain, the wind was whipping it into a small holocaust.

" Reports of everything you have done for the past month have been smuggled out of the country," he said. " There is a man who has been here for some time. He is waiting to take a specimen of the bacteria to London."

She wheeled on him. " You will stop him, of course," she warned.

He shook his head. " I shall not." His voice was almost gentle as he went on, " You are not sane. You would lead us all into destruction."

" You poor little man." She showed no anger, only contempt. " You are like all the rest. You have not the imagination to see. Come here! "

Abruptly she walked to the glass door leading to the balcony and turned the handle. She had to lean against it with all her weight to force it open against the wind.

" Come! " she repeated. " Come and see the elements at work. Working for me! " He stayed stubbornly where he was.

" You are frightened? " she laughed. " There is no need. It will not touch us. It cannot."

She walked majestically on to the balcony, her hair blowing back from her forehead, and paused at the balustrade, stretching her arms towards the sky. Kaufman caught the sound of her ecstatic laughter in the howling wind.

On an impulse he crossed to the door and pulled it shut. The bedlam outside lessened as if it had moved away. Suddenly there was a crescendo of noise and the great old house shook. A piece of coping crashed on the balcony, smashing into a score of pieces.

He saw Gamboul stare down at a lump of jagged marble just as a cascade of sand struck her. She bent quickly, rubbing her fists in her eyes. Blindly she stumbled to the door and began beating on it. The thick, decorative glass broke. Her fist ran with blood. He could see her mouth opening and shutting as she screamed at him.

He backed into the gloom of the room, watching impassively. The bursts of wind were coming faster now, until one merged into another. The house groaned and trembled. At last it came: a roaring, crumbling mass of stone which crashed on to the balcony and, tearing it out by its concrete roots, hurled it down into the courtyard below. The dust of debris mixed with the sand like eddying smoke. Kaufman walked forward, pressing his face myopically against the glass to see what had happened.

It was all very indistinct, but he thought he could see a twisted body among the rubble below. He kept on looking for a minute or so. He felt none of the disquiet that the sight of the old Arab woman had given him. Eventually he sought a chair well away from the crumbling walls. With a completely steady hand he lighted a cigarello.

" When the storm is past," he said aloud to the empty room, " I shall make myself a call to London. There is the matter of relations with the English."

He frowned, hoping that this would not be too great a problem. Professor Dawnay might be amenable; but Fleming was a formidable adversary. There had, after all, been so many unfortunate incidents between them in the past. The English mentality when it got obstinate ideas was something he had never understood.

The storm weakened, the clouds thinned and light returned though the wind blew nearly as hard as before. He went down to the courtyard. Yusel had been taken into the cellars, a guard reported. Kaufman heard himself giving orders for him to be kept under guard but decently treated, and then went and looked at Gamboul's body. It lay, twisted and broken, among the fallen

165

stonework, and her dark eyes, rimmed with blood, stared life-lessly up at him.

One of her cars was undamaged, and Kaufman ordered the driver to take him to the computer compound. Damage on the route through the town's outskirts was appalling. A scattering of Arabs were looting destroyed shops; they fled at the sight of the car with the Intel insignia. There were no troops or police anywhere.

The squat, solid buildings inside the compound seemed reasonably intact; a few windows were blown in, and some of the garish, modernistic fripperies at the entrance to the executive building had toppled. Kaufman drove past them, straight to the laboratories.

Dawnay was alone, injecting bacteria into rows of test tubes. The disorderly array of apparatus occupying every bench and table she had been able to commandeer was strangely reassuring after the desolation outside.

"Ah, Professor Dawnay," Kaufman beamed, " you were not damaged by the storm, I trust? "

" No," she said shortly.

" I have to inform you," he went on, " that Fraulein Gamboul is dead." He enjoyed her look of amazement. " She was killed by the tornado. I am now the senior representative of Intel in this country. I ask you to help me. Our measures against the bacteria causing the storms: they are successful, yes? "

" It looks like it, for the moment, and in the sea here," she replied.

" Wonderbar! " he said. " Everywhere else things go from bad to worse—unless we give them your cure."

"And quickly."

Kaufman nodded. "That is what I have thought." He dropped his voice. " You know, Professor, Fraulein Gamboul was prepared to let it go on until the world accepted her terms, outrageous terms. She was insane, of course. Did you know that she killed Salim, shot him dead herself? She was a woman possessed. She would have left everything too late. We should all have perished."

Dawnay looked at him coldly. " We may still."

He licked his lips nervously and removed his glasses, polishing the lenses over and over again. " There has been an appeal from London over the radio. I shall answer it when communica-

166

tions are restored. And I shall prove we can help by sending your own personal report on the anti-bacterium. Professor Neilson shall take it on the first available plane."

He saw her startled look.

"Oh yes," he said triumphantly, replacing his glasses and staring at her. "I know all about Professor Neilson being here. He will not wish to trust me. He does not yet understand that I am just a business man, and a good business man sees through calamity to brighter things."

Dawnay could not disguise her relief. "So Neilson will explain how you can give bulk supplies to the world?"

He shook his head impatiently. "Not at once," he said. "People will be prepared to pay a great deal. I told you I am a business man." He turned to the door. His smile had gone. "You will have a typed report ready for despatch in an hour."

For a while Dawnay went on with her work like an automaton. She had not counted on Kaufman haggling over the price of life.

She crossed to the computer building in search of someone to talk to; there was superficial damage to the entrance bay and the cooling tower, but the computer appeared unharmed. No guards were left, but an electrician appeared from the staff rest room. He said he had no idea where Dr. Fleming was. Abu Zeki, he believed, had left immediately after the first of the afternoon's storms to visit his family.

Dawnay thanked him and made her way to the sick quarters.

The nurse had put up makeshift barricades of screens over the broken windows. The girl smiled with relief at seeing someone at last.

"Miss Andre has slept through it all," she whispered. "I think she is a little stronger."

Dawnay sat down by the bed. The nurse was right. Bad as the light was, Dawnay could see a better colour in Andre's cheeks.

"Is it—is it working?" Andre had not opened her eyes or moved when she whispered her question.

Dawnay clasped the fragile hand. "Yes, it's working," she murmured. "The barograph in the lab is still going up. How long it will last I don't know."

Andre struggled to sit up. "It was not in the message that we must . . ." She stopped and lay back, exhausted. "I tried to tell her. She would not listen. She came last night. I told her to listen to me, not to the computer. But ——."

" Gamboul, you mean? " said Dawnay gently. " She's dead, Andre. Kaufman is now in charge."

Andre nodded slowly, as if she knew. Her fingers tried to find Dawnay's. " Do you believe me? " she asked. She saw Dawnay nod. The fingers relaxed and she lay back with her eyes closed once more. " Tell me all that has happened and I will tell you what to do."

As rapidly as she could, Dawnay gave a survey of the situation as far as she knew it. Before she had finished she thought Andre had fallen asleep or had lapsed into a coma, she was so utterly motionless. But after a full two minutes, the girl began speaking in a level monotone.

Dawnay listened intently. The responsibility Andre was thrusting on her shoulders was tremendous. It was intimidating; yet it was inspiring too. The rational, reasoned motives were all that her scientific mind needed. When Andre finished Dawnay made just one brief answer.

" I'll go right away," she said.

Half an hour later she was ordering a servant at the Presidential palace to take her immediately to his master. She had driven herself in a car she had found undamaged in the Intel parking lot. It was the first time she had been behind a car wheel since her young days as a student. Her erratic course did not matter. Flood water had destroyed the road in many places. Rubble from tottering houses had to be avoided or driven over. No guards stood outside the palace.

The President saw her immediately. He was seated in his high-backed chair, looking years older than when she had last taken her leave of him.

His ritualistic courtesy had not deserted him. He rose and bent over her hand, and indicated a chair. The faithful little negro boy was still there. The President told him to go and see if he could find someone to make coffee. Then he returned to his seat.

" The country is dying, Professor Dawnay," he said simply.

" The whole world may be," Dawnay replied. " That is why I have come. It is in your power to help. You have been informed that Miss Gamboul is dead? The President nodded. " So you are free."

" Free! " he said bitterly. " It is a little late."

" It may not be," she insisted. " It partly depends on you, your Excellency. If the anti-bacteria I have made is handled by Intel, and if it works, then it will be Intel's world. Kaufman will fix their price for them."

" I have been told very little, but I can gather the trend of events. And what can I do to stop this man Kaufman? He is like the others—Salim, Mm'selle Gamboul. . . ."

" We will deal with Kaufman," Dawnay promised. " While you send out the bacteria as a gift from Azaran. It will be the first action of a free nation."

He gazed at her with his sad, intelligent eyes. " Or the last," he suggested.

" Not if every laboratory in the world receives a supply. Then we've got a chance. If we can do it in the right way, through the right people." She thought back to their long battles with the authorities at Thorness. " Ever since the message was first picked up and a computer built to handle it, a few people have been struggling to keep this power out of the wrong hands and put it into the right ones."

"And what are mine? " he asked mildly.

" What we will make them for you! "

The boy entered with a tray. The President poured out some coffee and handed Dawnay a cup. He slowly sipped his own before he spoke again.

" So you are right? " he murmured, eyeing her keenly. "And to whom will you be responsible? Hundreds of thousands of people have died because—you will forgive me—of these experiments of yours."

Dawnay felt blood flooding into her neck and cheeks: a visible sign of her feeling of enormous guilt. " It was an accident," she said inadequately. " It could have happened with any experiment. I made a mistake."

Some of the fire of the revolutionary of years before flamed briefly in the President's face as he stood up and confronted her.

" Hundreds of thousands more may have to die correcting your mistake," he said. " The errors of politicians are sometimes expensive, and business men sometimes do their best to profit from them. But you scientists, you kill half the world. And the other half cannot live without you."

169

His anger faded. He sighed and permitted himself a slight smile. " I am in your hands, Professor Dawnay. You will forgive me if I add that I wish I were not."

Dawnay drove back to the compound determined to mould events the way she knew they had to be; but the responsibility appalled her. She badly needed the catharsis of Fleming's critical mind.

She found him in the servicing bay behind the computer. He was working at the desk, which was a litter of papers.

" Hello," he said lazily. " I holed up here—safe from the desert breezes and from interruption." He glanced at his wrist watch. " God, is that the time? I've been trying to work out this thing for Andre. I've done most of the chemical conversions. They don't make a hell of a lot of sense."

He threw across some calculations. She read them cursorily. " It would be lethal if it's wrong," she said shortly.

" She's dying anyway, isn't she? I've been trying all ways . . . ."

She interrupted him impatiently. " John, there isn't time for that."

He looked up at her. " Make 'em and break 'em, eh? "

Dawnay flushed. " There's something else that comes first. Or have you forgotten what's still raging over the greater part of the world? "

" No, I haven't forgotten," he said.

" We've made a lot of mistakes," she went on. " Both of us. I'm trying to get things right because it's the only hope we have. What happens to the world depends on us, on whether we take over or whether Kaufman does."

His grin was sardonic. " Have you been having the treatment, like Gamboul? "

" Gamboul is dead," she said evenly.

" Dead? " Fleming jumped to his feet. " Then the machine misfired! It's had a go at us and it's failed."

Dawnay shook her head.

" It hasn't done either. Gamboul was only supposed to protect us until we were in a position to use our own judgment."

He nodded towards the massive panels of the computer. " Or its . . . ."

" Our own judgment, John," she repeated. " We make the decisions now. Don't you see that this can be the beginning of a new life?"

He gathered the papers on the desk into an untidy pile. " Except for Andre," he said harshly.

" She'll have to wait. There are other people dying besides her."

He had to accept the logic of the statement. It did not make him dislike it less. He admired and was fond of Madeleine Dawnay, and was all the more nauseated by the familiar, corrupting scent of power which he now sensed around her.

" To hell with everything," he said. " I can't think any more tonight. We may as well try to get a little sleep before the wind decides to blow the roof off."

They walked from the building together. The residential area was a shambles of mud and rubble. But their quarters provided makeshift shelter. Fleming wished Dawnay good-night and went to his own chalet. The windows had gone and he could look past the shattered palm trees to the building opposite where the sick quarters were. The nurse had found a hurricane lamp from somewhere. It was the only light in the pitch black darkness—a dull yellow blob which drew his eyes like a magnet, mesmerising his mind. He fell into a half sleep, thinking of the life that still flickered near that puny flame.

He was roused by Abu Zeki.

" Much has happened," Abu said, struggling to control his emotions. " The storm, yesterday, it was very bad in the mountains. My home has gone."

" Your family? " Fleming sat up.

" Lemka and Jan—they are alive. My mother-in-law. She is dead." Abu's voice faltered. " She had laid down with little Jan in her arms, beneath her. When I arrived—I, I thought they were both dead. Then Jan began crying. He was saturated in blood, his grandmother's blood."

" Where is Lemka? "

" She was in the cave with Professor Neilson. She'd gone up with food. Neilson made her stay when the storm came. They came down just after I'd rescued Jan. I'm afraid Lemka is very bitter—about all that Professor Dawnay and you—all that we have been doing here."

" Not bitter, Abu; just right." Fleming felt the familiar hopelessness closing down on him. " It's no use saying I'm sorry. What about Yusel and Neilson? "

" Yusel is safe, so far. He had gone to my house to talk to Neilson about taking out the bacteria on his next flight. But Kaufman followed him. Yusel was beaten up. Then they took him back to Baleb. I suppose he'd have been killed in the house if they hadn't. Then in the early hours, while we were getting my wife and the child settled in a neighbour's house, he arrived in an Intel car. Kaufman had sent him back, with a note for Neilson. Yusel gave us the news that Mm'selle Gamboul was dead."

"A note for Neilson!" Fleming exclaimed. " What did it say? "

" Kaufman wanted to see him. He promised there would be no danger. Yusel insisted it was a trap, but Mr. Neilson said he wanted to go. I brought him down with me. He's waiting in the reception building now for Kaufman to come from town."

Fleming sprang off the bed. " I'll get over there. You'd better come too, Abu. If it's one of Kaufman's usual pistol and dagger efforts I want to be around."

Both men hurried to the executive building. In the keen light of dawn the damaged facade looked cheap and tawdry. There had also been considerable damage in the vast entrance hall, some of it the obvious results of looting by the demoralised guards.

" Kaufman will be sitting in the seat of the mighty—in Gamboul's office. You'd better wait down here, Abu. Warn us if anyone arrives," Fleming ordered.

He ran lightly up the staircase. One of the double doors of the director's office was slightly ajar, and he sidled along the wall until he could listen.

Kaufman's guttural voice was unctuous and polite. " The plane is coming from Vienna, I hope, Herr Neilson," he was saying. " It should arrive very soon. It will be loaded immediately. You must expect an uncomfortable flight. Conditions are still bad everywhere."

"And some written proof of your proposals? " Neilson asked coldly.

" I have obtained a letter from the President," said Kaufman. " That makes this matter official, but of course, everything will be done by us."

172

It was the comment Fleming had expected; had been waiting for. He pushed open the door and walked in. Kaufman looked up, startled, and then went on talking as if he had seen no one.

" We, that is to say Intel, will make the anti-bacteria and market it, though we will not hold our fellow human beings to ransom. That was Fraulein Gamboul's idea. I stopped it."

Fleming strode forward. " You're not in a position to dispense charity, Kaufman."

"And you are not entitled to be in this office without permission," retorted Kaufman.

" There are no Azaran guards to protect you now," Fleming said; " not even a receptionist." He moved closer to Neilson so that they both faced the German.

Kaufman picked up his case and extracted a cigarello. He kept the match against the glowing end for longer than necessary. His hand was shaking a little.

" It is no use bearing old grudges," he said, removing the cigarello. " One does what one has to do for the superiors one works for. One does as they order. But at the same time one tries to do good." There was a whine in his voice as he uneasily watched his visitors.

Neilson stood up, clenching the edge of the desk. His knuckles were white with the pressure he put into the grip. " You killed my son," he said with deceptive quietness. " He was shot before the eyes of his mother and myself at your order. If I'd had the means and if you weren't still essential to fly me out I'd have killed you the moment I entered this office."

" Please! " said Kaufman.

" How did Gamboul die? " Fleming snapped.

" The balcony of her house. It fell. I was there. I saw it. She was mad, completely mad. I couldn't save her."

" Did you try? "

" No," the German yelled. " I could have dragged her inside when the building started to fall. But I didn't. I chose to save —"

"— Your own skin! "

" The world! " Kaufman stood up and faced them defiantly across the desk. He saw a faint derisive smile on Fleming's face and no smile at all on Neilson's, and before either man could move he had dodged round the chair and darted to a small door that led to a private staircase. He tore it open and then backed away. Yusèl was standing there, expressionless, with a small

173

curved Bedouin knife in his hand. Kaufman moved back to the desk. " You cannot get in my way like this! " His voice rose. " I am doing business fairly. I'm trying to help you all! "

Fleming moved nearer the window. " The weather is holding up," he said. " The plane should get through on time. Before it arrives, you'll provide the help you talk about. You'll confirm your orders for Professor Neilson's flight. You'll make quite certain that it flies to London. That's the last thing you'll organise here. Get on with it."

Kaufman hesitated, then nodded. He picked up a pen and reached to a side drawer in the desk as if to take a noteheading.

He moved amazingly quickly. In a split second he had leaped up, a gun in his hand, and moved backwards to the outer door.

" This is not your game, gentlemen," he taunted them. " You should not try it." Then he turned and ran for the stairs.

Fleming and Neilson were close on his heels, but he gained his lead as he leaped recklessly downstairs. Fleming saw Abu look up and start running towards the foot of the staircase. Fleming's shout of warning coincided with the bark of the pistol shot. Abu crumpled in a heap. Such was the onrush of Kaufman's flight that he was unable to stop in time, and he fell headlong over his victim's body.

Before he could rise Neilson was on him, quickly followed by Yusel. Fleming's thoughts were for Abu and he knelt down and lifted the Arab in his arms. The head fell backwards, blood vomiting from the mouth. Fleming could not be certain whether the staring eyes were sightless or trying to send him a message. Very gently he let the body rest prone on the floor.

Neilson was insanely pummelling into Kaufman. " Leave him," Fleming shouted. He went up to the weeping, yammering German. " We're not going to kill you," he said. " There's a murder charge for you to answer in Geneva and in other places, if the courts aren't all destroyed."

" I do not make these things happen," Kaufman whined. " I have to obey."

Fleming turned away, unable to stomach any more. " Keep hold of him, Yusel," he ordered. " Get him down to the airport. Take his gun. He'll give you no trouble."

" Wait! "

They spun around and saw Dawnay standing in the entrance.

"What are you all doing here?" she asked. Then she saw Abu's body. Fleming explained, and then allowed her to lead him back upstairs to the main offices.

"You come too," she commanded Neilson and Kaufman. Yusel had gone out and now returned with a white robe with which he covered the body of his dead cousin. They all went into Gamboul's room and Dawnay sat at Gamboul's desk with Kaufman facing her and guarded by Yusel. Fleming wandered uneasily over to the window, but she called him back.

"John," she said. "It's not as simple as you may think: we haven't finished with Herr Kaufman yet."

She looked up into Kaufman's bruised and dejected face. "To whom did you report in Vienna?"

Kaufman did not answer at once, but when Dawnay shifted her gaze from him to Yusel he changed his mind.

"The Board of Directors," he said sulkily.

"To whom you reported Gamboul's death?"

"Yes"

"And who is taking over here?"

Kaufman glanced away for a moment. "I am."

"But you are not a director."

He drew himself up with a return of assurance: "I am temporarily in charge."

"Until?" Dawnay asked. There was another pause.

"You'd better tell us the easy way," said Fleming.

"Or perhaps," Neilson added, "you'd rather I broke your neck."

"There are three directors coming on the plane to-day, from Vienna." Kaufman addressed himself entirely to Dawnay, as if to a judge whom he might expect to be lenient. Dawnay looked only mildly surprised.

"Three?"

"They should have come before!" He began to speak quickly, with mounting passion. "Fraulein Gamboul was not equal to it. It deranged her, but she would not have anyone else. We have been ridiculously understaffed for so great a project; but she had considerable influence with the Chairman." He gave a knowing, leering wink. "She was an attractive woman. But now it is different; I have put it all on proper business footings. We will have directors, and executives and assistants —they are bringing many to-day."

175

"Are they?" said Dawnay with interest.

"Oh yes. And any kind of reinforcements we need. So—" He turned triumphantly to Fleming and Neilson, but Dawnay cut him short.

"So we shall have to put you all under guard," she said calmly. "That can be arranged for. Meanwhile, as soon as the aircraft is in, you'll help us send a Telex in your own code to Vienna."

"To say what?"

"That they have arrived safely and that all is well and you need no further help. You will also give us the names and full particulars of your chairman and other directors in Europe, and all addresses and telephone numbers you can find here in the office." She turned to her American colleague. "I'll give you a report to take to London, Professor Neilson, and as much of the anti-bacterium as I can. They should be able to get you there by nightfall."

12

CLEAR SKY

THE Prime Minister received the emergency committee in his private study on the first floor of 10, Downing Street. Although he had insisted on the fact being kept secret, he had been in bed for two days. His doctors diagnosed the trouble as cardiac asthma, which was as good a description as any for the strain felt by everyone of more than middle age as breathing became more and more difficult. The news of Dawnay's miracle in Azaran had now reached Whitehall, but its effects were still unfelt.

However, he insisted on rising to greet the Minister of Science and Osborne when they arrived.

" Glad you made it," he wheezed. "Are things still bad? "

"A nightmare, sir," said the Minister. "All the low ground beyond Hammersmith is flooded; the roads are under water." He began coughing.

" It's no good for us, this business," said the Prime Minister. " We'll be the first to succumb. Which will solve many a political problem. We shall soon have the youngest cabinet in history, called The Survivors."

The Minister of Science managed a polite laugh. " One worrying matter, sir, is that London Airport is flooded out. Gatwick's been unserviceable for some time, of course. And Civil Aviation isn't too happy about Hurn. I'd like your authority to get the R.A.F. to clear Lyneham for a priority landing. With at least two helicopters standing by for a run direct to us here. Hyde Park is still fairly clear despite the feeding centres and casualty stations."

" This means you have more news, Bertie," said the Prime Minister. " I do wish you could restrain your sense of melodrama."

177

"We've picked up a signal from Azaran, sir," Osborne inter-posed. "Professor Neilson's on his way. He and Professor Dawnay have taken over from a Herr Kaufman, who we believe was involved in the security leak at Thorness."

"Quite so, Osborne," said the Prime Minister with an amused smile. That was an old wound now and, like Osborne's other wounds, it was healing over and being forgotten. Osborne had more than redeemed himself since then. "Thorness. But the anti-bacterium?"

"He's bringing all he can carry, sir. Not much because of the flight difficulties these days, but enough to distribute to about a thousand breeding centres."

"Through the international organisation?"

"Yes," said the Minister of Science. "I may say, Prime Minister, that the will to co-operate has been magnificent. Japan suggested moving every oil tanker still afloat into mid-ocean, straddling marine currents like the Gulf Stream. The Soviet Union has completely cleared five state chemical plants. Fifty per cent. of the United States oil refineries are now cleaned and waiting. Here the Royal Engineers expect to have every gasometer on the coast patched up and ready by Saturday; the dairy and petroleum firms have had all their road tankers commandeered and marshalled at the various centres we decided on."

"Good," wheezed the Prime Minister. "Let's hope, dear boy, that it's happening in time for some of us. You will want to confer with Neilson, of course, when he gets here. Afterwards, send him round here. I shall want to discuss his plans. Then a broadcast. The people deserve a few words of encouragement and hope."

But it was not until the following night that the Prime Minister felt justified in telling the world that hope was returning. Throughout the previous twenty-four hours there had been frantic activity. The thousand activated test tubes Neilson brought seemed pathetically few when allocation began. A hundred of them were first distributed to British breeding centres. To save time the chemists concerned were briefed verbally by Neilson. Multi-language instructions were then prepared while Army Signals contacted all nations concerned to report details of samples and estimated time of arrival.

The R.A.F. and the United States Air Force handled transportation. A little slice of history was made as a U.S. long-range reconnaissance jet dropped towards Moscow's military airfield with Russian fighters doing welcoming victory rolls around her.

In a gesture to the almost unknown man who had had the titular responsibility of saving the world thrust upon him the Prime Minister insisted that the broadcast should open with the statement by the President of Azaran.

The radio link was difficult and tenuous, but over most of the globe it held.

"For many centuries we of Azaran have been considered a backward people," came the soft sing-song tones of the President. "But now, if we can bring salvation to the rest of the world it will be our privilege and joy. Already over our own country the weather is improving, and the air once more satisfies our lungs. This, we pray and believe, will spread to all the stricken peoples of the earth."

A resourceful radio station operator had dug up a recording of the Azarani national anthem. Its plaintive discord surged out and faded.

Then the Prime Minister made his historic broadcast from London. "Strains of a newly synthesised bacterium, which we have received from Azaran, can be the means of banishing the evil which has inflicted itself on mankind. With the help of the scientists, in whose hands our fate now lies, the governments of all nations are doing all they can. Already strains of the bacterium are being bred in the United Kingdom and pumped into the sea. First batches have arrived in the laboratories of our sister nations in this crusade against annihilation. More are coming from Azaran and will be distributed as fast as is humanly possible. With a concerted effort in every quarter of the globe we may hope the content of the sea will change, and we will breathe our native air again."

The Prime Minister leaned back in his chair, exhausted. Speaking had been a great effort and he rested while translations of his speech were broadcast in the five working languages of the United Nations. Then he called for his car. He turned to the officials gathered around him and spoke in a voice which was hardly more than a whisper. "I would like to see, gentlemen, if those promises I've made are reasonable. They tell me there's a breeding plant down at the London docks."

179

A police car escorted the Prime Minister's limousine through the darkened City past Tower Bridge. It nosed a way through piles of debris, detouring round many a barricaded street, until it pulled up on an old shabby wharf.

A sullen drizzle was falling, a respite from the interminable storms and gales. Two raincoated men were standing at the water's edge, watching a man in a police launch. They started when they recognised the bent elderly man beside them as the Prime Minister.

" We're testing for nitrogen content, sir," one of the men explained. "Anti-bacteria were pumped into this water six hours ago."

" How's it doing? " asked the Prime Minister.

" Fine, sir. Come and look."

In the headlight of the police launch the filthy river water looked black and sullen. But while they watched a bubble formed and burst. Nearby two more bubbles formed.

" It's happening right across the river, sir. Been noticeable for the last two and a half hours. It's the nitrogen being released as the new bacterium kills off the old one."

Another car drew up on the wharf. Osborne, alerted by the Premier's P.A., had brought Neilson to the site. The Prime Minister greeted them quietly with a smile and a half-raised hand.

" The cure is not, I hope, as bad as the disease," he inquired of the American.

Neilson shook his head. " No sir. The anti-bacterium does not survive the conditions it creates; Professor Dawnay has tested this fact very thoroughly. It has only one enemy, one source of food, the bacteria emerging from Thorness. Once it has exhausted the supply of those it languishes and dies itself."

" Just as an antibiotic destroys germs and then is itself destroyed," put in Osborne.

" Except that in this case we think that the end will be more complete —"

The Prime Minister interrupted Neilson with another smile. " I see you have it under control."

He stood a little longer, watching the bubbles come and go. " Thank God! Thank God! " he whispered as he returned to his car.

Conditions in Azaran were completely transformed within twenty-four hours of Neilson's arrival in Britain. Aircraft from a dozen nations flew in scientists and technicians to help Dawnay and to organise transportation and communications. A U.N. stand-by force was put on call but, by the President's wish, was only to enter Azaran in the event of a threat from Intel. Dawnay had engineered herself complete freedom.

But the whole entity of Intel was collapsing quietly and completely. The NKVD, Interpol and the FBI, working together on the report which Neilson had taken to London, raided and closed the main offices in Vienna and in Zurich and Hong Kong; and the names revealed in the documents they captured caused consternation in a dozen chancelleries. By general agreement among the great powers, no pressure was brought to force dismissal and arrest, but all the consortium's trading licences were withdrawn. There were a couple of suicides and a whole series of resignations on health grounds, hardly noticed in the worldwide drama of retreat from chaos, and what was left came rapidly to a standstill, leaving empty trading posts all over the world without credentials or trade, and useless unclaimed millions in safe deposits in Swiss banks. In Azaran, the main centre of anti-bacteria production and the computer which had evolved it were left respectively in the hands of Madeleine Dawnay and her associate, John Fleming, who had both become world-famous characters overnight.

The atmosphere of super-efficiency and the constant flattery bestowed on Dawnay and himself repelled Fleming. He wanted no part of it; nor, indeed, was there anything for him usefully to do. He avoided the eager, enthusiastic groups who gathered in the makeshift canteen. He evaded invitations to parties which were soon organised in Baleb.

Soon after he had seen Kaufman into Interpol's custody, Fleming had suffered an experience which he found he could not dismiss from his mind. He had collected the handful of personal things in Abu's desk and driven to Lemka's village, glad that an officer of the President's personal staff had gone earlier to break the news of Abu's death to her.

It was very quiet inside the ruined courtyard of the house. A line of washing fluttered in the wind. The baby's cot stood in the shade of a crumbling wall. A spiral of smoke eddied away from a cluster of faggots in a makeshift grate. He called and

181

waited until Lemka appeared at the shattered doorway at the sound of footsteps.

" I came to say —" Fleming began.

" Do not tell me that you are sorry," she interrupted, moving to the clothes line and keeping her face averted. "And do not tell me it was not your fault."

" I didn't want to involve your husband," he muttered.

She turned round angrily. " You involved us all."

" I liked him, you know. Very much. I came to see what I could do," he pleaded.

She was fighting back her tears. " You've done enough. You've saved the world—from your own muddle. So now you think it is all right. How can you—all of you—be so arrogant? You don't believe in God. You don't accept life as His gift. You want to change it because you think you're greater than God."

" I tried to stop . . ." His voice trailed away.

" You tried, and we suffer. The girl—your girl—was right when she said you condemn us. Why don't you go back and listen to her? "

" She is dying."

" You kill her too? " She looked at him more with pity than with hatred. He could not answer. He laid the little parcel of Abu's possessions at the foot of the child's cot and walked away.

Back at the compound, he stole like an interloper by a round-about route to his own quarters. He took out the computer print-out and his own calculations from a drawer and began studying them.

He had put them away when Dawnay had refused to help him, because he felt that he could not possibly do them himself. He simply did not know enough bio-chemistry. For what seemed a lifetime he had avoided Andre's room, because he could no longer face the fact of her dying, and by now he had given up all hope of Dawnay having the time, energy or will to be able to help him.

Dawnay now was installed in the executive block, at the centre of a quickly-spun web of radio and cable communications, directing and advising struggling scientists all round the world. He did not know how she managed it, or whether she ever slept; he didn't even see her.

He sat in his little room and stared glumly at the mass of

182

figures. Then he opened a fresh bottle of whisky and started to try to make head or tail of them. It was close on midnight when he walked a little unsteadily across the deserted clearing to the laboratory.

With the experimental work over, the master breeding tanks had been transferred to the executive building where there was room for the regiments of assistants Dawnay could now direct. The laboratory where it had all begun was neat and lifeless. He groped for a switch. The light came on. Most of the circuits had been restored during the previous day.

Hardly knowing from what recesses of memory of his student days they came, or how much was inspired by the neat Scotch, he began to find the facts he needed arranging themselves in his mind. Slowly and laboriously, and a little drunkenly, he started to make a chemical synthesis out of the mass of calculation he had written down.

His own training kept him roughly on the right path, but he ruefully had to face the fact that the ordinary, plebeian routine of practical chemistry was really beyond him. He lacked patience and accuracy; but obstinacy, and the memory of Lemka's pitying eyes, drove him on. He did not notice that morning sunlight was outshining the bare electric bulbs, nor did he hear the door open.

" What a hell of a mess! " said Dawnay's voice. " Look at my laboratory. What do you think you're doing? "

He dropped off the high stool at the bench and stretched. " Hello, Madeleine," he said. " I've been trying to synthesise this thing for Andre. Most of the main chain seems to have jelled. But the side chains are all to hell."

Dawnay ran an expert eye over his work amid the litter spread across bench and desks. " I'm not surprised," she exclaimed. " You've achieved a glorious mess. Better leave it to me."

" I thought you hadn't time. I thought you were too busy setting the world to rights."

She ignored what he was saying and went on looking at the equations he had written down.

"Admittedly," she said slowly, " if there's a chemical deficiency in her blood or endocrine glands there must be a chemical answer, but we can't know whether this is it."

" It has to be, doesn't it? " he suggested. " Our electronic boss says so."

She considered for a time. " Why do you want to do this, John? " she enquired. " You've always been afraid of her. Always wanted her out of the way."

" Now I want her to live! "

She eyed him speculatively, a smile hovering around her mouth. " Because you're a scientist and you want to know what the message is really all about? You can't bear to think that Gamboul knew and you don't? That's really the reason, isn't it? "

" You've some funny old ideas," he smiled.

" Maybe," she answered, " maybe." She reached for an overall on the wall hook. " Go and get some breakfast, John. Then come back here. I'll have some work for you to do."

The two of them worked in perfect, almost instinctive co-operation, carefully avoiding any kind of moral or emotional argument. They were like enemies who were forced to live in the same cell. They talked of nothing but the enormous complication of the job, and for ten solid days, and most of the nights, they carried on. Messages about the world-wide improvements in barometric pressure, news bulletins reporting a noticeable lessening of wind violence, were just noted and then forgotten.

Because of her own forebodings of failure, Dawnay did not even tell Fleming that even before the checking was complete she had started injections on Andre. The ethics did not bother her. Andre's life was hovering near its end in any case.

Fleming still avoided the girl's sick room. He told himself that he would not see her until he could give her hope. He knew Dawnay was visiting her regularly, but he deliberately refrained from asking how she was.

And Dawnay, noting the slow improvement in her patient, hardly dared to believe that she had succeeded. Only when the doctor came and made prolonged and successful tests of muscular reflexes did she admit even to herself that the near-impossible had happened.

It was Andre herself who settled the matter. " I am getting well," she said one morning as she waited for another injection. " You have saved my life."

" You have saved yourself," Dawnay said gently. " You and John and the computer calculations."

" What will he do now—now that I'm to go on? " Andre asked.

" I don't know." Dawnay had wondered so much herself that she had been awaiting and dreading this question. " He's divided. One part wants to go on. The other is frightened. We're all like that. But fear doesn't entirely stop us going forward."

"And I stand for going forward? " Andre asked.

" For much more. Down here on our cosy little earth we used to think we were protected from the outside by sheer distance. Now we see that intelligence—pure, raw intelligence—can cross great gulfs of space and threaten us."

" You still think of me as a threat from outside? "

" No," Dawnay answered. " No, I don't."

Andre smiled. " Thank you for that. Can't I see him soon? "

" You're strong enough to get up," Dawnay agreed. " He should see you. Yes," she went on after a pause. " We'll go together when you can walk."

One evening the following week Fleming went back to the computer block. Partly to ease his conscience, and partly because he needed some fairly unskilled help, he had invited Yusel to work on the computer. The salary was good, which would help Lemka and the child.

When Dawnay found them there, the Arab excused himself and she was left alone with Fleming.

" John," she said, "Andre's here."

Fleming looked up in surprise.

" Where? "

" Outside." She smiled a little grimly at Fleming's amazement. " She's cured, John. We've done it. She'll be all right now."

At first she thought he was not going to say anything at all. Then he asked, in a hurt voice. " Why couldn't you have told me? "

" I wasn't sure which way it was going."

He stared at her with amazement. " So you've repaired her, and the first thing you do is to bring her here—back to the machine! It's all so easy, so planned, just as if we're being used." He turned away with a frown. " How can we go on competing with her, with this? "

" That depends on you," Dawnay replied. " I can't help you. My job here is finished. I'm flying home tomorrow."

" You can't! " he exclaimed.

" You wanted her well," she reminded him, but he looked at her and through her as though at a ghost.

" You can't leave me like this," he implored. " Not with her *here*."

She had never before seen him plead for help. " Look, John," she said kindly. " You're not a child that hides behind its mother's skirts. You're supposed to be a scientist. Andre didn't use you or me. It was we who turned the world upside down. It was Andre who saved it." She moved to the door, beckoning to the waiting girl. " I'll see you before I go."

Andre walked quickly towards Fleming, stopping before him and smiling like a happy schoolgirl. She was still thin and pale, and her eyes looked very big above her high, sharp cheek-bones; but she no longer looked ill. She was alive and vibrant, with a kind of fined-down beauty which touched him in spite of himself.

" I can hardly believe that you're like this," he said.

" You're not glad? "

" Of course I'm glad . . . ."

"Are you afraid of me? "

" So long as you're a puppet, a mechanical doll."

Colour suffused her cheeks and she tossed her hair away from her face. "And you're not? You still think of yourself as a divine, unique creation. Three thousand millions of you on this earth alone. They—we—are all puppets, dancing on strings."

" Let's dance then." He kept his hands in his pockets, his body motionless.

" I will do whatever you wish," she told him. "All I know is one certain thing. We cannot go separate ways."

He put out his hand and brushed it against hers. " Then let's leave here," he said. He turned and looked at the grey bulk of the computer. "After we've destroyed this. We'll make a real job of it this time. Then we'll find somewhere with peace, like that island we were on with old what-was-his-name—Preen."

"All right," she said. " We will do as you want. I have often told you that. But have you thought? Have you really thought? Do you think we'd be allowed to live in peace any more than Preen was? The only safe place for us is here. If we accept this and its protection we accept what is planned."

" Planned! That damned word. And what *is* planned? "

" What you want. It will be done here and in the rest of the world."

186

" I'm afraid I'm not cut out to be a dictator."

" The only possible sort of dictator is someone who is not cut out for it," she said. " Someone who knows."

" Knows what? " he asked.

She took hold of his arm and began to lead him across to the observation bay of the computer.

" I'll show you what I showed Mm'selle Gamboul," she said. " Stand close beside me."

Obediently he stood by the panel and brought in the phase switches as she called the numbers. She sat down, alert and expectant, with a hand on his.

The computer began to purr. Relays snicked into operation, the screen glowed. Like a film coming into focus the shadows grew smaller and sharper as they took form and perspective.

" It looks like the moon," Fleming murmured. " Dead mountains, dust-filled valleys."

" It isn't," Andre whispered, without looking away from the screen. " It isn't the moon. It's the planet from which the message came."

" You mean they're showing us themselves? " Fleming stared at the bizarre shadows and reflections. " The lighting's completely weird."

" Because of the source," she explained, " the light from their sun is blue."

She concentrated on the tube and the picture began to shift. The scenery moved horizontally at increasing speed until the screen became a blur of dazzling light. Again the scene slowed down and became stationary. There was a terrible stillness about it this time, the absolutely rigidity of timeless age.

An enormous plain stretched into the background where it merged with the dark sky. In the foreground stood monstrous elongated shapes, placed haphazardly and apparently half buried in the level, soft-looking surface.

Fleming felt the skin on the back of his neck prickling. " My God," he whispered, " what are they? "

" They are the ones," said Andre. " The ones who sent it. The ones I'm supposed to be like."

" But they're lifeless." He corrected himself. " They're immobile."

She nodded, her eyes wide and fixed on the screen. " Of

187

course," she said. " Really big brains cannot move around any more than this computer. There's no need."

" The surface of them seems solid. How do they see? "

" Eyes would be useless. The blue light would destroy all tissue and nerve fibre as you know them. They see by other means, just as their other senses are different from those people—" she hesitated " —people like us—have developed."

The picture began to crumble. Sections detached themselves and spun off the screen. Quickly everything faded.

" Is that all there is? " Fleming felt deprived of something.

Andre turned her face to him. It glistened with perspiration; her eyes were enormous, the pupils distended. " Yes," she smiled. " That's all. They are the ones. They wanted us to see their planet. They believed it would be enough. Perhaps as a warning. Perhaps to show what time brings and how to survive. How we could do the same."

Fleming glanced back at the dark screen. To him those shapes still stood clear and definite in their piteous immobility against the glass. " No," he said.

" Is it so much worse than the human race? " she asked him. " Which lives and reproduces and works and struggles by animal instinct. That's all human beings are—animals who spend their time competing for existence, keeping their bodies alive. And when the earth gets too crowded there is a holocaust and the survivors begin the cycle over again, and the brain never develops."

" Oh no? "

" Not really. Not fast enough. By the time the earth becomes no longer fit to live on, the human race will still be little struggling animals who die out."

" Unless we change? "

She nodded. " The brain from out there can guide us, and we can guide others. So long as we keep hold of the authority it gives us."

"And impose what it wants us to on the rest of the world? "

" We can only start to point a possible way," Andre answered. " It will be millions of years before the earth . . . ."

" We haven't the right," he said.

" To use knowledge of what could be? " They argued for a long while, but in the end she said, "All right, then you're

188

quite clear in your mind? You want to destroy all this? " She waved an expressive hand along the machine.

" Yes," he said firmly. " That's what I want."

She got up and crossed to the record cabinets. From the rear of a drawer she took a small roll of film and held it out to him.

" What's that? " he demanded, refusing to touch it.

" It's a roll of input negative. It writes zeros throughout the whole of the memory section. The computer has no will to stop it now. Feed this film in and in a few minutes it will be nothing but a mass of metal and glass."

He followed her to the programming console. He watched her slip the film on the spool holder and snap the flange shut. His eyes travelled upwards to the red button on the control panel. He was moving his hand to press it when Andre gently but firmly clasped his fingers.

" I'd rather that it wasn't you who did that," she said. " You see, I know it's a mistake. And I'd rather it wasn't yours."

He let his arm drop and stepped away from the panel. Andre bent over the operating desk and began writing on the memo pad clamped to one side.

" We'll leave a note," she explained. " But who for? "

He grinned happily. " For Yusel."

" Yes," she agreed. " Yusel. He'll start the input motor quite innocently when he sees this." In big capitals she wrote Yusel's name. " Now take me away please," she whispered, " if that's what you really want."

He did not move as she came close to him. Then very lightly he bent his head and kissed her, full on the mouth.

As he felt her lips warm and full against his, he sensed suddenly her full humanity. All the fear and strain of the past months fell away from him and he was simply alone at last with the woman he wanted.

He withdrew his mouth gently from hers and held her away from him at arms' length, and smiled at her. When she smiled back the grey panels of the computer cabinets became dim, unimportant shadows. He laughed out loud and took one of her hands in his.

" Now, let's go. I can get Kaufman's car. There's a place I'd like you to see."

She followed him unquestioningly. Outside it was dark and cool. The wind was just the night breeze of the desert. No clouds marred the serenity of the pale, peaceful light from an almost full moon.

In the car she snuggled against him. He drove steadily along the route which held such memories for him. When he neared the mountains he drove off the road, anxious to avoid arousing the sleeping people in Lemka's village. He stopped the car in the shadow of a great boulder.

Hand in hand they clambered up a goat track, making for the white mass of the temple ruins. The air became colder. Both of them panted with the effort, and the blood tingled in their faces and hands.

In silence Fleming stopped when his feet were on the great flight of steps which led up to the ruined portico. He kept his grip firmly on Andre's hand, making her stop too.

" Why have we come here? " she whispered.

" To breathe," he said, tilting his head back and inhaling deeply.

She looked upwards, too—into the vault of the sky, darkening at the edge of the mountain crest where the moonshine weakened. The Pole Star hung there like a brilliant lamp. Not far from it another star twinkled.

" Beta Cassiopeiae, it's called," said Fleming, knowing that their minds were so attuned that there was no need to doubt that she was looking just where he was. "A nicer name is the Lady in the Chair. Can you make out the shape? "

She laughed. " No, I can't." She continued looking upwards. " But now I know why you brought me here. That glimmer between the Pole Star and your Chair Lady."

" Yes," he said, putting his arm protectively around her.

"Andromeda," she whispered, " my namesake."

" The place where they are, the creatures without movement, without eyes; just with brains." He deliberately turned his head away from the stars. " It doesn't make sense. Think of the machine they made us build at Thorness. Remember what it did to you? Your hands? "

She nodded. " I remember. But if it had been very reasonable, very wise, would you have opposed it? " She saw him shake his head. " Then you'd have really fallen under its spell. You and everybody else. Just like Mademoiselle Gamboul."

" I suppose so."

" Therefore what are you afraid of? By making it brutal and

savage they forced you to take the control yourself. That's why we changed the decision circuits in this Azaran model. And that was intended too. It was all predictable."

" The nitrogen bug too? "

" Of course. That was to make absolutely sure that the control would be changed. That the decisions would not be the machine's."

Fleming was almost convinced. " But why run so close? It nearly did for us."

" That was a miscalculation."

" Don't kid yourself," he grinned. " That thing never made a mistake."

" They made just one; they hadn't reckoned on someone like you. They never thought that the first computer would be destroyed, only that it would be changed. If you hadn't done what you did that night in Scotland the marine bacteria could have been coped with much sooner."

" You've no proof," he protested lamely.

" I do know," she said softly. " I know you destroyed the only means of saving everything. At least that's what would have happened if your friend Bridger hadn't sold the design to Intel."

He was delighted with that. " Good old Denis," he exclaimed. " They ought to bury him in Westminster Abbey." He turned and put his hands on her shoulders. "And you, what was your purpose? To establish it here in a position of absolute power? "

" No. My job was to find someone who would understand how to use it." She fingered the button on his coat. " You wouldn't trust me. And yet—you expected a breakthrough into new knowledge."

Abruptly she stepped away.

" This is it, John. It's in your hands now."

"And you? " he asked, keeping his distance.

" I'm in your hands too."

" But what are you? "

She came back to him. " Flesh and blood," she said happily. " Dawnay's mixture."

He put his hands on either side of her face and tilted it so that the waning moon shone full on her. " It's the nearest thing to a miracle I've ever seen," he said.

They turned and walked down the mountain path, hand in hand. " I remember the night the message first came through,"

Fleming said thoughtfully. " I started burbling about a New Renaissance. I was a bit tight. Old Bridger wasn't so cocky about it as I was. He said, ' When all the railings are down you have to have something to hang on to '."

His arm went round her waist, pulling her body close against his. " I'd better get used to hanging on to you, hadn't I? "

She smiled up at him, but she was not quite content.

"And the message? " she asked.

They had reached level ground, and he quickened his pace, once again taking her hand and pulling her along as he took long strides towards the car.

" Where are we going now? " she asked.

He looked back to her and laughed out loud again.

" To save it! " He shouted so that the hillside rang with his voice. " We've just about time to beat Yusel in to work. The new Renaissance begins in about an hour from now—if we get cracking."

He bundled Andre into the car. After he had walked round to the driving seat he paused for a second, looking up to the sky, already paling with the false dawn. The stars were going out. Very dimly, between the Lady in the Chair and the Pole Star he could make out the hazy light of the great Andromeda galaxy across the immensity of space.